A CLASSIC SCIENCE–FICTION NOVEL

The Best of Both Worlds . . .

When Martin Padway suddenly finds himself a reluctant time-traveler in ancient Rome, he sets out to make the world a better place. In order to reverse the course of history and prevent the encroaching Dark Ages, Padway must first stem the tide of barbarism that threatens Italy and, indeed, all western civilization. Relying on his 20th-century expertise, Padway "invents" and/or introduces:

- Printing and newspapers
- Arabic numerals
- Double-entry bookkeeping
- Copernican astronomy
- Distilling

to the ancient world, shattering much of the established social order.

A rousing romp through time!

"A work of real and stimulating imagination."

—*Saturday Review of Literature*

"Good fun!"

—*The New Yorker*

Lest Darkness Fall

L. SPRAGUE de CAMP

BALLANTINE BOOKS ● NEW YORK

SBN 345-24139-8-125

First Printing: August, 1974

Cover art by Stivers

Printed in the United States of America

BALLANTINE BOOKS
A Division of Random House, Inc.
201 East 50th Street, New York, N.Y. 10022
Simultaneously published by
Ballantine Books, Ltd., Toronto Canada

To Catherine

Lest Darkness Fall

CHAPTER I

TANCREDI TOOK HIS hands off the wheel again and waved them. "—so I envy you, Dr. Padway. Here in Rome we have still some work to do. But *pah!* It is all filling in little gaps. Nothing big, nothing new. And restoration work. Building contractor's work. Again, *pah!*"

"Professor Tancredi," said Martin Padway patiently, "as I said, I am not a doctor. I hope to be one soon, if I can get a thesis out of this Lebanon dig." Being himself the most cautious of drivers, his knuckles were white from gripping the side of the little Fiat, and his right foot ached from trying to shove it through the floor boards.

Tancredi snatched the wheel in time to avoid a lordly Isotta by the thickness of a razor blade. The Isotta went its way thinking dark thoughts. "Oh, what is the difference? Here everybody is a doc-tor, whether he is or not, if you understand me. And such a smart young man as you— What was I talking about?"

"That depends." Padway closed his eyes as a pedestrian just escaped destruction. "You were talking about Etruscan inscriptions, and then about the nature of time, and then about Roman archaeol—"

"Ah, yes, the nature of time. This is just a silly idea of mine, you understand. I was saying all these people who just disappear, they have slipped back down the suitcase."

"The what?"

"The trunk, I mean. The trunk of the tree of time. When they stop slipping, they are back in some former time. But as soon as they do anything, they change all subsequent history."

"Sounds like a paradox," said Padway.

"No-o. The trunk continues to exist. But a new branch starts out where they come to rest. It has to, otherwise we

1

would all disappear, because history would have changed and our parents might not have met."

"That's a thought," said Padway. "It's bad enough knowing the sun might become a nova, but if we're also likely to vanish because somebody has gone back to the twelfth century and stirred things up——"

"No. That has never happened. We have never vanished, that is. You see, doc-tor? We continue to exist, but another history has been started. Perhaps there are many such, all existing somewhere. Maybe, they aren't much different from ours. Maybe the man comes to rest in the middle of the ocean. So what? The fish eat him, and things go on as before. Or they think he is mad, and shut him up or kill him. Again, not much difference. But suppose he becomes a king or a *duce?* What then?

"Presto, we have a new history! History is a four-dimensional web. It is a tough web. But it has weak points. The junction places—the focal points, one might say—are weak. The backslipping, if it happens, would happen at these places."

"What do you mean by focal points?" asked Padway. It sounded to him like polysyllabic nonsense.

"Oh, places like Rome, where the world-lines of many famous events intersect. Or Istanbul. Or Babylon. You remember that archaeologist, Skrzetuski, who disappeared at Babylon in 1936?"

"I thought he was killed by some Arab holdup men."

"Ah. They never found his body! Now, Rome may soon again be the intersection point of great events. That means the web is weakening again here."

"I hope they don't bomb the Forum," said Padway.

"Oh, nothing like that. There will be no more great wars; everybody knows it is too dangerous. But let us not talk politics. The web, as I say, is tough. If a man did slip back, it would take a terrible lot of work to distort it. Like a fly in a spider web that fills a room."

"Pleasant thought," said Padway.

"Is it not, though?" Tancredi turned to grin at him, then trod frantically on the brake. The Italian leaned out and showered a pedestrian with curses.

He turned back to Padway. "Are you coming to my house for dinner tomorrow?"

"Wh-what? Why yes, I'll be glad to. I'm sailing next—"

"*Si, si.* I will show you the equations I have worked out. Energy must be conserved, even in changing one's time. But nothing of this to my colleagues, please. You understand." The sallow little man took his hands off the wheel to wag both forefingers at Padway. "It is a harmless eccentricity. But one's professional reputation must not suffer."

"*Eek!*" said Padway.

Tancredi jammed on the brake and skidded to a stop behind a truck halted at the intersection of the Via del Mare and the Piazza Aracoeli. "What was I talking about?" he asked.

"Harmless eccentricities," said Padway. He felt like adding that Professor Tancredi's driving ranked among his less harmless ones. But the man had been very kind to him.

"Ah, yes. Things get out, and people talk. Archaeologists talk even worse than most people. Are you married?"

"What?" Padway felt he should have gotten used to this sort of thing by now. He hadn't. "Why—yes."

"Good. Bring your wife along. Then you see some real Italian cooking, not this spaghetti-and-meat-balls stuff."

"She's back in Chicago." Padway didn't feel like explaining that he and his wife had been separated for over a year.

He could see, now, that it hadn't been entirely Betty's fault. To a person of her background and tastes he must have seemed pretty impossible: a man who danced badly, refused to play bridge, and whose idea of fun was to get a few similar creatures in for an evening of heavy talk on the future of capitalism and the love life of the bullfrog. At first she had been thrilled by the idea of traveling in far places, but one taste of living in a tent and watching her husband mutter over the inscriptions on potsherds had cured that.

And he wasn't much to look at—rather small, with outsize nose and ears and a diffident manner. At college they had called him Mouse Padway. Oh, well, a man in exploratory work was a fool to marry, anyway. Just look at the divorce rate among them—anthropologists, paleontologists, and such—

"Could you drop me at the Pantheon?" he asked. "I've never examined it closely, and it's just a couple of blocks to my hotel."

"Yes, doc-tor, though I am afraid you will get wet. It looks like rain, does it not?"

"That's all right. This coat will shed water."

Tancredi shrugged. They bucketed down the Corso Vittorio Emanuele and screeched around the corner into the Via Cestari. Padway got out at the Piazza del Pantheon, and Tancredi departed, waving both arms and shouting: "Tomorrow at eight, then? *Si*, fine."

Padway looked at the building for a few minutes. He had always thought it a very ugly one, with the Corinthian front stuck on the brick rotunda. Of course that great concrete dome had taken some engineering, considering when it had been erected. Then he had to jump to avoid being spattered as a man in a military uniform tore by on a motorcycle.

Padway walked over to the portico, round which clustered men engaged in the national sport of loitering. One of the things that he liked about Italy was that here he was, by comparison, a fairly tall man. Thunder rumbled behind him, and a raindrop struck his hand. He began to take long steps. Even if his trench coat would shed water, he didn't want his new twelve-thousand-lire Borsalino soaked. He liked that hat.

His reflections were cut off in their prime by the granddaddy of all lightning flashes, which struck the Piazza to his right. The pavement dropped out from under him like a trapdoor.

His feet seemed to be dangling over nothing. He could not see anything for the reddish-purple after-images in his retinas. The thunder rolled on and on.

It was a most disconcerting feeling, hanging in the midst of nothing. There was no uprush of air as in falling down a shaft. He felt somewhat as Alice must have felt on her leisurely fall down the rabbit-hole, except that his senses gave him no clear information as to what was happening. He could not even guess how fast it was happening.

Then something hard smacked his soles. He almost fell. The impact was about as strong as that resulting from a two-foot fall. As he staggered by he hit his shin on something. He said "Ouch!"

His retinas cleared. He was standing in the depression caused by the drop of a roughly circular piece of pavement.

The rain was coming down hard, now. He climbed out of the pit and ran under the portico of the Pantheon. It was so dark that the lights in the building ought to have been switched on. They were not.

Padway saw something curious: the red brick of the rotunda was covered by slabs of marble facing. That, he thought, was one of the restoration jobs that Tancredi had been complaining about.

Padway's eyes glided indifferently over the nearest of the loafers. They switched back again sharply. The man, instead of coat and pants, was wearing a dirty white woolen tunic.

It was odd. But if the man wanted to wear such a getup, it was none of Padway's business.

The gloom was brightening a little. Now Padway's eyes began to dance from person to person. They were all wearing tunics. Some had come under the portico to get out of the rain. These also wore tunics, sometimes with poncho-like cloaks over them.

A few of them stared at Padway without much curiosity. He and they were still staring when the shower let up a few minutes later. Padway knew fear.

The tunics alone would not have frightened him. A single incongruous fact might have a rational if recondite explanation. But everywhere he looked more of these facts crowded in on him. He could not concisely notice them all at once.

The concrete sidewalk had been replaced by slabs of slate.

There were still buildings around the Piazza, but they were not the same buildings. Over the lower ones Padway could see that the Senate House and the Ministry of Communications—both fairly conspicuous objects—were missing.

The sounds were different. The honk of taxi horns was absent. There were no taxis to honk. Instead, two oxcarts creaked slowly and shrilly down the via della Minerva.

Padway sniffed. The garlic-and-gasoline aroma of modern Rome had been replaced by a barnyard-and-backhouse symphony wherein the smell of horse was the strongest and also the most mentionable motif. Another ingredient was incense, wafting from the door of the Pantheon.

The sun came out. Padway stepped out into it. Yes, the portico still bore the inscription crediting the construction of the building to M. Agrippa.

Glancing around to see that he was not watched, Padway stepped up to one of the pillars and slammed his fist into it. It hurt.

"Hell," said Padway, looking at his bruised knuckles.

He thought, I'm not asleep. All this is too solid and consistent for a dream. There's nothing fantastic about the early afternoon sunshine and the beggars around the Piazza.

But if he was not asleep, what? He might be crazy . . . But that was a hypothesis difficult to build a sensible course of action on.

There was Tancredi's theory about slipping back in time. Had he slipped back, or had something happened to him to make him imagine he had? The time-travel idea did not appeal to Padway. It sounded metaphysical, and he was a hardened empiricist.

There was the possibility of amnesia. Suppose that flash of lightning had actually hit him and suppressed his memory up to that time; then suppose something had happened to jar it loose again . . . He would have a gap in his memory between the first lightning flash and his arrival in this archaistic copy of old Rome. All sorts of things might have happened in the meantime. He might have blundered into a movie set. Mussolini, having long secretly believed himself a reincarnation of Julius Cæsar, might have decided to make his people adopt classical Roman costume.

It was an attractive theory. But the fact that he was wearing exactly the same clothes, and had the same things in his pockets as before the flash, exploded it.

He listened to the chatter of a couple of the loafers. Padway spoke fair, if pedantic, Italian. He could not quite get the substance of these men's talk. In the rush of syllables he would often catch a familiar sound-group, but never enough at one time. Their speech had the tantalizing pseudo familiarity of Plattdeutsch to an English-speaking person.

He thought of Latin. At once the loafers' speech became more familiar. They were not speaking classical Latin. But Padway found that if he took one of their sentences and matched it first against Italian and then against Latin, he could understand most of it.

He decided that they were speaking a late form of Vulgar Latin, rather more than halfway from the language of Cicero to that of Dante. He had never even tried to speak this hybrid. But by dredging his memory for his knowledge of sound changes, he could make a stab at it: *Omnia Gallia e devisa en parte trei, quaro una encolont Belge, alia* . . .

The two loafers had observed his eavesdropping. They frowned, lowered their voices, and moved off.

No, the hypothesis of delirium might be a tough one, but it offered fewer difficulties than that of the time-slip.

If he was imaging things, was he really standing in front of the Pantheon and imaging that the people were dressed and speaking in the manner of the period 300-900 A.D.? Or was he lying in a hospital bed recovering from near-electrocution and imaging he was in front of the Pantheon? In the former case he ought to find a policeman and have himself taken to a hospital. In the latter this would be waste motion. For safety's sake he had better assume the former.

No doubt one of these people was really a policeman complete with shiny hat. What did he mean "really"? Let Bertrand Russell and Alfred Korzybski worry about that. How to find . . .

A beggar had been whining at him for a couple of minutes. Padway gave such a perfect impression of deafness that the ragged little hunchback moved off. Now another man was speaking to him. On his left palm the man held a string of beads with a cross, all in a heap. Between his right thumb and forefinger he held the clasp of the string. He raised his right hand until the whole string hung from it, then lowered it back onto his left palm, then raised it again, talking all the while.

Whenever and however all this was, that gesture assured Padway that he was still in Italy.

Padway asked in Italian: "Could you tell me where I could find a policeman?"

The man stopped his sales talk, shrugged, and replied, *"Non compr' endo."*

"Hey!" said Padway. The man paused. With great concentration Padway translated his request into what he hoped was Vulgar Latin.

The man thought, and said he didn't know.

Padway started to turn elsewhere. But the seller of beads called to another hawker: *"Marco!* The gentleman wants to find a police agent."

"The gentleman is brave. He is also crazy," replied Marco.

The bead-seller laughed. So did several people. Padway grinned a little; the people were human if not very helpful. He said: "Please, I—really—want—to—know."

The second hawker, who had a tray full of brass knickknacks tied around his neck, shrugged. He rattled off a paragraph that Padway could not follow.

Padway slowly asked the bead-seller: "What did he say?"

"He said he didn't know," replied the bead-seller. "I don't know either."

Padway started to walk off. The bead-seller called after him: "Mister."

"Yes?"

"Did you mean an agent of the municipal prefect?"

"Yes."

"Marco, where can the gentleman find an agent of the municipal prefect?"

"I don't know," said Marco.

The bead-seller shrugged. "Sorry, I don't know either."

If this were twentieth-century Rome, there would be no difficulty about finding a cop. And not even Benny the Moose could make a whole city change its language. So he must be in (a) a movie set, (b) ancient Rome (the Tancredi hypothesis), or (c) a figment of his imagination.

He started walking. Talking was too much of a strain.

It was not long before any lingering hopes about a movie set were dashed by the discovery that this alleged ancient city stretched for miles in all directions, and that its street plan was quite different from that of modern Rome. Padway found his little pocket map nearly useless.

The signs on the shops were in intelligible classical Latin. The spelling had remained as in Cæsar's time, if the pronunciation had not.

The streets were narrow, and for the most part not very crowded. The town had a drowsy, shabby-genteel, rundown personality, like that of Philadelphia.

At one relatively busy intersection Padway watched a man on a horse direct traffic. He would hold up a hand to stop an oxcart, and beckon a sedan chair across. The man wore a gaudily striped shirt and leather trousers. He looked like a central or northern European rather than an Italian.

Padway leaned against a wall, listening. A man would say a sentence just too fast for him to catch. It was like having your hook nibbled but never taken. By terrific concentration, Padway forced himself to think in Latin. He mixed his cases and numbers, but as long as he confined himself to simple sentences he did not have too much trouble with vocabulary.

A couple of small boys were watching him. When he looked at them they giggled and raced off.

It reminded Padway of those United States Government projects for the restoration of Colonial towns, like Williamsburg. But this looked like the real thing. No restoration included all the dirt and disease, the insults and altercations, that Padway had seen and heard in an hour's walk.

Only two hypotheses remained: delirium and time-slip. Delirium now seemed the less probable. He would act on the assumption that things were in fact what they seemed.

He couldn't stand there indefinitely. He'd have to ask questions and get himself oriented. The idea gave him gooseflesh. He had a phobia about accosting strangers. Twice he opened his mouth, but his glottis closed up tight with stage fright.

Come on, Padway, get a grip on yourself. "I beg your pardon, but could you tell me the date?"

The man addressed, a mild-looking person with a loaf of bread under his arm, stopped and looked blank. *"Qui' e'?* What is it?"

"I said, could you tell me the date?"

The man frowned. Was he going to be nasty? But all he said was, *"Non compr' endo."* Padway tried again, speaking very slowly. The man repeated that he did not understand.

Padway fumbled for his date-book and pencil. He wrote his request on a page of the date-book, and held the thing up.

The man peered at it, moving his lips. His face cleared. "Oh, you want to know the *date?*" said he.

"Sic, the date."

The man rattled a long sentence at him. It might as well have been in Trabresh. Padway waved his hands despairingly, crying, *"Lento!"*

The man backed up and started over. "I said I understood you, and I thought it was October 9th, but I wasn't sure because I couldn't remember whether my mother's wedding anniversary came three days ago or four."

"What year?"

"What *year?*"

"Sic, what year?"

"Twelve eighty-eight *Anno Urbis Conditae.*"

It was Padway's turn to be puzzled. "Please, what is that in the Christian era?"

"You mean, how many years since the birth of Christ?"

"Hoc ille—that's right."

"Well, now—I don't know; five hundred and something. Better ask a priest, stranger."

"I will," said Padway. "Thank you."

"It's nothing," said the man, and went about his business. Padway's knees were weak, though the man hadn't bitten him, and had answered his question in a civil enough manner. But it sounded as though Padway, who was a peaceable man, had not picked a very peaceable period.

What was he to do? Well, what would any sensible man do under the circumstances? He'd have to find a place to sleep and a method of making a living. He was a little startled when he realized how quickly he had accepted the Tancredi theory as a working hypothesis.

He strolled up an alley to be out of sight and began going through his pockets. The roll of Italian bank notes would be about as useful as a broken five-cent mousetrap. No, even less; you might be able to fix a mousetrap. A book of American Express traveler's checks, a Roman street-car transfer, an Illinois driver's license, a leather case full of keys—all ditto. His pen, pencil, and lighter would be useful as long as ink, leads, and lighter fuel held out. His pocketknife and his watch would undoubtedly fetch good prices, but he wanted to hang onto them as long as he could.

He counted the fistful of small change. There were just twenty coins, beginning with four ten-lire silver cartwheels. They added up to forty-nine lire, eight centesimi, or about five dollars. The silver and bronze should be exchangeable. As for the nickel fifty-centesimo and twenty-centesimo pieces, he'd have to see. He started walking again.

He stopped before an establishment that advertised itself as that of S. Dentatus, goldsmith and money changer. He took a deep breath and went in.

S. Dentatus had a face rather like that of a frog. Padway laid out his change and said: "I . . . I should like to change this into local money, please." As usual he had to repeat the sentence to make himself understood.

S. Dentatus blinked at the coins. He picked them up, one by one, and scratched at them a little with a pointed instrument. "Where do these—you—come from?" he finally croaked.

"America."

"Never heard of it."

"It is a long way off."

"Hm-m-m. What are these made of? Tin?" The money changer indicated the four nickel coins.

"Nickel."

"What's that? Some funny metal they have in your country?"

"Hoc ille."

"What's it worth?"

Padway thought for a second of trying to put a fantasti-
cally high value on the coins. While he was working up his
courage, S. Dentatus interrupted his thoughts:

"It doesn't matter, because I wouldn't touch the stuff.
There wouldn't be any market for it. But these other pieces
—let's see—" He got out a balance and weighed the
bronze coins, and then the silver coins. He pushed counters
up and down the grooves of a little bronze abacus, and
said: "They're worth just under one solidus. Give you a solidus even for them."

Padway didn't answer immediately. Eventually he'd have
to take what was offered, as he hated the idea of bargaining and didn't know the values of the current money. But
to save his face he had to appear to consider the offer
carefully.

A man stepped up to the counter beside him. He was a
heavy, ruddy man with a flaring brown mustache and his
hair in a long or Ginger Rogers bob. He wore a linen
blouse and long leather pants. He grinned at Padway, and
reeled off: *"Ho, frijond, habais faurthei! Alai skalljans
sind waidedjans."*

Oh, Lord, another language! Padway answered: "I . . .
I am sorry, but I do not understand."

The man's face fell a little; he dropped into Latin: "Sorry, thought you were from the Chersonese, from your
clothes. I couldn't stand around and watch a fellow Goth
swindled without saying anything, ha, ha!"

The Goth's loud, explosive laugh made Padway jump a
little; he hoped nobody noticed. "I appreciate that. What is
this stuff worth?"

"What has he offered you?" Padway told him. "Well,"
said the man, "even I can see that you're being hornswog-
gled. You give him a fair rate, Sextus, or I'll make you eat
your own stock. That would be funny, ha, ha!"

S. Dentatus sighed resignedly. "Oh, very well, a solidus
and a half. How am I to live, with you fellows interfering
with legitimate business all the time? That would be, at the
current rate of exchange, one solidus thirty-one sesterces."

"What is this about a rate of exchange?" asked Padway.

The Goth answered: "The gold-silver rate. Gold has
been going down the last few months."

Padway said: "I think I will take it all in silver."

While Dentatus sourly counted out ninety-three sesterces, the Goth asked: "Where do you come from? Somewhere up in the Hunnish country?"

"No," said Padway, "a place farther than that, called America. You have never heard of it, have you?"

"No. Well now, that's interesting. I'm glad I met you, young fellow. It'll give me something to tell the wife about. She thinks I head for the nearest brothel every time I come to town, ha, ha!" He fumbled in his handbag and brought out a large gold ring and an unfaceted gem. "Sextus, this thing came out of its setting again. Fix it up, will you? And no substitutions, mind."

As they went out the Goth spoke to Padway in a lowered voice. "The real reason I'm glad to come to town is that somebody put a curse on my house."

"A curse? What kind of a curse?"

The Goth nodded solemnly. "A shortness-of-breath curse. When I'm home I can't breathe. I go around like this —" He gasped asthmatically. "But as soon as I get away from home I'm all right. And I think I know who did it."

"Who?"

"I foreclosed a couple of mortgages last year. I can't prove anything against the former owners, *but*—" He winked ponderously at Padway.

"Tell me," said Padway, "do you keep animals in your house?"

"Couple of dogs. There's the stock, of course, but we don't let them in the house. Though a shoat got in yesterday and ran away with one of my shoes. Had to chase it all over the damned farm. I must have been a sight, ha, ha!"

"Well," said Padway, "try keeping the dogs outside all the time and having your place well swept every day. That might stop your—uh—wheezing."

"Now, that's interesting. You really think it would?"

"I do not know. Some people get the shortness of breath from dog hairs. Try it for a couple of months and see."

"I still think it's a curse, young fellow, but I'll try your scheme. I've tried everything from a couple of Greek physicians to one of St. Ignatius' teeth, and none of them works." He hesitated. "If you don't mind, what were you in your own country?"

Padway thought quickly, then remembered the few acres he owned in down-state Illinois. "I had a farm," he said.

"That's fine," roared the Goth, clapping Padway on the back with staggering force. I'm a friendly soul but I don't want to get mixed up with people too far above or below my own class, ha, ha! My name is Nevitta; Nevitta Gummund's son. If you're passing up the Falminian Way sometime, drop in. My place is about eight miles north of here."

"Thanks. My name is Martin Padway. Where would be a good place to rent a room?"

"That depends. If I didn't want to spend too much money I'd pick a place farther down the river. Plenty of boarding houses over toward the Viminal Hill. Say, I'm in no hurry; I'll help you look." He whistled sharply and called: *"Hermann, hiri her!"*

Hermann, who was dressed much like his master, got up off the curb and trotted down the street leading two horses, his leather pants making a distinctive *flop-flop* as he ran.

Nevitta set out a brisk walk, Hermann leading the horses behind. Nevitta said: "What did you say your name was?"

"Martin Padway—Martinus is good enough." (Padway properly pronounced it Mar*tee*no.)

Padway did not want to impose on Nevitta's good nature, but he wanted the most useful information he could get. He thought a minute, then asked: "Could you give me the names of a few people in Rome, lawyers and physicians and such, to go to when I need them?"

"Sure. If you want a lawyer specializing in cases involving foreigners, Valerius Mummius is your man. His office is alongside of the Aemilian Basilica. For a physician try my friend Leo Vekkos. He's a good fellow as Greeks go. But personally I think the relic of a good Arian saint like Asterius is as effective as all their herbs and potations."

"It probably is at that," said Padway. He wrote the names and addresses in his date-book. "How about a banker?"

"I don't have much truck with them; hate the idea of getting in debt. But if you want the name of one, there's

Thomasus the Syrian, near the Aemilian Bridge. Keep your eyes open if you deal with him."

"Why, isn't he honest?"

"Thomasus? Sure he's honest. You just have to watch him, that's all. Here, this looks like a place you could stay." Nevitta pounded on the door, which was opened by a frowsy superintendent.

This man had a room, yes. It was small and ill-lighted. It smelled. But then so did all of Rome. The superintendent wanted seven sesterces a day.

"Offer him half," said Nevitta to Padway in a stage whisper.

Padway did. The superintendent acted as bored by the ensuing haggling as Padway was. Padway got the room for five sesterces.

Nevitta squeezed Padway's hand in his large red paw. "Don't forget, Martinus, come see me some time. I always like to hear a man who speaks Latin with a worse accent than mine, ha, ha!" He and Hermann mounted and trotted off.

Padway hated to see them go. But Nevitta had his own business to tend to. Padway watched the stocky figure round a corner, then entered the gloomy, creaking boarding house.

CHAPTER II

PADWAY AWOKE EARLY with a bad taste in his mouth, and a stomach that seemed to have some grasshopper in its ancestry. Perhaps that was the dinner he'd eaten—not bad, but unfamiliar—consisting mainly of stew smothered in leeks. The restaurateur must have wondered when Padway made plucking motions at the table top; he was unthinkingly trying to pick up a knife and fork that weren't there.

One might very well sleep badly the first night on a bed consisting merely of a straw-stuffed mattress. And it had cost him an extra sesterce a day, too. An itch made him pull up his undershirt. Sure enough, a row of red spots on his midriff showed that he had not, after all, slept alone.

He got up and washed with the soap he had bought the previous evening. He had been pleasantly surprised to find that soap had already been invented. But when he broke a piece off the cake, which resembled a slightly decayed pumpkin pie, he found that the inside was soft and gooey because of incomplete potash-soda metathesis. Moreover, the soap was so alkaline that the thought he might as well have cleaned his hands and face by sandpapering.

Then he made a determined effort to shave with olive oil and a sixth-century razor. The process was so painful that he wondered if it mightn't be better to let nature take its course.

He was in a tight fix, he knew. His money would last about a week—with care, perhaps a little longer.

If a man knew he was going to be whisked back into the past, he would load himself down with all sorts of useful junk in preparation, an encyclopedia, texts on metallurgy, mathematics, and medicine, a slide rule, and so forth. And a gun, with plenty of ammunition.

But Padway had no gun, no encyclopedia, nothing but what an ordinary twentieth-century man carries in his pockets. Oh, a little more, because he'd been traveling at the time: such useful things as the traveler's checks, a hopelessly anachronistic street map, and his passport. And he had his wits. He'd need them.

The problem was to find a way of using his twentieth-century knowledge that would support him without getting him into trouble. You couldn't, for example, set out to build an automobile. It would take several lifetimes to collect the necessary materials, and several more to learn how to handle them and to worry them into the proper form. Not to mention the question of fuel.

The air was fairly warm, and he thought of leaving his hat and vest in the room. But the door had the simplest kind of ward lock, with a bronze key big enough to be presented by a mayor to a visiting dignitary. Padway was sure he could pick the lock with a knife blade. So he took all his clothes along. He went back to the same restaurant for breakfast. The place had a sign over the counter reading, "RELIGIOUS ARGUMENTS NOT ALLOWED." Padway asked the proprietor how to get to the address of Thomasus the Syrian.

The man said: "You follow along Long Street down to the Arch of Constantine, and then New Street to the Julian Basilica, and then you turn left onto Tuscan Street, and—" and so on.

Padway made him repeat it twice. Even so, it took most of the morning to find his objective. His walk took him past the Forum area, full of temples, most of whose columns had been removed for use in the five big and thirty-odd little churches scattered around the city. The temples looked pathetic, like a Park Avenue doorman bereft of his pants.

At the sight of the Ulpian Library, Padway had to suppress an urge to say to hell with his present errand. He loved burrowing into libraries, and he definitely did not love the idea of bearding a strange banker in a strange land with a strange proposition. In fact, the idea scared him silly, but his was the kind of courage that shows itself best when its owner is about to collapse from blue funk. So he grimly kept on toward the Tiber.

Thomasus hung out in a shabby two-story building. The Negro at the door—probably a slave—ushered Padway into what he would have called a living room. Presently the banker appeared. Thomasus was a paunchy, bald man with a cataract on his left eye. He gathered his shabby robe about him, sat down, and said: "Well, young man?"

"I"—Padway swallowed and started again—"I'm interested in a loan."

"How much?"

"I don't know yet. I want to start a business, and I'll have to investigate prices and things first."

"You want to start a new business? In Rome? *Hm-m-m.*" Thomasus rubbed his hands together. "What security can you give?"

"None at all."

"*What?*"

"I said, none at all. You'd just have to take a chance on me."

"But . . . but, my dear sir, don't you know anybody in town?"

"I know a Gothic farmer named Nevitta Gummund's son. He sent me hither."

"Oh, yes, Nevitta. I know him slightly. Would he go your note?"

Padway thought. Nevitta, despite his expansive gestures, had impressed him as being pretty close where money was concerned. "No," he said, "I don't think he would."

Thomasus rolled his eyes upward. "Do You hear that, God? He comes in here, a barbarian who hardly knows Latin, and admits that he has no security and no guarantors, and still he expects me to lend him money! Did You ever hear the like?"

"I think I can make you change your mind," said Padway.

Thomasus shook his head and made clucking noises. "You certainly have plenty of self-confidence, young man; I admit as much. What did you say your name was?" Padway told him what he had told Nevitta. "All right, what's your scheme?"

"As you correctly inferred," said Padway, hoping he was showing the right mixture of dignity and cordiality, "I'm a foreigner. I just arrived from a place called America. That's a long way off, and naturally it has a lot of customs and features different from those of Rome. Now, if you could back me in the manufacture of some of our commodities that are not known here—"

"Ai!" yelped Thomasus, throwing up his hands. "Did You hear that, God? He doesn't want me to back him in some well-known business. Oh, no. He wants me to start some newfangled line that nobody ever heard of! I couldn't think of such a thing, Martinus. What was it you had in mind?"

"Well, we have a drink made from wine, called brandy, that ought to go well."

"No, I couldn't consider it. Though I admit that Rome needs manufacturing establishments badly. When the capital was moved to Ravenna all revenue from Imperial salaries was cut off, which is why the population has shrunk so the last century. The town is badly located, and hasn't any real reason for being any more. But you can't get anybody to do anything about it. King Thiudahad spends his time writing Latin verse. Poetry! But no, young man, I couldn't put money into a wild project for making some weird barbarian drink."

Padway's knowledge of sixth-century history was beginning to come back to him. He said: "Speaking of Thiudahad, has Queen Amalaswentha been murdered yet?"

"Why"—Thomasus looked sharply at Padway with his good eye—"yes, she has." That meant that Justinian, the "Roman" emperor of Constantinople, would soon begin his disastrously successful effort to reconquer Italy for the Empire. "But why did you put your question that way?"

Padway asked. "Do—do you mind if I sit down?"

Thomasus said he didn't. Padway almost collapsed into a chair. His knees were weak. Up to now his adventure had seemed like a complicated and difficult masquerade party. His own question about the murder of Queen Amalaswentha had brought home to him all at once the fearful hazards of life in this world.

Thomasus repeated: "I asked why, young sir, you put your question that way?"

"What way?" asked Padway innocently. He saw where he'd made a slip.

"You asked whether she had been murdered *yet*. That sounds as though you had known ahead of time that she would be killed. Are you a soothsayer?"

There were no flies on Thomasus. Padway remembered Nevitta's advice to keep his eyes open.

He shrugged. "Not exactly. I heard before I came here that there had been trouble between the two Gothic sovereigns, and that Thiudahad would put his co-ruler out of the way if he had a chance. I—uh—just wondered how it came out, that's all."

"Yes," said the Syrian. "It was a shame. She was quite a woman. Good-looking, too, though she was in her forties. They caught her in her bath last summer and held her head under. Personally I think Thiudahad's wife Gudelinda put the old jelly-fish up to it. He wouldn't have nerve enough by himself."

"Maybe she was jealous," said Padway. "Now, about the manufacture of that barbarian drink, as you call it—"

"What? *You* are a stubborn fellow. It's absolutely out of the question, though. You have to be careful, doing business here in Rome. It's not like a growing town. Now, if this were Constantinople—" he sighed. "You can really make money in the East. But I don't care to live there, with Justinian making life exciting for the heretics, as he calls them. What's your religion, by the way?"

"What's yours? Not that it makes any difference to me."

"Nestorian."

"Well," said Padway carefully, "I'm what we call a Congregationalist." (It was not really true, but he guessed an agnostic would hardly be popular in this theology-mad world.) "That's the nearest thing we have to Nestorianism in my country. But about the manufacture of brandy—"

"Nothing doing, young man. Absolutely not. How much equipment would you need to start?"

"Oh, a big copper kettle and a lot of copper tubing, and a stock of wine for the raw material. It wouldn't have to be good wine. And I could get started quicker with a couple of men to help me."

"I'm afraid it's too much of a gamble. I'm sorry."

"Look here, Thomasus, if I show you how you can halve the time it takes you to do your accounts, would you be interested?"

"You mean you're a mathematical genius or something?"

"No, but I have a system I can teach your clerks."

Thomasus closed his eyes like some Levantine Buddha. "Well—if you don't want more than fifty solidi—"

"All business is a gamble, you know."

"That's the trouble with it. But—I'll do it, *if* your accounting system is as good as you say it is."

"How about interest?" asked Padway.

"Three per cent."

Padway was startled. Then he asked. "Three per cent per what?"

"Per month, of course."

"Too much."

"Well, what do you expect?"

"In my country six per cent per year is considered fairly high."

"You mean you expect *me* to lend you money at that rate? *Ai!* Did You hear that, God? Young man, you ought to go live among the wild Saxons, to teach them something about piracy. But I like you, so I'll make it twenty-five per year."

"Still too much. I might consider seven and a half."

"You're being ridiculous. I wouldn't consider less than twenty for a minute."

"No. Nine per cent, perhaps."

"I'm not even interested. Too bad; it would have been nice to do business with you. Fifteen."

"That's out, Thomasus. Nine and a half."

"Did You hear that, God? He wants me to make him a present of my business! Go away, Martinus. You're wasting your time here. I couldn't possibly come down any more. Twelve and a half. That's absolutely the bottom."

"Ten."

"Don't you understand Latin? I said that was the bottom. Good day; I'm glad to have met you." When Padway got up, the banker sucked his breath through his teeth as though he had been wounded unto death, and rasped: "Eleven."

"Ten and a half."

"Would you mind showing your teeth? My word, they are human after all. I thought maybe they were shark's teeth. Oh, very well. This sentimental generosity of mine will be my ruin yet. And now let's see that accounting system of yours."

An hour later three chagrined clerks sat in a row and regarded Padway with expressions of, respectively, wonderment, apprehension, and active hatred. Padway had just finished doing a simple piece of long division with Arabic numerals at the time when the three clerks, using Roman numerals, had barely gotten started on the interminable trial-and-error process that their system required. Padway translated his answers back into Roman, wrote it out on his tablet, and handed the tablet to Thomasus.

"There you are," he said. "Have one of the boys check it by multiplying the divisor by the quotient. You might as well call them off their job; they'll be at it all night."

The middle-aged clerk, the one with the hostile expression, copied down the figures and began checking grimly. When after a long time he finished, he threw down his stylus. "That man's a sorcerer of some sort," he growled. "He does the operations in his head, and puts down all those silly marks just to fool us."

"Not at all," said Padway urbanely. "I can teach you to do the same."

"What? *Me* take lessons from a long-trousered barbarian? I—" he started to say more, but Thomasus cut him off by saying that he'd do as he was told, and no back talk. "Is that so?" sneered the man. "I'm a free Roman citizen, and I've been keeping books for twenty years. I guess I know my business. If you want a man to use that heathen system, go buy yourself some cringing Greek slave. I'm through!"

"Now see what you've done!" cried Thomasus when the clerk had taken his coat off the peg and marched out. "I shall have to hire another man, and with this labor shortage—"

"That's all right," soothed Padway. "These two boys will be able to do all the work of three easily, once they learn American arithmetic. And that isn't all; we have something called double-entry bookkeeping, which enables you to tell any time how you stand financially, and to catch errors—"

"Do You hear that, God? He wants to turn the whole banking business upside down! Please, dear sir, one thing at a time; or you'll drive us mad! I'll grant your loan, I'll help you buy your equipment. Only don't spring any more of your revolutionary methods just now!" He continued more calmly: "What's that bracelet I see you looking at from time to time?"

Padway extended his wrist. "It's a portable sundial, of sorts. We call it a watch."

"A *vatcha,* hm? It looks like magic. Are you sure you aren't a sorcerer after all?" He laughed nervously.

"No," said Padway. "It's a simple mechanical device, like a—a water clock."

"Ah. I see. But why a pointer to show sixtieths of an hour? Surely nobody in his right mind would want to know the time as closely as that?"

"We find it useful."

"Oh, well, other lands, other customs. How about giving my boys a lesson in your American arithmetic now? Just to assure us that it is as good as you claim."

"All right. Give me a tablet." Padway scratched the numerals 1 to 9 in the wax, and explained them. "Now," he said, "this is the important part." He drew a circle. "This is our character meaning *nothing*."

The younger clerk scratched his head. "You mean it's a symbol without meaning? What would be the use of that?"

"I didn't say it was without meaning. It means nil, zero —what you have left when you take two away from two."

The older clerk looked skeptical. "It doesn't make sense to me. What is the use of a symbol for what does not exist?"

"You have a *word* for it, haven't you? Several words, in fact. And you find them useful, don't you?"

"I suppose so," said the older clerk. "But we don't use *nothing* in our calculations. Whoever heard of figuring the interest on a loan at no per cent? Or renting a house for no weeks?"

"Maybe," grinned the younger clerk, "the honorable sir can tell us how to make a profit on no sales—"

Padway snapped: "And we'll get through this explanation sooner with no interruptions. You'll learn the reason for the zero symbol soon enough."

It took an hour to cover the elements of addition. Then Padway said the clerks had had enough for one day; they should practice addition for a while every day until they could do it faster than by Roman numerals. Actually he was worn out. He was naturally a quick speaker, and to have to plod syllable by syllable through this foul language almost drove him crazy.

"Very ingenious, Martinus," wheezed the banker. "And now for the details of that loan. Of course you weren't serious in setting such an absurdly low figure as ten and a half per cent—"

"What? You're damn right I was serious! And you agreed—"

"Now, Martinus. What I meant was that *after* my clerks had learned your system, if it was as good as you claimed, I'd consider lending you money at that rate. But meanwhile you can't expect me to give you my—"

Padway jumped up. "You—you wielder of a—oh, hell, what's Latin for *chisel?* If you won't—"

"Don't be hasty, my young friend. After all, you've given my boys their start; they can go alone from there if need be. So you might as well—"

"All right, you just let them try to go on from there. I'll find another banker and teach his clerks properly. Subtraction, multiplication, div—"

"*Ai!*" yelped Thomasus. "You can't go spreading this secret all over Rome! It wouldn't be fair to me!"

"Oh, can't I? Just watch. I could even make a pretty good living teaching it. If you think—"

"Now, now, let's not lose our tempers. Let's remember Christ's teachings about patience. I'll make a special concession because you're just starting out in business . . ."

Padway got his loan at ten and a half. He agreed grudgingly not to reveal his arithmetic elsewhere until the first loan was paid off.

Padway bought a copper kettle at what he would have called a junk shop. But nobody had ever heard of copper tubing. After he and Thomasus had exhausted the second-hand metal shops between the latter's house and the warehouse district at the south end of town, he started in on coppersmith's places. The coppersmiths had never heard of copper tubing, either. A couple of them offered to try to turn out some, but at astronomical prices.

"Martinus!" wailed the banker. "We've walked at least five miles, and my feet are giving out. Wouldn't lead pipe do just as well? You can get all you want of that."

"It would do fine except for one thing," said Padway, "we'd probably poison our customers. And that *might* give the business a bad name, you know."

"Well, I don't see that you're getting anywhere as it is."

Padway thought a minute while Thomasus and Ajax, the Negro slave, who was carrying the kettle, watched him. "If I could hire a man who was generally handy with tools, and had some metal-working experience, I could show him how to make copper tubing. How do you go about hiring people here?"

"You don't," said Thomasus. "It just happens. You could buy a slave—but you haven't enough money. I shouldn't care to put up the price of a good slave into your venture. And it takes a skilled foreman to get enough work out of a slave to make him a profitable investment."

Padway said, "How would it be to put a sign in front of your place, stating that a position is open?"

"What?" squawked the banker. "Do You hear that, God? First he seduces my money away from me on this wild plan. Now he wants to plaster my house with signs! Is there no limit—"

"Now, Thomasus, don't get excited. It won't be a big sign, and it'll be very artistic. I'll paint it myself. You want me to succeed, don't you?"

"It won't work, I tell you. Most workmen can't read. And I won't have you demean yourself by manual labor that way. It's ridiculous; I won't consider it. About how big a sign did you have in mind?"

Padway dragged himself to bed right after dinner. There was no way, as far as he knew, of getting back to his own time. Never again would he know the pleasures of the *American Journal of Archaeology,* of Mickey Mouse, of flush toilets, of speaking the simple, rich, sensitive English language . . .

Padway hired his man the third day after his first meeting with Thomasus the Syrian. The man was a dark, cocky little Sicilian named Hannibal Scipio.

Padway had meanwhile taken a short lease on a tumble-down house on the Quirinal, and collected such equipment and personal effects as he thought he would need. He bought a short-sleeved tunic to wear over his pants, with the idea of making himself less conspicuous. Adults seldom paid much attention to him in this motley town, but he was tired of having small boys follow him through the streets.

He did, however, insist on having ample pockets sewn into the tunic, despite the tailor's shocked protests at ruining a good, stylish garment with this heathen innovation.

He whittled a mandrel out of wood and showed Hannibal Scipio how to bend the copper stripping around it. Hannibal claimed to know all that was necessary about soldering. But when Padway tried to bend the tubing into shape for his still, the seams popped open with the greatest of ease. After that Hannibal was a little less cocky—for a while.

Padway approached the great day of his first distillation with some apprehension. According to Tancredi's ideas this was a new branch of the tree of time. But mightn't the professor have been wrong, so that, as soon as Padway did anything drastic enough to affect all subsequent history, he would make the birth of Martin Padway in 1908 impossible, and disappear?

"Shouldn't there be an incantation or something?" asked Thomasus the Syrian.

"No," said Padway. "As I've already said three times, this isn't magic." Looking around though, he could see how some mumbo-jumbo might have been appropriate: running his first large batch off at night in a creaky old house, illuminated by flickering oil lamps, in the presence of only Thomasus, Hannibal Scipio, and Ajax. All three looked apprehensive, and the Negro seemed all teeth and eyeballs. He stared at the still as if he expected it to start producing demons in carload lots any minute.

"It takes a long time, doesn't it?" said Thomasus, rubbing his pudgy hands together nervously. His good eye glittered at the nozzle from which drop after yellow drop slowly dripped.

"I think that's enough," said Padway. "We'll get mostly water if we continue the run." He directed Hannibal to remove the kettle and poured the contents of the receiving flask into a bottle. "I'd better try it first," he said. He poured out a little into a cup, sniffed, and took a swallow. It was definitely not good brandy. But it would do.

"Have some?" he said to the banker.

"Give some to Ajax first."

Ajax backed away, holding his hands in front of him, yellow palms out. "No, please, master——"

He seemed so alarmed that Thomasus did not insist. "Hannibal, how about you?"

"Oh, no," said Hannibal. "Meaning no disrespect, but I've got a delicate stomach. The least little thing upsets it. And if you're all through, I'd like to go home. I didn't sleep well last night." He yawned theatrically. Padway let him go, and took another swallow.

"Well," said Thomasus, "if you're sure it won't hurt me, I might take just a little." He took just a little, then coughed violently, spilling a few drops from the cup. "Good God, man, what are your insides made of? That's volcano juice!" As his coughing subsided, a saintlike expression appeared. "It does warm you up nicely inside, though, doesn't it?" He screwed up his face and his courage, and finished the cup in one gulp.

"Hey," said Padway. "Go easy. That isn't wine."

"Oh, don't worry about me. Nothing makes me drunk."

Padway got out another cup and sat down. "Maybe you can tell me one thing that I haven't got straight yet. In my country we reckon years from the birth of Christ. When I asked a man, the day I arrived, what year it was, he said 1288 after the founding of the city. Now, can you tell me how many years before Christ Rome was founded? I've forgotten."

Thomasus took another slug of brandy and thought. "Seven hundred and fifty-four—no, 753. That means that this is the year of our Lord 535. That's the system the church uses. The Goths say the second year of Thiudahad's reign, and the Byzantines the first year of the consulship of Flavius Belisarius. Or the somethingth year of Justinian *imperium*. I can see how it might confuse you." He drank some more. "This is a wonderful invention, isn't it?" He held his cup up and turned it this way and that. "Let's have some more. I think you'll make a success, Martinus."

"Thanks. I hope so."

"Wonderful invention. Course it'll be a success. Couldn't help being a success. A big success. Are You listening, God? Well, make sure my friend Martinus has a big success.

"I know a successful man when I see him, Martinus. Been picking them for years. That's how I'm such a success in the banking business. Success—success—let's drink to success. Beautiful success. Gorgeous success.

"I know what, Martinus. Let's go some place. Don't like drinking to success in this old ruin. You know, atmosphere. Some place where there's music. How much brandy have you got left? Good, bring the bottle along."

The joint was in the theater district on the north side of the Capitoline. The "music" was furnished by a young woman who twanged a harp and sang songs in Calabrian dialect, which the cash customers seemed to find very funny.

"Let's drink to—" Thomasus started to say "success" for the thirtieth time, but changed his mind. "Say, Martinus, we'd better buy some of this lousy wine, or he'll have us thrown out. How does this stuff mix with wine?" At Padway's expression, he said: "Don't worry, Martinus, old friend, this is on me. Haven't made a night of it in years. You know, family man." He winked and snapped his fingers for the waiter. When he had finally gotten through his little ceremony, he said: "Just a minute, Martinus, old friend, I see a man who owes me money. I'll be right back." He waddled unsteadily across the room.

A man at the next table asked Padway suddenly: "What's that stuff you and old one-eye have been drinking, friend?"

"Oh, just a foreign drink called brandy," said Padway uneasily.

"That's right, you're a foreigner, aren't you? I can tell by your accent." He screwed up his face, and then said: "I know; you're a Persian. I know a Persian accent."

"Not exactly," said Padway. "Farther away than that."

"That so? How do you like Rome?" The man had very large and very black eyebrows.

"Fine, so far," said Padway.

"Well, you haven't seen anything," said the man. "It hasn't been the same since the Goths came." He lowered his voice conspiratorially: "Mark my words, it won't be like this always, either!"

"You don't like the Goths?"

"No! Not with the persecution we have to put up with!"

"Persecution?" Padway raised his eyebrows.

"Religious persecution. We won't stand for it forever."

"I thought the Goths let everybody worship as they pleased."

"That's just it! We Orthodox are forced to stand around and watch Arians and Monophysites and Nestorians and Jews going about their business unmolested, as if they owned the country. If that isn't persecution, I'd like to know what is!"

"You mean that you're persecuted because the heretics and such are not?"

"Certainly, isn't that obvious? We won't stand—What's your religion, by the way?"

"Well," said Padway, "I'm what in my country is called a Congregationalist. That's the nearest thing to Orthodoxy that we have."

"*Hm-m-m.* We'll make a good Catholic out of you, perhaps. So long as you're not one of these Maronites or Nestorians—"

"What's that about Nestorians?" said Thomasus, who had returned unobserved. "We who have the only logical view of the nature of the Son—that He was a man in whom the Father indwelt—"

"Nonsense!" snapped Eyebrows. "That's what you expect of half-baked amateur theologians. Our view—that of the dual nature of the Son—has been irrefutably shown—"

"Hear that, God? As if one person could have more than one nature—"

"You're all crazy!" rumbled a tall, sad-looking man with thin yellow hair, watery blue eyes, and a heavy accent. "We Arians abhor theological controversy, being sensible men. But if you want a sensible view of the nature of the Son—"

"You're a Goth?" barked Eyebrows tensely.

"No, I'm a Vandal, exiled from Africa. But as I was saying" —he began counting on his fingers—"either the Son was a man, or He was a god, or He was something in between. Well, now, we admit He wasn't a man. And there's only one God, so He wasn't a god. So He must have been—"

About that time things began to happen too fast for Padway to follow them all at once. Eyebrows jumped up and began yelling like one possessed. Padway couldn't follow him, except to note that the term "infamous heretics" occurred about once per sentence. Yellow Hair roared back at him, and other men began shouting from various parts of the room: "Eat him up, barbarian!" "This is an Orthodox country, and those who don't like it can go back where they——" "Damned nonsense about dual natures! We Monophysites——" "I'm a Jacobite, and I can lick any man in the place!" "Let's throw all the heretics out!" "I'm a Eunomian, and I can lick any *two* men in the place!"

Padway saw something coming and ducked, the mug missed his head by an inch and a half. When he looked up the room was a blur of action. Eyebrows was holding the self-styled Jacobite by the hair and punching his face; Yellow Hair was swinging four feet of bench around his head and howling a Vandal battle song. Padway hit one champion of Orthodoxy in the middle; his place was immediately taken by another who hit Padway in the middle. Then they were overborne by a rush of men.

As Padway struggled up through the pile of kicking, yelling humanity, like a swimmer striking for the surface, somebody got hold of his foot and tried to bite it off. As Padway was still wearing a pair of massive and practically indestructible English walking shoes, the biter got nowhere. So he shifted his attack to Padway's ankle. Padway yelped with pain, yanked his foot free, and kicked the biter in the face. The face yielded a little, and Padway wondered whether he'd broken a nose or a few teeth. He hoped he had.

The heretics seemed to be in a minority, that shrank as its members were beaten down and cast forth into darkness. Padway's eye caught the gleam of a knife blade and he thought it was well past his bedtime. Not being a religious man, he had no desire to be whittled up in the cause of the single, dual, or any other nature of Christ. He located Thomasus the Syrian under a table. When he tried to drag him out, the banker shrieked with terror and hugged the table leg as if it were a woman and he a sailor who had been six months at sea. Padway finally got him untangled.

The yellow-haired Vandal was still swinging his bench. Padway shouted at him. The man couldn't have understood in the uproar, but his attention was attracted, and when Padway pointed at the door he got the idea. In a few seconds he had cleared a path. The three stumbled out, pushed through the crowd that was beginning to gather outside, and ran. A yell behind them made them run faster, until they realized that it was Ajax, and slowed down to let him catch up.

They finally sat down on a park bench on the edge of the Field of Mars, only a few blocks from the Pantheon, where Padway had his first sight of post-Imperial Rome. Thomasus, when he got his breath, said: "Martinus, why did you let me drink so much of that heathen drink? Oh, my head! If I hadn't been drunk, I'd have had more sense than to start a theological argument."

"I tried to slow you down," said Padway mildly, "but you—"

"I know, I know. But you should have prevented me from drinking so much, forcibly if necessary. My head! What will my wife say? I never want to see that lousy barbarian drink again! What did you do with the bottle, by the way?"

"It got lost in the scuffle. But there wasn't much left in it anyway." Padway turned to the Vandal. "I guess I owe you some thanks for getting us out of there so quickly."

The man pulled his drooping mustache. "I was glad to do it, friend. Religious argument is no occupation for decent people. Permit me; my name is Fritharik Staifan's son." He spoke slowly, fumbling for words occasionally. "Once I was counted a man of noble family. Now I am merely a poor wanderer. Life holds nothing for me any more." Padway saw a tear glistening in the moonlight.

"You said you were a Vandal?"

Fritharik sighed like a vacuum cleaner. "Yes, mine was one of the finest estates in Carthage, before the Greeks came. When King Gelimer ran away, and our army scattered, I escaped to Spain, and thence I came hither last year."

"What are you doing now?"

"Alas, I am not doing anything now. I had a job as

bodyguard to a Roman patrician until last week. Think of it—a noble Vandal serving as bodyguard! But my employer got set on the idea of converting me to Orthodoxy. That," said Fritharik with dignity, "I would not allow. So here I am. When my money is gone, I don't know what will become of me. Perhaps I will kill myself. Nobody would care." He sighed some more, then said: "You aren't looking for a good, reliable bodyguard, are you?"

"Not just now," said Padway, "but I may be in a few weeks. Do you think you can postpone your suicide until then?"

"I don't know. It depends on how my money holds out. I have no sense about momey. Being of noble birth, I never needed any. I don't know whether you'll ever see me alive again." He wiped his eyes on his sleeve.

"Oh, for heaven's sake," said Thomasus, "there are plenty of things you could do."

"No," said Fritharik tragically. "You wouldn't understand, friend. There are considerations of honor. And anyway, what has life to offer me? Did you say you might be able to take me on later?" he asked Padway. Padway said yes, and gave him his address. "Very well, friend, I shall probably be in a nameless lonely grave before two weeks have passed. But if not, I'll be around."

CHAPTER III

AT THE END of the week, Padway was gratified not only by the fact that he had not vanished into thin air, and by the appearance of the row of bottles on the shelf, but by the state of his finances. Counting the five solidi for the first month's rent on the house, the six more that had gone into his apparatus, and Hannibal's wages and his own living expenses, he still had over thirty of his fifty borrowed solidi left. The first two items wouldn't recur for a couple of weeks, anyway.

"How much are you going to charge for that stuff?" asked Thomasus.

Padway thought. "It's a luxury article, obviously. If we can get some of the better-class restaurants to stock it, I don't see why we shouldn't get two solidi per bottle. At least until somebody discovers our secret and begins competing with us."

Thomasus rubbed his hands together. "At that rate, you could practically pay back your loan with the proceeds of the first week's sales. But I'm in no hurry; it might be better to reinvest them in the business. We'll see how things turn out. I think I know the restaurant we should start with."

Padway experienced a twinge of dread at the idea of trying to sell the restaurateur the idea. He was not a born salesman, and he knew it.

He asked: "How should I go about getting him to buy some of the stuff? I'm not very familiar with your Roman business methods."

"That's all right. He won't refuse, because he owes me money, and he's behind in his interest payments. I'll introduce you."

It came about as the banker had said. The restaurant owner, a puffy man named Gaius Attalus, glowered a bit at first. The entrepreneur fed him a little brandy by way of a sample, and he warmed up. Thomasus had to ask God whether He was listening only twice before Attalus agreed to Padway's price for half a dozen bottles.

Padway, who had been suffering from one of his periodic fits of depression all morning, glowed visibly as they emerged from the restaurant, his pockets pleasantly heavy with gold.

"I think," said Thomasus, "you had better hire that Vandal chap, if you're going to have money around the house. And I'd spend some of it on a good strong box."

So when Hannibal Scipio told Padway "There's a tall, gloomy-looking bird outside who says you said to come see you," he had the Vandal sent in and hired him almost at once.

When Padway asked Fritharik what he proposed to do his bodyguarding with, Fritharik looked embarrassed, chewed his mustache, and finally said: "I had a fine sword, but I hocked it to keep alive. It was all that stood between me and a nameless grave. Perhaps I shall end in one yet," he sighed.

"Stop thinking about graves for a while," snapped Padway, "and tell me how much you need to get your sword back."

"Forty solidi."

"Whew! Is it made of solid gold, or what?"

"No. But it's good Damascus steel, and has gems in the handle. It was all that I saved from my beautiful estate in Africa. You have no idea what a fine place I had—"

"Now, now!" said Padway. "For heaven's sake don't start crying! Here's five solidi; go buy yourself the best sword you can with that. I'm taking it out of your salary. If you want to save up to get this bejeweled cheese knife of yours back, that's your business." So Fritharik departed, and shortly thereafter reappeared with a secondhand sword clanking at his side.

"It's the best I could do for the money," he explained. "The dealer claimed it was Damascus work, but you can tell that the Damascus marks on the blade are fakes. This local steel is soft, but I suppose it will have to do. When I had my beautiful estate in Africa, the finest steel was none too good." He sighed gustily.

Padway examined the sword, which was a typical sixth-century *spatha* with a broad single-edged thirty-inch blade. It was, in fact, much like a Scotch broadsword without the fancy knuckle-guard. He also noticed that Fritharik Staifan's son, though as mournful as ever, stood straighter and walked with a more determined stride when wearing the sword. He must, Padway thought, feel practically naked without it.

"Can you cook?" Padway asked Fritharik.

"You hired me as a bodyguard, not as a housemaid, my lord Martinus. I have my dignity."

"Oh, nonsense, old man. I've been doing my own cooking, but it takes too much of my time. If I don't mind, you shouldn't. Now, can you cook?"

Fritharik pulled his mustache. "Well—yes."

"What, for instance?"

"I can do a steak. I can fry bacon."

"What else?"

"Nothing else. That is all I ever had occasion to do. Good red meat is the food for a warrior. I can't stomach these greens the Italians eat."

Padway sighed. He resigned himself to living on an unbalanced diet until—well, why not? He could at least inquire into the costs of domestic help.

Thomasus found a serving-wench for him who would cook, clean house, and make beds for an absurdly low wage. The wench was named Julia. She came from Apulia and talked dialect. She was about twenty, dark, stocky, and gave promise of developing tremendous heft in later years. She wore a single shapeless garment and padded about the house on large bare feet. Now and then she cracked a joke too rapidly for Padway to follow and shook with peals of laughter. She worked hard, but Padway had to teach her his ideas from the ground up. The first time he fumigated his house he almost frightened her out of her wits. The smell of sulphur dioxide sent her racing out the door shrieking that Satanas had come.

Padway decided to knock off on his fifth Sunday in Rome. For almost a month he had been working all day and most of the night, helping Hannibal to run the still, clean it, and unload casks of wine; and seeing restaurateurs who had received inquiries from their customers about this remarkable new drink.

In an economy of scarcity, he reflected, you didn't have to turn handsprings finding customers, once your commodity caught on. He was meditating striking Thomasus for a loan to build another still. This time he'd build a set of rolls and roll his own copper sheeting out of round stock, instead of trying to patch together this irregular hand-hammered stuff.

Just now, though, he was heartily sick of the business. He wanted fun, which to him meant the Ulpian Library. As he looked in the mirror, he thought he hadn't changed much inside. He disliked barging in on strangers and bargaining as much as ever. But outside none of his former friends would have known him. He had grown a short reddish beard. This was partly because he had never in his other life shaved with a guardless razor, and it gave him the jitters to do so; and partly because he had always secretly coveted a beard, to balance his oversized nose.

He wore another new tunic, a Byzantine-style thing with ballooning sleeves. The trousers of his tweed suit gave an incongruous effect, but he didn't fancy the short pants of the country, with winter coming on. He also wore a cloak, which was nothing but a big square blanket with a hole in the middle to put his head through. He had hired an old woman to make him socks and underwear.

Altogether he was pretty well pleased with himself. He admitted he had been lucky in finding Thomasus; the Syrian had been an enormous help to him.

He approached the library with much the same visceral tingle that a lover gets from the imminence of a meeting with his beloved. Nor was he disappointed. He felt like shouting when a brief nosing about the shelves showed him Berosus' *Chaldean History,* the complete works of Livius, Tacitus' *History of the Conquest of Britain,* and Cassiodorus' recently published *Gothic History* complete. Here was stuff for which more than one twentieth-century historian or archaeologist would cheerfully commit murder.

For a few minutes he simply dithered, like the proverbial ass between two haystacks. Then he decided that Cassiodorus would have the most valuable information to impart, as it dealt with an environment in which he himself was living. So he lugged the big volumes out and set to work. It was hard work, too, even for a man who knew Latin. The books were written in a semi-cursive minuscule hand with all the words run together. The incredibly wordy and affected style of the writer didn't bother him as it would have if he had been reading English; he was after facts.

"Excuse me, sir," said the librarian, "but is that tall barbarian with the yellow mustache your man?"

"I suppose so," said Padway. "What is it?"

"He's gone to sleep in the Oriental section, and he's snoring so that the readers are complaining."

"I'll tend to him," said Padway.

He went over and awakened Fritharik. "Can't you read?" he asked.

"No," said Fritharik quite simply. "Why should I? When I had my beautiful estate in Africa, there was no occasion—"

"Yes, I know all about your beautiful estate, old man. But you'll have to learn to read, or else do your snoring outside."

Fritharik went out somewhat huffily, muttering in his own East-German dialect. Padway's guess was that he was calling reading a sissy accomplishment.

When Padway got back to his table, he found an elderly Italian dressed with simple elegance going through his Cassiodorus. The man looked up and said: "I'm sorry; were you reading these?"

"That's all right," said Padway. "I wasn't reading all of them. If you're not using the first volume . . ."

"Certainly, certainly, my dear young man. I ought to warn you, though, to be careful to put it back in its proper place. Scylla cheated of her prey by Jason has no fury like that of our esteemed librarian when people misplace his books. And what, may I ask, do you think of the work of our illustrious pretorian prefect?"

"That depends," said Padway judiciously. "He has a lot of facts you can't get elsewhere. But I prefer my facts straight."

"How do you mean?"

"I mean with less flowery rhetoric."

"Oh, but my dear, dear young man! Here we moderns have at last produced a historian to rank with the great Livius, and you say you don't like—" He glanced up, lowered his voice, and leaned forward. "Just consider the delicate imagery, the glorious erudition! Such style! Such wit!"

"That's just the trouble. You can't give me Polybius, or even Julius Cæsar—"

"Julius Cæsar! Why everybody knows *he* couldn't write! They use his *Gallic War* as an elementary Latin text for foreigners! All very well for the skin-clad barbarian, who through the gloomy fastnesses of the northern forests pursues the sanguinary boar and horrid bear. But for cultivated men like ourselves—I ask you, my dear young man! Oh"—he looked embarrassed—"you will understand that in my remarks on foreigners I meant nothing personal. I perceive that you are an outlander, despite your obvious breeding and erudition. Are you by any chance from the fabled land of Hind, with its pearl-decked maidens and its elephants?"

"No, farther away than that," said Padway. He knew he had flushed a literary Roman patrician, of the sort who couldn't ask you to pass the butter without wrapping the request in three puns, four mythological illusions, and a dissertation on the manufacture of butter in ancient Crete. "A place called America. I doubt whether I should ever return, though."

"Ah, how right you are! Why should one live anywhere but in Rome if one can? But perhaps you can tell me of the wonders of far-off China, with its gold-paved streets!"

"I can tell you a little about it," said Padway cautiously. "For one thing, the streets aren't gold-paved. In fact they're mostly not paved at all."

"How disappointing! But I daresay that a truthful traveler returning from heaven would pronounce its wonders grossly overrated. We must get together, my excellent young sir. I am Cornelius Anicius."

Evidently, Padway thought, he was expected to know who Cornelius Anicius was. He introduced himself. Ah, he thought, enter romance. A pretty slim dark girl approached, addressed Anicius as "Father," and said that she had not been able to find the Sabellian edition of Persius Flaccus.

"Somebody is using it, no doubt," said Anicius. "Martinus, this is my daughter Dorothea. A veritable pearl from King Khusrau's headdress of a daughter, though I as her father may be prejudiced." The girl smiled sweetly at Padway and excused herself.

Anicius asked: "And now, my dear young man, what is your occupation?"

Without thinking, Padway said he was in business.

"Indeed? What sort of business?"

Padway told him. The patrician froze up as he digested

the information. He was still polite and smiling, but with a smile of a different sort.

"Well, well, that's interesting. Very interesting. I daresay you'll make a good financial success of your busines." He spoke the sentence with a slight difficulty, like a Y.M.C.A. secretary talking about the facts of life. "I suppose we aren't to blame for the callings wherein God stations us. But it's too bad you haven't tried the public service. That is the only way to rise above one's class, and an intelligent young man like you deserves to do so. And now, if you'll excuse me, I'll do some reading."

Padway had been hoping for an invitation to Anicius' house. But now that Anicius knew him to be a mere vulgar manufacturer, no invitation would be forthcoming. Padway looked at his watch; it was nearly lunch time. He went out and awoke Fritharik.

The Vandal yawned. "Find all the books you wanted, Martinus? I was just dreaming of my beautiful estate—"

"To hell with—" barked Padway, then shut his mouth.

"What?" said Fritharik. "Can't I even dream about the time I was rich and respected? That's not very—"

"Nothing, nothing. I didn't mean you."

"I'm glad of that. My one consolation nowadays is my memories. But what are you so angry at, Martinus? You look as if you could bite nails in two." When there was no answer, he went on: "It must have been something in those books. I'm glad I never learned to read. You get all worked up over things that happened long ago. I'd rather dream about my beaut—*oop!* I'm sorry, boss; I won't mention it again."

Padway and Thomasus the Syrian sat, along with several hundred naked Romans, in the steam room of the Baths of Diocletian. The banker looked around and leered: "I hear that in the old days they let the women into these baths, too. Right mixed in with the men. Of course that was in pagan times; there's nothing like that now."

"Christian morality, no doubt," said Padway dryly.

"Yes," chuckled Thomasus. "We moderns are *such* a moral people. You know what the Empress Theodora used to complain about?"

"Yes," said Padway, and told Thomasus what the empress used to complain about.

"Damn it!" cried Thomasus. "Every time I have a dirty story, either you've heard it, or you know a better one."

Padway didn't see fit to tell the banker that he had read that bit of dirt in a book that hadn't yet been written, namely, the *Anecdotes* by Procopius of Cæsarea.

Thomasus went on: "I've got a letter from my cousin Antiochus in Naples. He's in the shipping business. He has news from Constantinople." He paused impressively. "War."

"Between us and the Empire?"

"Between the Goths and the Empire, anyway. They've been carrying on mysterious dickerings ever since Amalaswentha was killed. Thiudahad has tried to duck responsibility for the murder, but I think our old poet-king has come to the end of his rope."

Padway said: "Watch Dalmatia and Sicily. Before the end of the year—" He stopped.

"Doing a bit of soothsaying?"

"No, just an opinion."

The good eye sparkled at Padway through the steam, very black and very intelligent. "Martinus, just who are you?"

"What do you mean?"

"Oh, there's something about you—I don't know how to put it—not just your funny way of putting things. You produce the most astonishing bits of knowledge, like a magician pulling rabbits out of his cap. And when I try to pump you about your own country or how you came hither, you change the subject."

"Well—" said Padway, wondering just how big a lie to risk. Then he thought of the perfect answer—a truthful one that Thomasus would be sure to misconstrue. "You see, I left my own country in a great hurry."

"Oh. For reasons of health, eh? I don't blame you for being cagy in that case." Thomasus winked.

When they were walking up Long Street toward Padway's house, Thomasus asked how the business was. Padway told him: "Pretty good. The new still will be ready next week. And I sold some copper strip to a merchant leaving for Spain. Right now I'm waiting for the murder."

"The *murder?*"

"Yes, Fritharik and Hannibal Scipio didn't get along. Hannibal's been cockier than ever since he's had a couple of men under him. He rides Fritharik."

"*Rides* him?"

"American vernacular, literally translated. Meaning that he subjects him to constant and subtle ridicule and insult. By the way, I'm going to pay off your loan when we get home."

"Entirely?"

"That's right. The money's in the strong box waiting for you."

"Splendid, my dear Martinus! But won't you need another?"

"I'm not sure," said Padway, who was sure that he would. "I was thinking of expanding my distillery."

"That's a great idea. Of course now that you're established we'll put our loans on a business basis—"

"Meaning?" said Padway.

"Meaning that the rate of interest will have to be adjusted. The normal rate, you know, is much higher—"

"Ha, ha," said Padway. "That's what I thought you had in mind. But now that you know the business is a sure one, you can afford to give me a lower rate."

"*Ai*, Martinus, that's absurd! Is that any way to treat me after all I've done for you?"

"You don't have to lend it if you don't want to. There are other bankers who'd be glad to learn American arithmetic—"

"Listen to him, God! It's robbery! It's extortion! I'll never give in! Go to your other bankers, see if I care!"

Three blocks of argument brought the interest rate down to ten per cent, which Thomasus said was cutting his own heart out and burning it on the altar of friendship.

When Padway had spoken of an impending murder, he had neither been passing off hindsight as foresight, nor trying to be literally prophetic. He was more astonished than Thomasus, when they entered his big workshop, to find Fritharik and Hannibal glaring like a couple of dogs who dislike each other's smell. Hannibal's two assistants were looking on with their backs to the door; thus nobody saw the newcomers.

Hannibal snarled: "What do you mean, you big cotton-head? You lie around all day, too lazy to turn over, and then you dare criticize me—"

"All I said," growled the Vandal in his clumsy, deliberate Latin, "was that the next time I caught you, I'd report it. Well I did, and I'm going to."

"I'll slit your lousy throat if you do!" yelled Hannibal.

Fritharik cast a short but pungent aspersion on the Sicilian's sex life. Hannibal whipped out a dagger and lunged at Fritharik. He moved with rattlesnake speed, but he used the instinctive but tactically unsound overhand stab. Fritharik, who was unarmed, caught his wrist with a smack of flesh on flesh, then lost it as Hannibal dug his point into the Vandal's forearm.

When Hannibal swung his arm up for another stab, Padway arrived and caught his arm. He hauled the little man away from his opponent, and immediately had to hang on for dear life to keep from being stabbed himself. Hannibal was shrieking in Sicilian patois and foaming a little at the mouth. Padway saw that he wanted to kill him. He jerked his face back as the dirty fingernails of Hannibal's left hand raked his nose, which was a target hard to miss.

Then there was a thump, and Hannibal collapsed, dropping his dagger. Padway let him slide to the floor, and saw that Nerva, the older of the two assistants, was holding a stool by one leg. It had all happened so quickly that Fritharik was just bending over to pick up a short piece of board for a weapon, and Thomasus and Carbo, the other workman, were still standing just inside the door.

Padway said to Nerva: "I think you're the man for my next foreman. What's this about, Fritharik?"

Fritharik didn't answer, he stalked toward the unconscious Hannibal with plain and fancy murder in his face.

"That's enough, Fritharik!" said Padway sharply. "No more rough stuff, or you're fired, too!" He planted himself in front of the intended victim. "What was he doing?"

The Vandal came to himself. "He was stealing bits of copper from stock and selling them. I tried to get him to stop without telling you; you know how it is if your fellow employees think you're spying on them. Please, boss, let me have one whack at him. I may be a poor exile, but no little Greek catamite—"

Padway refused permission. Thomasus suggested swearing out a complaint and having Hannibal arrested; Padway said no, he didn't want to get mixed up with the law. He did allow Fritharik to send Hannibal, when the Sicilian came to, out the front door with a mighty kick in the fundament. Exit villain, sneering, thought Padway as he watched the ex-foreman slink off.

Fritharik said: "I think that was a mistake, Martinus. I could have sunk his body in the Tiber without anybody's knowing. He'll make trouble for us."

Padway suspected that the last statement was correct. But he merely said: "We'd better bind your arm up. Your whole sleeve is blood-soaked. Julia, get a strip of linen and boil it. Yes, *boil* it!"

CHAPTER IV

PADWAY HAD RESOLVED not to let anything distract him from the task of assuring himself a livelihood. Until that was accomplished, he didn't intend to stick his neck out by springing gunpowder or the law of gravitation on the unsuspecting Romans.

But the banker's war talk reminded him that he was, after all, living in a political and cultural as well as an economic world. He had never, in his other life, paid more attention to current events than he had to. And in post-Imperial Rome, with no newspapers or electrical communication, it was even easier to forget about things outside one's immediate orbit.

He was living in the twilight of western classical civilization. The Age of Faith, better known as the Dark Ages, was closing down. Europe would be in darkness, from a scientific and technological aspect, for nearly a thousand years. That aspect was, to Padway's naturally prejudiced mind, the most, if not the only, important aspect of a civilization. Of course, the people among whom he was living had no conception of what was happening to them. The process was too slow to observe directly, even over the span of a life-time. They took their environment for granted, and even bragged about their modernity.

So what? Could one man change the course of history to the extent of preventing this interregnum? One man had changed the course of history before. Maybe. A Carlylean would say yes. A Tolstoyan or Marxist would say no; the environment fixes the pattern of a man's accomplishments and throws up the man to fit that pattern. Tancredi had expressed it differently by calling history a tough web, which would take a huge effort to distort.

How would one man go about it? Invention was the mainspring of technological development. But even in his own time, the lot of the professional inventor had been hard, without the handicap of a powerful and suspicious ecclesiasticism. And how much could he accomplish by simply "inventing," even if he escaped the unwelcome attentions of the pious? The arts of distilling and metal rolling were launched, no doubt, and so were Arabic numerals. But there was so much to be done, and only one lifetime to do it in.

What then? Business? He was already in it; the upper classes were contemptuous of it; and he was not naturally a businessman, though he could hold his own well enough in competition with these sixth-century yaps. Politics? In an age when victory went to the sharpest knife, and no moral rules of conduct were observable? *Br-r-r-r!*

How to prevent darkness from falling?

The Empire might have been together longer if it had had better means of communication. But the Empire, at least in the west, was hopelessly smashed, with Italy, Gaul, and Spain under the muscular thumbs of their barbarian "garrisons."

The answer was *Rapid communication and the multiple record*—that is, printing. Not even the most diligently destructive barbarian can extirpate the written word from a culture wherein the *minimum* edition of most books is fifteen hundred copies. There are just too many books.

So he would be a printer. The web might be tough, but maybe it had never been attacked by a Martin Padway.

"Good morning, my dear Martinus," said Thomasus. "How is the copper-rolling business?"

"So-so. The local smiths are pretty well stocked with strip, and not many of the shippers are interested in paying my prices for such a heavy commodity. But I think I'll clean up that last note in a few weeks."

"I'm glad to hear that. What will you do then?"

"That's what I came to see you about. Who's publishing books in Rome now?"

"Books? Books? Nobody, unless you count the copyists who replace worn-out copies for the libraries. There are a couple of bookstores down in the Agiletum, but their stock is all imported. The last man who tried to run a publishing business in Rome went broke years ago. Not enough demand, and not enough good authors. You're not thinking of going into it, I hope?"

"Yes, I am. I'll make money at it, too."

"What? You're crazy, Martinus. Don't consider it. I don't want to see you go broke after making such a fine start."

"I shan't go broke. But I'll need some capital to start."

"What? Another loan? But I've just told you that nobody can make money publishing in Rome. It's a proven fact. I won't lend you an as on such a harebrained scheme. How much do you think you'd need?"

"About five hundred solidi."

"*Ai, ai!* You've gone mad, my boy! What would you need such a lot for? All you have to do is buy or hire a couple of scribes—"

Padway grinned. "Oh, no. That's the point. It takes a scribe months to copy out a work like Cassiodorus' *Gothic History* by hand, and that's only one copy. No wonder a work like that costs fifty solidi per copy! I can build a machine that will turn out five hundred or a thousand copies in a few weeks, to retail for five or ten solidi. But it will take time and money to build the machine and teach an operator how to run it."

"But that's real money! God, are You listening? Well, please make my misguided young friend listen to reason! For the last time, Martinus, I won't consider it! How does the machine work?"

If Padway had known the travail that was in store for him, he might have been less confident about the possibilities of starting a printshop in a world that knew neither printing presses, type, printer's ink, nor paper. Writing ink was available, and so was papyrus. But it didn't take Padway long to decide that these would be impractical for his purposes.

His press, seemingly the most formidable job, proved the easiest. A carpenter down in the warehouse district promised to knock one together for him in a few weeks, though he manifested a not unnatural curiosity as to what Padway proposed to do with the contraption. Padway wouldn't tell him.

"It's not like any press I ever saw," said the man. "It doesn't look like a felt press. I know! You're the city's new executioner, and this is a newfangled torture instrument! Why didn't you want to tell me, boss? It's a perfectly respectable trade! But say, how about giving me a pass to the torture chamber the first time you use it? I want to be sure my work holds up, you know!"

For a bed they used a piece sawn off the top of a section of a broken marble column and mounted on wheels. All Padway's instincts revolted at this use of a monument of antiquity, but he consoled himself with the thought that one column mattered less than the art of printing.

For type, he contracted with a seal cutter to cut him a set of brass types. He had, at first, been appalled to discover that he would need ten to twelve thousand of the little things, since he could hardly build a type-casting machine, and would therefore have to print directly from the types. He had hoped to be able to print in Greek and Gothic as well as in Latin, but the Latin types alone set him back a round two hundred solidi. And the first sample set that the seal cutter ran off had the letters facing the wrong way and had to be melted up again. The type was what a twentieth-century printer would have called fourteen-point Gothic, and an engraver would have called sans-serif. With such big type he would not be able to get much copy on a page, but it would at least, he hoped, be legible.

Padway shrank from the idea of making his own paper. He had only a hazy idea of how it was done, except that it was a complicated process. Papyrus was too glossy and brittle, and the supply in Rome was meager and uncertain.

There remained vellum. Padway found that one of the tanneries across the Tiber turned out small quantities as a side line. It was made from the skins of sheep and goats by extensive scraping, washing, stretching, and paring. The price seemed reasonable. Padway rather staggered the owner of the tannery by ordering a thousand sheets at one crack.

He was fortunate in knowing that printer's ink was based on linseed oil and lampblack. It was no great trick to buy a bag of flaxseed and run it through a set of rolls like those he used for copper rolling, and to rig up a contraption consisting of an oil lamp, a water-filled bowl suspended and revolved over it, and a scraper for removing the lampblack. The only thing wrong with the resulting ink was that it wouldn't print. That is, it either made no impression or came off the type in shapeless gobs.

Padway was getting nervous about his finances; his five hundred solidi were getting low, and this seemed a cruel joke. His air of discouragement became so obvious that he caught his workers remarking on it behind their hands. But he grimly set out to experiment on his ink. Sure enough, he found that with a little soap in it, it would work fairly well.

In the middle of February Nevitta Grummund's son wandered in through the raw drizzle. When Fritharik showed him in, the Goth slapped Padway on the back so hard as to send him halfway across the room. "Well, well!" he bellowed. "Somebody gave me some of that terrific drink you've been selling, and I remembered your name. So I thought I'd look you up. Say, you got yourself well established in record time, for a stranger. Pretty smart young man, eh? Ha, ha!"

"Would you like to look around?" invited Padway.

"Only I'll have to ask you to keep my methods confidential. There's no law here protecting ideas, so I have to keep my things secret until I'm ready to make them public property."

"Sure, you can trust me. I wouldn't understand how your devices work anyhow."

In the machine shop Nevitta was fascinated by a crude wire-drawing machine that Padway had rigged up. "Isn't that pretty?" he said, picking up the roll of brass wire. "I'd like to buy some for my wife. It would make nice bracelets and earrings."

Padway hadn't anticipated that use of his products, but said he would have some ready in a week.

"Where do you get your power?" asked Nevitta.

Padway showed him the work-horse in the back yard walking around a shaft in the rain.

"Shouldn't think a horse would be efficient," said the Goth. "You could get a lot more power out of a couple of husky slaves. That is, if your driver knew his whip. Ha, ha!"

"Oh, no," said Padway. "Not this horse. Notice anything peculiar about his harness?"

"Well, yes, it *is* peculiar. But I don't know what's wrong with it."

"It's that collar over his neck. You people make your horses pull against a strap around the throat. Every time he pulls, the strap cuts into his windpipe and shuts off the poor animal's breath. That collar puts the load on his shoulders. If you were going to pull a load, you wouldn't hitch a rope around your neck to pull it with, would you?"

"Well," said Nevitta dubiously, "maybe you're right. I've been using my kind of harness for a long time, and I don't know that I'd care to change."

Padway shrugged. "Any time you want one of these outfits, you can get it from Metellus the Saddler on the Appian Way. He made this to my specifications. I'm not making them myself; I have too much else to do."

Here Padway leaned against the doorframe and closed his eyes.

"Aren't you feeling well?" asked Nevitta in alarm.

"No. My head weighs as much as the dome of the Pantheon. I think I'm going to bed."

"Oh, my word, I'll help you. Where's that man of mine? *Hermann!*" When Hermann appeared, Nevitta rattled a sentence of Gothic at him wherein Padway caught the name of Leo Vekkos.

Padway protested: "I don't want a physician—"

"Nonsense, my boy, it's no trouble. You were right about keeping the dogs outside. It cured my wheezes. So I'm glad to help you."

Padway feared the ministrations of a sixth-century physician more than he feared the grippe with which he was coming down. He did not know how to refuse gracefully. Nevitta and Fritharik got him to bed with rough efficiency.

Fritharik said: "It looks to me like a clear case of elf-shot."

"What?" croaked Padway.

"Elf-shot. The elves have shot you. I know, because I had it once in Africa. A Vandal physician cured me by drawing out the invisible darts of the elves. When they become visible they are little arrowheads made of chipped flint."

"Look," said Padway, "I know what's wrong with me. If everybody will let me alone, I'll get well in a week or ten days."

"We couldn't think of that!" cried Nevitta and Fritharik together. While they were arguing, Hermann arrived with a sallow, black-beared, sensitive-looking man.

Leo Vekkos opened his bag. Padway got a glimpse into the bag, and shuddered. It contained a couple of books, an assortment of weeds, and several small bottles holding organs of what had probably been small mammals.

"Now then, excellent Martinus," said Vekkos, "let me see your tongue. Say ah." The physician felt Padway's forehead, poked his chest and stomach, and asked him intelligent-sounding questions about his condition.

"This is a common condition in winter," said Vekkos in a didactic tone. "It is something of a mystery. Some hold it to be an excess of blood in the head, which causes that stuffy feeling whereof you complain. Others assert that it is an excess of black bile. I hold the view that it is caused by the conflict of the natural spirits of the liver with the animal spirits of the nervous system. The defeat of the animal spirits naturally reacts on the respiratory system—"

"It's nothing but a bad cold—" said Padway.

Vekkos ignored him. "—since the lungs and throat are under their control. The best cure for you is to rouse the vital spirits of the heart to put the natural spirits in their place." He began fishing weeds out of the bag.

"How about elf-shot?" asked Fritharik.

"What?"

Fritharik explained the medical doctrine of his people.

Vekkos smiled. "My good man, there is nothing in Galen about elf-shot. Nor in Celsus. Nor in Asclepiades. So I cannot take you seriously—"

"Then you don't know much about doctoring," growled Fritharik.

"Really," snapped Vekkos. "Who is the physician?"

"Stop squabbling, or you'll make me worse," grumbled Padway. "What are you going to do to me?"

Vekkos held up a bunch of weeds. "Have these herbs stewed and drink a cupful every three hours. They include a mild purgative, to draw off the black bile through the bowels in case there should be an excess."

"Which is the purgative?" asked Padway.

Vekkos pulled it out. Padway's thin arm shot out and grabbed the weed. "I just want to keep this separate from the rest, if you don't mind."

Vekkos humored him, told him to keep warm and stay in bed, and departed. Nevitta and Hermann went with him.

"Calls himself a physician," grumbled Fritharik, "and never heard of elf-shot."

"Get Julia," said Padway.

When the girl came, she set up a great to-do: "Oh, generous master, whatever is wrong with you? I'll get Father Narcissus—"

"No, you won't," said Padway. He broke off a small part of the purgative weed and handed it to her. "Boil this in a kettle of water, and bring me a cup of the water." He handed her the rest of the bunch of greenery. "And throw these out. Somewhere where the medicine man won't see them."

A slight laxative should be just the thing, he thought. If they would only leave him alone . . .

Next morning his head was less thick, but he felt very tired. He slept until eleven, when he was wakened by Julia. With Julia was a dignified man wearing an ordinary civilian cloak over a long white tunic with tight sleeves. Padway guessed that he was Father Narcissus by his tonsure.

"My son," said the priest. "I am sorry to see that the Devil had set his henchmen on you. This virtuous young woman besought my spiritual aid . . ."

Padway resisted a desire to tell Father Narcissus where to go. His one constant principle was to avoid trouble with the Church.

"I have not seen you at the Church of the Angel Gabriel," continued Father Narcissus. "You are one of us, though, I hope?"

"American rite," mumbled Padway.

The priest was puzzled by this. But he went on. "I know that you have consulted the physician Vekkos. How much better it is to put your trust in God, compared to whose power these bleeders and stewers of herbs are impotent! We shall start with a few prayers . . . ."

Padway lived through it. Then Julia appeared stirring something.

"Don't be alarmed," said the priest. "This is one cure that never fails. Dust from the tomb of St. Nereus, mixed with water."

There was nothing obviously lethal about the combination, so Padway drank it. Father Narcissus asked conversationally: "You are not, then, from Padua?"

Fritharik put his head in. "That so-called physician is here again."

"Tell him just a moment," said Padway. God, he was tired. "Thanks a lot, Father. It's nice to have seen you."

The priest went out, shaking his head over the blindness of mortals who trusted in *materia medica*.

Vekkos came in with an accusing look. Padway said: "Don't blame me. The girl brought him."

Vekkos sighed. "We physicians spend our lives in hard scientific study, and then we have to compete with these alleged miracle-workers. Well, how's my patient today?"

While he was still examining Padway, Thomasus the Syrian appeared. The banker waited around nervously until the Greek left. Then Thomasus said: "I came as soon as I heard you were sick, Martinus. Prayers and medicines are all very well, but we don't want to miss any bets. My colleague, Ebenezer the Jew, knows a man, one of his own sect named Jeconias of Naples, who is pretty good at curative magic. A lot of these magicians are frauds; I don't believe in them for a minute. But this man has done some remarkable—"

"I don't want him," groaned Padway. "I'll be all right if everybody will stop trying to cure me . . ."

"I brought him along, Martinus. Now do be reasonable. He won't hurt you. And I couldn't afford to have you die with those notes outstanding—of course that's not the only consideration; I'm fond of you personally . . ."

Padway felt like one in the grip of a nightmare. The more he protested, the more quacks they sicked on him.

Jeconias of Naples was a little fat man with a bouncing manner, more like a high-pressure salesman than the conventional picture of a magician.

He chanted: "Now, just leave everything to me, excellent Martinus. Here's a little cantrip that'll scare off the weaker spirits." He pulled out a piece of papyrus and read off something in an unknown language. "There, that didn't hurt, did it? Just leave it all to old Jeconias. He knows what he's doing. Now we'll put this charm under the bed, so-o-o! There, don't you feel better already? Now we'll cast your horoscope. If you'll give me the date and hour of your birth . . ."

How the hell, thought Padway, could he explain to this damned little quack that he was going to be born 1,373 years hence? He threw his reserve to the winds. He heaved himself up in bed and shouted feebly: "Presumptious slave, know you not that I am one of the hereditary custodians of the Seal of Solomon? That I can shuffle your silly planets around the sky with a word, and put out the sun with a sentence? And you talk of casting *my* horoscope?"

The magician's eyes were popping. "I—I'm sorry, sir, I didn't know . . ."

"Shemkhamphoras!" yelled Padway. "Ashtaroth!

Baâl-Marduk! St. Frigidaire! Tippecanoe and Tyler too! Begone, worm! One word from you of my true identity, and I'll strike you down with the foulest form of leprosy! Your eyeballs will rot, your fingers will drop off joint by joint—" But Jeconias was already out the door. Padway could hear him negotiate the first half of the stairway three steps at a time, roll head over heels the rest of the way, and race out of the front door.

Padway chuckled. He told Fritharik, who had been attracted by the noise: "You park yourself at the door with your sword, and say that Vekkos has given orders to let nobody see me. And I mean *nobody*. Even if the Holy Ghost shows up, keep him out."

Fritharik did as ordered. Then he craned his neck around the doorframe. "Excellent boss! I found a Goth who knows the theory of elf-shot. Shall I have him come up and—"

Padway pulled the covers over his head.

It was now April, 536. Sicily had fallen to General Belisarius in December. Padway had heard this weeks after it happened. Except for business errands, he had hardly been outside his house in four months in his desperate anxiety to get his press going. And except for his workers and his business contacts he knew practically nobody in Rome, though he had a speaking acquaintance with the librarians and two of Thomasus' banker friends, Ebenezer the Jew and Vardan the Armenian.

The day the press was finally ready he called his workers together and said: "I suppose you know that this is likely to be an important day for us. Fritharik will give each of you a small bottle of brandy to take home when you leave. And the first man who drops a hammer or anything on those little brass letters gets fired. I hope none of you do, because you've done a good job and I'm proud of you. That's all."

"Well, well," said Thomasus, "that's splendid. I always knew you'd get your machine to run. Said so right from the start. What are you going to print? The *Gothic History*? That would flatter the pretorian prefect, no doubt."

"No. That would take months to run off, especially as my men are new at the job. I'm starting off with a little alphabet book. You know, A is for *asinus* (ass), B is for *braccae* (breeches), and so on."

"That sounds like a good idea. But, Martinus, can't you let your men handle it, and take a rest? You look as if you haven't had a good night's sleep in months."

"I haven't, to tell the truth. But I can't leave; every time something goes wrong I have to be there to fix it. And I've got to find outlets for this first book. Schoolmasters and such people. I have to do everything myself, sooner or later. Also, I have an idea for another kind of publication."

"What? Don't tell me you're going to start another wild scheme—"

"Now, now, don't get excited, Thomasus. This is a weekly booklet of news."

"Listen, Martinus, don't overreach yourself. You'll get the scribes' guild down on you. As it is, I wish you'd tell me more about yourself. You're the town's great mystery, you know. Everybody asks about you."

"You just tell them I'm the most uninteresting bore you ever met in your life."

There were only a little over a hundred free-lance scribes in Rome. Padway disarmed any hostility they might have had for him by the curious expedient of enlisting them as reporters. He made a standing offer of a couple of sesterces per story for acceptable accounts of news items.

When he came to assemble the copy for his first issue, he found that some drastic censorship was necessary. For instance, one story read:

Our depraved and licentious city governor, Count Honorius, was seen early Wednesday morning being pursued down Broad Way by a young woman with a butcher's cleaver. Because this cowardly wretch was not encumbered by a decent minimum of clothing, he outdistanced his pursuer. This is the fourth time in a month that the wicked and corrupt count has created a scandal by his conduct with women. It is rumored that King Thiudahad will be petitioned to remove him by a committee of the outraged fathers of daughters whom he has dishonored. It is to be hoped that the next time the diabolical count is chased with a cleaver, his pursuer will catch him.

Somebody, thought Padway, doesn't *like* our illustrious count. He didn't know Honorius, but whether the story was true or not, there was no free-press clause in the Italian constitutions between Padway and the city's torture chambers.

So the first eight-page issue said nothing about young women with cleavers. It had a lot of relatively innocuous news items, one short poem contributed by a scribe who fancied himself a second Ovid, an editorial by Padway in which he said briefly that he hoped the Romans would find his paper useful, and a short article—also by Padway—on the nature and habits of the elephant.

Padway turned the crackling sheepskin pages of the proof copy, was proud of himself and his men, a pride not much diminished by the immediate discovery of a number of glaring typographical errors. One of these, in a story about a Roman mortally wounded by robbers on High Path a few nights back, had the unfortunate effect of turning a harmless word into an obscene one. Oh, well, with only two hundred and fifty copies he could have somebody go through them and correct the error with pen and ink.

Still, he could not help being a little awed by the importance of Martin Padway in this world. But for pure good luck, it might have been he who had been fatally stabbed on High Path—and behold, no printing press, none of the inventions he might yet introduce, until the slow natural process of technical development prepared the way for them. Not that he deserved too much credit—Gutenberg ought to have some for the press, for instance.

Padway called his paper *Tempora Romae* and offered it at ten sesterces, about the equivalent of fifty cents. He was surprised when not only did the first issue sell out, but Fritharik was busy for three days turning away from his door people who wanted copies that were not to be had.

A few scribes dropped in every day with more news items. One of them, a plump cheerful-looking fellow about Padway's age, handed in a story beginning:

The blood of an innocent man has been sacrificed to the lusts of our vile monster of a city governor, Count Honorius.

Reliable sources have revealed that Q. Aurelius Galba, crucified on a charge of murder last week, was the husband of a wife who had long been adulterously coveted by our villainous count. At Galba's trial there was much comment among the spectators on the flimsiness of the evidence . . .

"Hey!" said Padway. "Aren't you the man who handed in that other story about Honorius and a cleaver?"

"That's right," said the scribe. "I wondered why you didn't publish it."

"How long do you think I'd be allowed to run my paper without interference if I did?"

"Oh, I never thought of that."

"Well, remember next time. I can't use this story either. But don't let it discourage you. It's well done; a lead sentence and everything. How do you get all this information?"

The man grinned. "I hear things. And what I don't hear, my wife does. She has women friends who get together for games of backgammon, and they talk."

"It's too bad I don't dare run a gossip column," said Padway. "But you would seem to have the makings of a newspaper man. What's your name?"

"George Menandrus."

"That's Greek, isn't it?"

"My parents were Greek; I am Roman."

"All right, George, keep in touch with me. Some day I may want to hire an assistant to help run the thing."

Padway confidently visited the tanner to place another order for vellum.

"When will you want it?" said the tanner. Padway told him in four days.

"That's impossible. I might have fifty sheets for you in that time. They'll cost you five times as much apiece as the first ones."

Padway gasped. "In God's name, why?"

"You practically cleaned out Rome's supply with that first order," said the tanner. "All of our stock, and all the rest that was floating around, which I went out and bought

up for you. There aren't enough skins left in the whole city
to make a hundred sheets. And making vellum takes time,
you know. If you buy up the last fifty sheets, it will be
weeks before you can prepare another large batch."

Padway asked: "If you expanded your plant, do you
suppose you could eventually get up to a capacity of two
thousand a week?"

The tanner shook his head. "I should not want to spend
the money to expand in such a risky business. And, if I
did, there wouldn't be enough animals in Central Italy to
supply such a demand."

Padway recognized when he was licked. Vellum was es-
sentially a by-product of the sheep-and-goat industry.
Therefore a sudden increase in demand would skyrocket
the price without much increasing the output. Though the
Romans knew next to nothing of economics, the law of
supply and demand worked here just the same.

It would have to be paper after all. And his second edition was going to be very, very late.

For paper, he got hold of a felter and told him that he
wanted him to chop up a few pounds of white cloth and
make them into the thinnest felt that anybody had ever
heard of. The felter dutifully produced a sheet of what
looked like exceptionally thick and fuzzy blotting paper.
Padway patiently insisted on finer breaking up of the cloth,
on a brief boiling before felting, and on pressing after. As
he went out of the shop he saw the felter tap his forehead
significantly. But after many trials the man presented him
with a paper not much worse for writing than a twentieth-
century paper towel.

Then came the heartbreaking part. A drop of ink applied to this paper spread out with the alacrity of a picnic
party that has discovered a rattlesnake in their midst. So
Padway told the felter to make up ten more sheets, and
into the mush from which each was made to introduce one
common substance—soap, olive oil, and so forth. At this
point the felter threatened to quit, and had to be appeased
by a raise in price. Padway was vastly relieved to discover
that a little clay mixed with the pulp made all the difference between a fair writing paper and an impossible one.

By the time Padway's second issue had been sold out, he had ceased to worry about the possibility of running out of paper. But another thought moved into the vacated worrying compartment in his mind: What should he do when the Gothic War really got going? In his own history it had raged for twenty years up and down Italy. Nearly every important town had been besieged or captured at least once. Rome itself would be practically depopulated by sieges, famine, and pestilence. If he lived long enough he might see the Lombard invasion and the near-extinction of Italian civilization. All this would interfere dreadfully with his plans.

He tried to shake off the mood. Probably the weather was responsible; it had rained steadily for two days. Everything in the house was dank. The only way to cure that would be to build a fire, and the air was too warm for that already. So Padway sat and looked out at the leaden landscape.

He was surprised when Fritharik brought in Thomasus' colleague, Ebenezer the Jew. Ebenezer was a frail-looking, kindly oldster with a long white beard. Padway found him distressingly pious; when he ate with the other bankers he did not eat at all, to put it Irishly, for fear of transgressing one of the innumerable rules of his sect.

Ebenezer took his cloak off over his head and asked: "Where can I put this where it won't drip, excellent Martinus? Ah. Thank you. I was this way on business, and I thought I'd look your place over, if I may. It must be interesting, from Thomasus' accounts." He wrung the water from his beard.

Padway was glad of something to take his mind off the ominous future. He showed the old man around.

Ebenezer looked at him from under bushy white eyebrows. "Ah. Now I can believe that you are from a far country. From another world, almost. Take that system of arithmetic of yours; it has changed our whole concept of banking—"

"What?" cried Padway. "What do you know about it?"

"Why," said Ebenezer, "Thomasus sold the secret to Vardan and me. I thought you knew that."

"He *did?* How much?"

"A hundred and fifty solidi apiece. Didn't you—"

Padway growled a resounding Latin oath, grabbed his hat and cloak, and started for the door.

"Where are you going, Martinus?" said Ebenezer in alarm.

"I'm going to tell that cutthroat what I think of him!" snapped Padway. "And then I'm going to—"

"Did Thomasus promise you not to reveal the secret? I cannot believe that he violated—"

Padway stopped with his hand on the door handle. Now that he thought, the Syrian had never agreed not to tell anybody about Arabic numerals. Padway had taken it for granted that he would not want to do so. But if Thomasus got pressed for ready cash, there was no legal impediment to his selling or giving the knowledge to whom he pleased.

As Padway got his anger under control, he saw that he had not really lost anything, since his original intention had been to spread Arabic numerals far and wide. What really peeved him was that Thomasus should chisel such a handsome sum out of the science without even offering Padway a cut. It was like Thomasus. He was all right, but as Nevitta had said you had to watch him.

When Padway did appear at Thomasus' house, later that day, he had Fritharik with him. Fritharik was carrying a strong box. The box was nicely heavy with gold.

"Martinus," cried Thomasus, a little appalled, "do you really want to pay off all your loans? Where did you get all this money?"

"You heard me," grinned Padway. "Here's an accounting of principal and interest. I'm tired of paying ten per cent when I can get the same for seven and a half."

"What? Where can you get any such absurd rate?"

"From your esteemed colleague, Ebenezer. Here's a copy of the new note."

"Well, I must say I wouldn't have expected that of Ebenezer. If all this is true, I suppose I could meet his rate."

"You'll have to better it, after what you made from selling my arithmetic."

"Now, Martinus, what I did was strictly legal—"

"Didn't say it wasn't."

"Oh, very well. I suppose God planned it this way. I'll give you seven and four tenths."

Padway laughed scornfully.

"Seven, then. But that's the lowest, absolutely, positively, finally."

When Padway had received his old notes, a receipt for the old loans, and a copy of the new note, Thomasus asked him, "How did you get Ebenezer to offer you such an unheard-of figure?"

Padway smiled. "I told him that he could have had the secret of the new arithmetic from me for the asking."

Padway's next effort was a clock. He was going to begin with the simplest design possible: a weight on the end of a rope, a ratchet, a train of gears, the hand and dial from a battered old clepsydra or water clock he picked up secondhand, a pendulum, and an escapement. One by one he assembled these parts—all but the last.

He had not supposed there was anything so difficult about making an escapement. He could take the back cover off his wrist-watch and see the escapement-wheel there, jerking its merry way around. He did not want to take his watch apart for fear of never getting it together again. Besides, the parts thereof were too small to reproduce accurately.

But he could *see* the damned thing; why couldn't he make a large one? The workmen turned out several wheels, and the little tongs to go with them. Padway filed and scraped and bent. But they would not work. The tongs caught the teeth of the wheels and stuck fast. Or they did not catch at all, so that the shaft on which the rope was wound unwound itself all at once. Padway at last got one of the contraptions adjusted so that if you swung the pendulum with your hand, the tongs would let the escapement-wheel revolve one tooth at a time. Fine. But the clock would not run under its own power. Take your hand off the pendulum, and it made a couple of half-hearted swings and stopped.

Padway said to hell with it. He'd come back to it some

day when he had more time and better tools and instruments. He stowed the mess of cog-wheels in a corner of his cellar. Perhaps, he thought, this failure had been a good thing, to keep him from getting an exaggerated idea of his own cleverness.

Nevitta popped in again. "All over your sickness, Martinus? Fine; I knew you had a sound constitution. How about coming out to the Flaminian racetrack with me now and losing a few solidi? Then come on up to the farm overnight."

"I'd like to a lot. But I have to put the *Times* to bed this afternoon."

"Put to bed?" queried Nevitta.

Padway explained.

Nevitta said: "I see. Ha, ha, I thought you had a girl friend named Tempora. Tomorrow for supper, then."

"How shall I get there?"

"You haven't a saddle horse? I'll send Hermann down with one tomorrow afternoon. But mind, I don't want to get him back with wings growing out of his shoulders!"

"It might attract attention," said Padway solemnly. "And you'd have a hell of a time catching him if he didn't want to be bridled."

So the next afternoon Padway, in a new pair of rawhide Byzantine jack boots, set out with Hermann up the Flaminan Way. The Roman Campagna, he noted, was still fairly prosperous farming country. He wondered how long it would take for it to become the desolate, malarial plain of the Middle Ages.

"How were the races?" he asked.

Hermann, it seemed, knew very little Latin, though that little was still better than Padway's Gothic. "Oh, my boss . . . he terrible angry. He talk . . . you know . . . hot sport. But hate lose money. Lose fifty sesterces on horse. Make noise like . . . you know . . . lion with gutache."

At the farmhouse Padway met Nevitta's wife, a pleasant, plump woman who spoke no Latin, and his eldest son, Dagalaif, a Gothic *scaio,* or marshal, home on vacation. Supper fully bore out the stories that Padway had heard about Gothic appetites. He was agreeably surprised to drink some fairly good beer, after the bilgewater that went by that name in Rome.

"I've got some wine, if you prefer it," said Nevitta.

"Thanks, but I'm getting a little tired of Italian wine. The Roman writers talk a lot about their different kinds, but it all tastes alike to me."

"That's the way I feel. If you really *want* some, I have some perfumed Greek wine."

Padway shuddered.

Nevitta grinned. "That's the way I feel. Any man who'd put perfume in his liquor probably swishes when he walks. I only keep the stuff for my Greek friends, like Leo Vekkos. Reminds me, I must tell him about your cure for my wheezes by having me put the dogs out. He'll figure out some fancy theory full of long words to explain it."

Dagalaif spoke up: "Say, Martinus, maybe you have inside information on how the war will go."

Padway shrugged. "All I know is what everybody else knows. I haven't a private wire—I mean a private channel of information to heaven. If you want a guess, I'd say that Belisarius would invade Bruttium this summer and besiege Naples about August. He won't have a large force, but he'll be infernally hard to beat."

Dagalaif said: "Huh! We'll let him up all right. A handful of Greeks won't get very far against the united Gothic nation."

"That's what the Vandals thought," answered Padway dryly.

"*Aiw*," said Dagalaif. "But we won't make the mistakes the Vandals made."

"I don't know, son," said Nevitta. "It seems to me we are making them already—or others just as bad. This king of ours—all he's good for is hornswoggling his neighbors out of land and writing Latin poetry. And digging around in libraries. It would be better if we had an illiterate one, like Theoderik. Of course," he added apologetically, "I admit I can read and write. My old man came from Pannonia with Theoderik, and he was always talking about the sacred duty of the Goths to preserve Roman civilization from savages like the Franks. He was determined that I would have a Latin education if it killed me. I admit I've found my education useful. But in the next few months it'll be more important for our leader to know how to lead a charge than to say *amo-amas-amat.*"

CHAPTER V

PADWAY RETURNED TO Rome in the best of humor. Nevitta was the first person, besides Thomasus the Syrian, who had asked him to his house. And Padway, despite his somewhat cool exterior, was a sociable fellow at heart. He was, in fact, so elated that he dismounted and handed the reins of the borrowed horse to Hermann without noticing the three tough-looking parties leaning against the new fence in front of the old house on Long Street.

When he headed for the gate, the largest of the three, a black-bearded man, stepped in front of him. The man was holding a sheet of paper—real paper, no doubt from the felter to whom Padway had taught the art—in front of him and reading out loud to himself:— "medium height, brown hair and eyes, large nose, short beard. Speaks with an accent." He looked up sharply. "Are you Martinus Paduei?"

"*Sic. Quis est?*"

"You're under arrest. Will you come along quietly?"

"*What?* Who—What for—"

"Order of the municipal perfect. Sorcery."

"But . . . but—*Hey!* You can't—"

"I said *quietly.*"

The other two men had moved up on each side of Padway, and each took an arm and started to walk him along the street. When he resisted, a short bludgeon appeared in the hand of one. Padway looked around frantically. Hermann was already out of sight. Fritharik was not to be seen; no doubt he was snoring as usual. Padway filled his lungs to shout; the man on his right tightened his grip and raised the bludgeon threateningly. Padway didn't shout.

They marched him down the Argiletum to the old jail below the Record Office on the Capitoline. He was still in somewhat of a daze as the clerk demanded his name, age, and address. All he could think of was that he had heard somewhere that you were entitled to telephone your lawyer before being locked up. And that information seemed hardly useful in the present circumstances.

A small, snapping Italian who had been lounging on a bench got up. "What's this, a sorcery case involving a foreigner? Sounds like a national case to me."

"Oh, no, it isn't," said the clerk. "You national officers have authority in Rome only in mixed Roman-Gothic cases. This man isn't a Goth; says he's an American, whatever that is."

"Yes, it is! Read your regulations. The pretorian prefect's office has jurisdiction in all capital cases involving foreigners. If you have a sorcery complaint, you turn it and the prisoner over to us. Come on, now." The little man moved possessively toward Padway. Padway did not like the use of the term "capital cases."

The clerk said: "Don't be a fool. Think you're going to drag him clear up to Ravenna for interrogation? We've got a perfectly good torture chamber here."

"I'm only doing my duty," snapped the state policeman. He grabbed Padway's arm and started to haul him toward the door. "Come along now, sorcerer. We'll show you some real, up-to-date torture at Ravenna. These Roman cops don't know anything."

"*Christus!* Are you crazy?" yelled the clerk. He jumped up and grabbed Padway's other arm; so did the black-bearded man who had arrested him. The state policemen pulled and so did the other two.

"Hey!" yelled Padway. But the assorted functionaries were too engrossed in their tug-of-war to notice.

The state policeman shouted in a painfully penetrating voice: "Justinius, run and tell the adjutant prefect that these municipal scum are trying to withhold a prisoner from us!" A man ran out the door.

Another door opened, and a fat, sleepy-looking man came in. "What's this?" he squeaked.

The clerk and the municipal policeman straightened up to attention, releasing Padway. The state policeman immediately resumed hauling him toward the door; the local cops abandoned their etiquette and grabbed him again. They all shouted at once at the fat man. Padway gathered that he was the municipal *commentariensius,* or police chief.

At that two more municipal policemen came in with a thin, ragged prisoner. They entered into the dispute with true Italian fervor, which meant using both hands. The ragged prisoner promptly darted out the door; his captors didn't notice his absence for a full minute.

They then began shouting at each other. "What did you let him go for?" "You brass-bound idiot, you're the one who let him go!"

The man called Justinius came back with an elegant person who announced himself as the *corniculatis,* or adjutant prefect. This individual waved a perfumed handkerchief at the struggling group and said: "Let him go, you chaps. Yes, you, too, Sulla." (This was the state policeman.) "There won't be anything left of him to interrogate if you keep that up."

From the way the others in the now-crowded room quieted, Padway guessed that the adjutant prefect was a pretty big shot.

The adjutant prefect asked a few questions, then said: "I'm sorry, my dear old *commentariensius,* but I'm afraid he's our man."

"Not yet he isn't," squeaked the chief. "You fellows can't just walk in here and grab a prisoner any time you feel like it. It would mean my job to let you have him."

The adjutant prefect yawned. "Dear, dear, you're *such* a bore. You forget that I represent the pretorian prefect, who represents the king, and if I order you to hand the prisoner over, you hand him over and that's the end of it. I so order you, now."

"Go ahead and order. You'll have to take him by force, and I've got more force than you have." The chief beamed

Billikenlike and twiddled his thumbs. "Clodianus, go fetch our illustrious city governor, if he's not too busy. We'll see whether we have authority over our own jail." The clerk departed. "Of course," the chief continued, "we *might* use Solomon's method."

"You mean cut him in two?" asked the adjutant prefect.

"That's it. Lord Jesus, that would be funny, wouldn't it? Ho, ho, ho, ho, ho!" The chief laughed shrilly until the tears ran down his face. "Would you prefer the head end or the legs end? Ho, ho, ho, ho, ho!" He rocked on his seat.

The other municipal officers dutifully laughed, also; the adjutant prefect permitted himself a wan, bored smile. Padway thought the chief's humor in questionable taste.

Eventually the clerk returned with the city governor. Count Honorius wore a tunic with the two purple stripes of a Roman senator, and walked with such a carefully measured tread that Padway wondered if his footsteps hadn't been laid out ahead of time with chalk marks. He had a square jaw and all the warmth of expression of a snapping turtle.

"What," he asked in a voice like a steel file, "is this all about? Quick, now, I'm a busy man." As he spoke, the little wattle under his jaw wobbled in a way that reminded Padway more than ever of a snapper.

The chief and the adjutant prefect gave their versions. The clerk dragged out a couple of law books; the three executive officers put their heads together and talked in low tones, turning pages rapidly and pointing to passages.

Finally the adjutant prefect gave in. He yawned elaborately. "Oh, well, it would be a dreadful bore to have to drag him up to Ravenna, anyway. Especially as the mosquito season will be starting there shortly. Glad to have seen you, my lord count." He bowed to Honorius, nodded casually to the chief, and departed.

Honorius said: "Now that we have him, what's to be done with him? Let's see that complaint."

The clerk dug out a paper and gave it to the count.

"*Hm-m-m.* '—and furthermore, that the said Martinus Paduei did most wickedly and feloniously consort with the Evil One, who taught him the diabolical arts of magic wherewith he has been jeopardizing the welfare of the citizens of the city of Rome—signed, Hannibal Scipio of Palermo.' Wasn't this Hannibal Scipio a former associate of yours or something?"

"Yes, my lord count," said Padway, and explaining the circumstances of his parting with his foreman. "If it's my printing press that he's referring to, I can easily show that it's a simple mechanical device, no more magical than one of your water clocks."

"*Hm-m-m,*" said Honorius, "that may or may not be true." He looked through narrowed eyes at Padway. "These new enterprises of yours have prospered pretty well, haven't they?" His faint smile reminded Padway of a fox dreaming of unguarded henroosts.

"Yes and no, my lord. I have made a little money, but I've put most of it back in the business. So I haven't more cash than I need for day-to-day expenses."

"Too bad," said Honorius. "It looks as though we'd have to let the case go through."

Padway was getting more and more nervous under that penetrating scrutiny, but he put up a bold front. "Oh, my lord, I don't think you have a case. If I may say so, it would be most unfortunate for your dignity to let the case come to trial."

"So? I'm afraid my good man, that you don't know what expert interrogators we have. You'll have admitted all sorts of things by the time they finish . . . ah . . . questioning you."

"Um-m-m. My lord, I said I didn't have much *cash.* But I have an idea that might interest you."

"That's better. Lutetius, may I use your private office?"

Without waiting for an answer, Honorius marched to the office, jerking his head to Padway to follow. The chief looked after them sourly, obviously resenting the loss of his share of the swag.

In the chief's office, Honorius turned to Padway. "You weren't proposing to bribe your governor by chance, were you?" he asked coldly.

"Well . . . uh . . . not exactly—"

The count shot his head forward. "How much?" he snapped. "And what's it in—jewels?"

Padway sighed with relief. "Please, my lord, not so fast. It'll take a bit of explaining."

"Your explanation had better be good."

"It's this way, my lord: I'm just a poor stranger in Rome, and naturally I have to depend on my wits for a living. The only really valuable thing I have is those wits. But, with reasonably kind treatment, they can be made to pay a handsome return."

"Get to the point, young man."

"You have a law against limited-liability corporations in other than public enterprises, haven't you?"

Honorius rubbed his chin. "We did have once. I don't know what its status is, now that the senate's authority is limited to the city. I don't think the Goths have made any regulations on that subject. Why?"

"Well if you can get the senate to pass an amendment to the old law—I don't think it would be necessary, but it would look better—I could show you how you and a few other deserving senators could benefit handsomely from the organization and operation of such a company."

Honorius stiffened. "Young man, that's a miserable sort of offer. You ought to know that the dignity of a patrician forbids him to engage in trade."

"You wouldn't engage in it, my lord. You'd be the stockholders."

"We'd be the what?"

Padway explained the operation of a stock corporation.

Honorius rubbed his chin again. "Yes, I see where something might be made of that plan. What sort of company did you have in mind?"

"A company for the transmission of information over long distances much more rapidly than a messenger can travel. In my country they'd call it a semaphore telegraph. The company gets its revenue from tolls on private messages. Of course, it wouldn't hurt if you could get a subsidy from the royal treasury, on the ground that the institution was valuable for national defense."

Honorius thought awhile. Then he said: "I won't commit myself now; I shall have to think about the matter and sound out my friends. In the meantime, you will, of course, remain in Lutetius' custody here."

Padway grinned. "My lord count, your daughter is getting married next week, isn't she?"

"What of it?"

"You want a nice write-up of the wedding in my paper, don't you? A list of distinguished guests, a wood-cut picture of the bride, and so forth."

"Hm-m-m. I shouldn't mind that; no."

"Well, then, you better not hold me, or I shan't be able to get the paper out. It would be a pity if such a gala event missed the news because the publisher was in jail at the time."

Honorius rubbed his chin and smiled thinly. "For a barbarian, you're not as stupid as one would expect. I'll have you released."

"Many thanks, my lord. I might add that I shall be able to write much more glowing paragraphs after that complaint has been dismissed. We creative workers, you know—"

When Padway was out of earshot of the jail, he indulged in a long "*Whew!*" He was sweating, and not with the heat, either. It was a good thing that none of the officials noticed how near he had been to collapse from sheer terror. The prospect of a stand-up fight wouldn't have bothered him more than most young men. But torture . . .

As soon as he had put his establishment in order, he went into a huddle with Thomasus. He was properly prepared when the procession of five sedan chairs, bearing Honorius and four other senators, crawled up Long Street to his place. The senators seemed not only willing but eager to lay their money on the line, especially after they saw the beautiful stock certificates that Padway had printed. But they didn't seem to have quite Padway's idea of how to run a corporation.

One of them poked him in the ribs and grinned. "My dear Martinus, you're not *really* going to put up those silly signal towers and things?"

"Well," said Padway cautiously, "that was the idea."

The senator winked. "Oh, I understand that you'll have to put up a couple to fool the middle class, so we can sell our stock at a profit. But *we* know it's all a fake, don't we?

You couldn't make anything with your signaling scheme in a thousand years."

Padway didn't bother to argue with him. He also didn't bother to explain the true object of having Thomasus the Syrian, Ebenezer the Jew, and Vardan the Armenian each take eighteen per cent of the stock. The senators might have been interested in knowing that these three bankers had agreed ahead of time to hold their stock and vote as Padway instructed, thereby giving him, with fifty-four per cent of the stock, complete control of the corporation.

Padway had every intention of making his telegraph company a success, starting with a line of towers from Naples to Rome to Ravenna, and tying its operation in with that of his paper. He soon ran into an elementary difficulty: If he wanted to keep his expenses down to somewhere within sight of income, he needed telescopes, to make possible a wide spacing of the towers. Telescopes meant lenses. Where in the world was there a lens or a man who could make one? True, there was a story about Nero's emerald lorgnette . . .

Padway went to see Sextus Dentatus, the froglike goldsmith who had changed his lire to sesterces. Dentatus croaked directions to the establishment of one Florianus the Glazier.

Florianus was a light-haired man with a drooping mustache and a nasal accent. He came to the front of his dark little shop smelling strongly of wine. Yes, he had owned his own glass factory once, at Cologne. But business was bad for the Rhineland glass industry; the uncertainties of life under the Franks, you know, my sir. He had gone broke. Now he made a precarious living mending windows and such.

Padway explained what he wanted, paid a little on account, and left him. When he went back on the promised day, Florianus flapped his hands as if he were trying to take off. "A thousand pardons, my sir! It has been hard to buy up the necessary cullet. But a few days more, I pray you. And if I could have a little more money on account —times are hard—I am poor—"

On Padway's third visit he found Florianus drunk. When Padway shook him, all the man could do was mumble Gallo-romance at him, which Padway did not understand. Padway went to the back of the shop. There was no sign of tools or materials for making lenses.

Padway left in disguest. The nearest real glass industry was at Puteoli, near Naples. It would take forever to get anything done by correspondence.

Padway called in George Menandrus and hired him as editor of the paper. For several days he talked himself hoarse and Menandrus deaf on How to Be an Editor. Then, with a sinking heart, he left for Naples. He experienced the famous canal-boat ride celebrated by Horace, and found it quite as bad as alleged.

Vesuvius was not smoking. But Puteoli, on the little strip of level ground between the extinct crater of Solfatara and the sea, was. Padway and Fritharik sought out the place recommended by Dentatus. This was one of the largest and smokiest of the glass factories.

Padway asked the doorman for Andronicus, the proprietor. Andronicus was a short, brawny man covered with soot. When Padway told who he was, Andronicus cried: "Ah! Fine! Come, gentlemen, I have just the thing."

They followed him into his private inferno. The vestibule, which was also the office, was lined with shelves. The shelves were covered with glassware. Andronicus picked up a vase. "Ah! Look! Such clearness! You couldn't get whiter glass from Alexandria! Only two solidi!"

Padway said: "I didn't come for a vase, my dear sir. I want—"

"No vase? No vase? Ah! Here is the thing." He picked up another vase. "Look! The shape! Such purity of line! It reminds you—"

"I said I didn't want to buy a vase. I want—"

"It reminds you of a beautiful woman! Of love!" Andronicus kissed his fingertips.

"I want some small pieces of glass, made specially—"

"Beads? Of course, gentlemen. Look." The glass manufacturer scooped up a handful of beads. "Look at the color! Emerald, turquoise, everything!" He picked up another bunch. "See here, the faces of the twelve apostles, one on each bead—"

"Not beads—"

"A beaker, then! Here is one. Look, it has the Holy Family in high relief—"

"Jesus!" yelled Padway. "Will you listen?"

When Andronicus let Padway explain what he wanted, the Neapolitan said: "Of course! Fine! I've seen ornaments shaped like that. I'll rough them out tonight, and have them ready day after tomorrow—"

"That won't quite do," said Padway. "These have to have an exactly spherical surface. You grind a concave against a convex with—what's your word for *emery?* The stuff you use in rough grinding? Some *naxium* to true them off . . ."

Padway and Fritharik went on to Naples and put up at the house of Thomasus' cousin, Antiochus the Shipper. Their welcome was less than cordial. It transpired that Antiochus was fanatically Orthodox. He loathed his cousin's Nestorianism. His pointed remarks about heretics made his guests so uncomfortable that they moved out on the third day. They took lodgings at an inn whose lack of sanitation distressed Padway's cleanly soul.

Each morning they rode out to Puteoli to see how the lenses were coming. Andronicus invariably tried to sell them a ton of glass junk.

When they left for Rome, Padway had a dozen lenses, half plano-convex and half plano-concave. He was skeptical about the possibility of making a telescope by holding a pair of lenses in line with his eye and judging the distances. It worked, though.

The most practical combination proved to be a concave lens for the eyepiece with a convex one about thirty inches in front of it. The glass had bubbles, and the image was somewhat distorted. But Padway's telescope, crude as it was, would make a two-to-one difference in the number of signal towers required.

About then, the paper ran its first advertisement. Thomasus had had to turn the screw on one of his debtors to make him buy space. The ad read:

DO YOU WANT A GLAMOROUS FUNERAL?

Go to meet your Maker in style! With one of our funer-
   als to look forward to, you will hardly mind dying!
Don't imperil your chances of salvation with a bungled
   burial!
Our experts have handled some of the noblest corpses in
   Rome.
Arrangements made with the priesthood of any sect.
   Special rates for heretics. Appropriately doleful music
   furnished at slight extra cost.

John the Egyptian, Genteel Undertaker
Near the Viminal Gate

CHAPTER VI

JUNIANUS, CONSTRUCTION MANAGER of the Roman Telegraph Co., panted into Padway's office. He said: "Work"
—stopped to get his breath, and started again—"work on
the third tower on the Naples line was stopped this morning by a squad of soldiers from the Rome garrison. I asked
them what the devil was up, and they said they didn't
know; they just had orders to stop construction. What,
most excellent boss, are you going to do about it?"

So the Goths objected? That meant seeing their higher-
ups. Padway winced at the idea of getting involved any further in politics. He sighed. "I'll see Linderis, I suppose."

The commander of the Rome garrison was a big, portly
Goth with the bushiest white whiskers Padway had ever
seen. His Latin was fair. But now and then he cocked a
blue eye at the ceiling and moved his lips silently, as if
praying; actually he was running through a declension or a
conjugation for the right ending.

He said: "My good Martinus, there is a war on. You
start erecting these . . . ah . . . mysterious towers without
asking our permission. Some of your backers are patricians
. . . ah . . . notorious for their pro-Greek sentiments.
What are we to think? You should consider yourself lucky
to have escaped arrest."

Padway protested: "I was hoping the army would find them useful for transmitting military information."

Liuderis shrugged. "I am merely a simple soldier doing my duty. I do not understand these . . . ah . . . devices. Perhaps they will work as you say. But I could not take the . . . ah . . . responsibility for permitting them."

"Then you won't withdraw your order?"

"No. If you want permission, you will have to see the king."

"But, my dear sir, I can't spare the time to go running up to Ravenna—"

Another shrug. "All one to me, my good Martinus. I know my duty."

Padway tried guile. "You certainly do, it seems. If I were the king, I couldn't ask for a more faithful soldier."

"You flatterer!" But Liuderis grinned, pleased. "I regret that I cannot grant your little request."

"What's the latest war news?"

Liuderis frowned. "Not very—But then I should be careful what I say. You are a more dangerous person than you look, I am sure."

"You can trust me. I'm pro-Gothic."

"Yes?" Liuderis was silent while the wheels turned. Then: "What is your religion?"

Padway was expecting that. "Congregationalist. That's the nearest thing to Arianism we have in my country."

"Ah, then perhaps you are as you say. The news is not good, what little there is. There is nobody in Bruttium but a small force under the king's son-in-law, Evermuth. And our good king—" He shrugged again, this time hopelessly.

"Now look here, most excellent Liuderis, won't you withdraw that order? I'll write Thiudahad at once asking his permission."

"No, my good Martinus, I cannot. You get the permission first. And you had better go in person, if you want action."

Thus it came about that Padway found himself, quite against his wishes, trotting an elderly saddle horse across the Apennines toward the Adriatic. Fritharik had been delighted at first to get any kind of a horse between his knees. Before they had gone very far his tone changed.

"Boss," he grumbled, "I'm not an educated man. But I know horseflesh. I always claimed that a good horse was a good investment." He added darkly: "If we are attacked by brigands, we'll have no chance with those poor old wrecks. Not that I fear death, or brigands either. But it would be sad for a Vandal knight to end in a nameless grave in one of these lonely valleys. When I was a noble in Africa—"

"We aren't running a racing stable," snapped Padway. At Fritharik's hurt look he was sorry he had spoken sharply. "Never mind, old man, we'll be able to afford good horses some day. Only right now I feel as if I had a pantsful of ants."

Brazilian army ants, he added to himself. He had done almost no riding since his arrival in old Rome, and not a great deal in his former life. By the time they reached Spoleto he felt as if he could neither sit nor stand, but would have to spend the rest of his life in a sort of semi-squat, like a rheumatic chimpanzee.

They approached Ravenna at dusk on the fourth day. The City in the Mist sat dimly astride the thirty-mile causeway that divided the Adriatic from the vast marshy lagoons to the west. A faint sunbeam lighted the gilded church domes. The church bells bonged, and the frogs in the lagoons fell silent; then resumed their croaking. Padway thought that anyone who visited this strange city would always be haunted by the bong of the bells, the croak of the frogs, and the thin, merciless song of the mosquitoes.

Padway decided that the chief usher, like Poo-Bah, had been born sneering. "My good man," said this being, "I couldn't possibly give you an audience with our lord king for three weeks at least."

Three weeks! In that time half of Padway's assorted machines would have broken down, and his men would be running in useless circles trying to fix them. Menandrus, who was inclined to be reckless with money, especially other people's, would have run the paper into bankruptcy. This impasse required thought. Padway straightened his aching legs and started to leave.

The Italian immediately lost some of his top-loftiness.

"But," he cried in honest amazement, "didn't you bring any *money?*"

Of course, Padway thought, he should have known that the man hadn't meant what he'd said. "What's your schedule of rates?"

The usher, quite seriously, began counting on his fingers. "Well, for twenty solidi I could give you your audience tomorrow. For the day after tomorrow, ten solidi is my usual rate; but that's Sunday, so I'm offering interviews on Monday at seven and a half. For one week in advance, two solidi. For two weeks——"

Padway interrupted to offer a five-solidi bribe for a Monday interview, and finally got it at that price plus a small bottle of brandy. The usher said: "You'll be expected to have a present for the king, too, you know."

"I know," said Padway wearily. He showed the usher a small leather case. "I'll present it personally."

Thiudahad Tharasmund's son, King of the Ostrogoths and Italians; Commander in Chief of the Armies of Italy, Illyria, and Southern Gaul; Premier Prince of the Amal Clan; Count of Tuscany; Illustrious Patrician; *ex-officio* President of the Circus; et cetera, et cetera, was about Padway's height, thin to gauntness, and had a small gray beard. He peered at his caller with watery gray eyes, and said in a reedy voice: "Come in, come in, my good man. What's *your* business? Oh, yes, Martinus Paduei. You're the publisher chap aren't you? Eh?" He spoke upper-class Latin without a trace of accent.

Padway bowed ceremoniously. "I am, my lord king. Before we discuss the business, I have——"

"Great thing, that book-making machine of yours. I've heard of it. Great thing for scholarship. You must see my man Cassiodorus. I'm sure he'd like you to publish his *Gothic History*. Great work. Deserves a wide circulation."

Padway waited patiently. "I have a small gift for you, my lord. A rather unusual——"

"Eh? Gift? By all means. Let's see it."

Padway took out the case and opened it.

Thiudahad piped: "Eh? What the devil is that?"

Padway explained the function of a magnifying glass. He didn't dwell on Thiudahad's notorious nearsightedness.

Thiudahad picked up a book and tried the glass on it. He squealed with delight. "Fine, my good Martinus. Shall I be able to read all I want without getting headaches?"

"I hope so, my lord. At least it should help. Now, about my business here——"

"Oh, yes, you want to see me about publishing Cassiodorus. I'll fetch him for you."

"No, my lord. It's about something else." He went on quickly before Thiudahad could interrupt again, telling him of his difficulty with Liuderis.

"Eh? I never bother my local military commanders. They know their business."

"But, my lord——" and Padway gave the king a little sales talk on the importance of the telegraph company.

"Eh? A money-making scheme, you say? If it's as good as all that, why wasn't I let in on it at the start?"

That rather jarred Padway. He said something vague about there not having been time. King Thiudahad wagged his head. "Still, that wasn't considerate of you, Martinus. It wasn't loyal. And if people aren't loyal to their king, where are we? If you deprive your king of an opportunity to make a little honest profit, I don't see why I should interfere with Liuderis on your account."

"Well, ahem, my lord, I did have an idea——"

"Not considerate at all. What were you saying? Come to the point, my good man, come to the point."

Padway resisted an impulse to strangle this exasperating little man. He beckoned Frithark, who was standing statuesquely in the background. Fritharik produced a telescope, and Padway explained *its* functions. . . .

"Yes, yes? Very interesting, I'm sure. Thank you, Martinus. I will say that you bring your king original presents."

Padway gasped; he hadn't intended giving Thiudahad his best telescope. But it was too late now. He said: "I thought that if my lord king saw fit to . . . ah . . . ease matters with your excellent Liuderis, I could insure your undying fame in the world of scholarship."

"Eh? What's that? What do you know about scholarship? Oh, I forgot; you're a publisher. Something about Cassiodorus?"

Padway repressed a sigh. "No, my lord. *Not* Cassiodorus. How would you like the credit for revolutionizing men's idea about the solar system?"

"I don't believe in interfering with my local commanders, Martinus. Liuderis is an excellent man. Eh? What were you saying. Something about the solar system? What's that got to do with Liuderis?"

"Nothing, my lord." Padway repeated what he had said.

"Well, maybe I'd consider it. What is this theory of yours?"

Little by little Padway wormed from Thiudahad a promise of a free hand for the telegraph company, in return for bits of information about the Copernican hypothesis, instructions for the use of the telescope to see the moons of Jupiter, and a promise to publish a treatise on astronomy in Thiudahad's name.

At the end of an hour he grinned and said, "Well, my lord, we seem to be in agreement. There's just one more thing. This telescope would be a valuable instrument of warfare. If you wanted to equip your officers with them—"

"Eh? Warfare? You'll have to see Wittigis about that. He's my head general."

"Where's he?"

"Where? Oh, dear me, I don't know. Somewhere up north, I think. There's been a little invasion by the Allemans or somebody."

"When will he be back?"

"How should I know, my good Martinus? When he's driven out these Allemans or Burgunds or whoever they are."

"But, most excellent lord, if you'll pardon me, the war with the Imperialists is definitely on. I think it's important to get these telescopes into the hands of the army as soon as possible. We'd be prepared to supply them at a reasonable—"

"Now, Martinus," snapped the king peevishly, "don't try to tell me how to run my kingdom. You're as bad as my Royal Council. Always 'Why don't you do this?', 'Why don't you do that?' I trust my commanders; don't bother myself with details. I say you'll have to see Wittigis, and that settles it."

Thiudahad was obviously prepared to be mulish, so Padway said a few polite nothings, bowed, and withdrew.

CHAPTER VII

WHEN PADWAY GOT BACK to Rome, his primary concern was to see how his paper was coming. The first issue that had been put out since his departure was all right. About the second, which had just been printed, Menandrus was mysteriously elated, hinting that he had a splendid surprise for his employer. He had. Padway glanced at a proof sheet, and his heart almost stopped. On the front page was a detailed account of the bribe which the new Pope, Silverius, had paid King Thiudahad to secure his election.

"Hell's bells!" cried Padway. "Haven't you any better sense than to print this, George?"

"Why?" asked Menandrus, crestfallen. "It's true, isn't it?"

"Of course, it's true! But you don't want us all hanged or burned at the stake, do you? The Church is already suspicious of us. Even if you find that a bishop is keeping twenty concubines, you're not to print a word of it."

Menandrus sniffled a little; he wiped away a tear and blew his nose on his tunic. "I'm sorry, excellent boss. I tried to please you; you have no idea how much trouble I went to to get the facts about that bribe. There *is* a bishop, too—not *twenty* concubines, but—"

"But we don't consider that news, for reasons of health. Thank heaven, no copies of this issue have gone out yet."

"Oh, but they have."

"*What?*" Padway's yell made a couple of workmen from the machine shop look in.

"Why, yes, John the Bookseller took the first hundred copies out just a minute ago."

John the Bookseller got the scare of his life when Padway, still dirty from days of travel, galloped down the street after him, dove off his horse, and grabbed his arm. Somebody set up a cry of "Thieves! Robbers! Help! Murder!" Padway found himself trying to explain to forty truculent citizens that everything was all right.

A Gothic soldier pushed through the crowd and asked what was going on here. A citizen pointed at Padway and shouted: "It's the fellow with the boots. I heard him say he'd cut the other man's throat if he didn't hand over his money!" So the Goth arrested Padway.

Padway kept his clutch on John the Bookseller, who was too frightened to speak. He went along quietly with the Goth until they were out of earshot of the crowd. Then he asked the soldier into a wineshop, treated him and John, and explained. The Goth was noncommittal, despite John's corroboration, until Padway tipped him liberally. Padway got his freedom and his precious papers. Then all he had to worry about was the fact that somebody had stolen his horse while he was in the Goth's custody.

Padway trudged back to his house with the papers under his arm. His household was properly sympathetic about the loss of the horse. Fritharik said: "There, illustrious boss, that piece of crow bait wasn't worth much anyhow."

Padway felt much better when he learned that the first leg of the telegraph ought to be completed in a week or ten days. He poured himself a stiff drink before dinner. After his strenuous day it made his head swim a little. He got Fritharik to join him in one of the latter's barbarian warsongs:

> "The black earth shakes
> As the heroes ride,
> And the ravens blood-
> Red sun will hide!
> The lances dip
> In a glittering wave,
> And the coward turns
> His gore to save . . ."

When Julia was late with the food, Padway gave her a playful spank. He was a little surprised at himself.

After dinner he was sleepy. He said to hell with the accounts and went upstairs to bed, leaving Fritharik already snoring on his mattress in front of the door. Padway would not have laid any long bets on Fritharik's ability to wake up when a burglar entered.

He had just started to undress when a knock startled him. He could not imagine . . .

"Fritharik?" he called.

"No. It's me."

He frowned and opened the door. The lamplight showed Julia from Apulia. She walked in with a swaying motion.

"What do you want, Julia?" asked Padway.

The stocky, black-haired girl looked at him in some surprise. "Why—uh—my lord wouldn't want me to say right out loud? That wouldn't be nice!"

"Huh?"

She giggled.

"Sorry," said Padway. "Wrong station. Off you go."

She looked baffled. "My—my master doesn't want me?"

"That's right. Not for that anyway."

Her mouth turned down. Two large tears appeared. "You don't like me? You don't think I'm nice?"

"I think you're a fine cook and a nice girl. Now out with you. Good night."

She stood solidly and began to sniffle. Then she sobbed. Her voice rose to a shrill wail: "Just because I'm from the country—you never looked at me—you never asked for me all this time—then tonight you were nice—I thought —I thought—boo-oo-oo . . ."

"Now, now . . . for heaven's sake stop crying! Here, sit down. I'll get you a drink."

She smacked her lips over the first swallow of diluted brandy. She wiped off the remaining tears. "Nice," she said. Everything was nice—*bonus, bona,* or *bonum,* as the case might be. "You are nice. Love is nice. Every man should have some love. Love—ah!" She made a serpentine movement remarkable in a person of her build.

Padway gulped. "Give me that drink," he said. "I need some too."

After a while. "Now," she said, "we make love?"

"Well—pretty soon. Yes, I guess we do." Padway hiccuped.

Padway frowned at Julia's large bare feet. "Just—*hic*—just a minute, my bounding hamadryad. Let's see those feet." The soles were black. "That won't do. Oh, it absolutely won't do, my lusty Amazon. The feet present an insur-insurmountable psychological obstacle."

"Huh?"

"They interpose a psychic barrier to the—*hic*—appropriately devout worship of Ashtaroth. We must have the pedal extremities—"

"I don't understand."

"Skip it; neither do I. What I mean is that we're going to wash your feet first."

"Is that a religion?"

"You might put it that way. Damn!" He knocked the ewer off its base, miraculously catching it on the way down. "Here we go, my Tritoness from the wine-dark, fish-swarming sea . . ."

She giggled. "You are the nicest man. You are a real gentleman. No man ever did *that* for me before . . ."

Padway blinked his eyes open. It all came back to him quickly enough. He tightened his muscles serratus. He felt fine. He prodded his conscience experimentally. It reacted not at all.

He moved carefully, for Julia was taking up two-thirds of his none-too-wide bed. He heaved himself on one elbow and looked at her. The movement uncovered her large breasts. Between them was a bit of iron, tied around her neck. This, she had told him, was a nail from the cross of St. Andrew. And she would not put it off.

He smiled. To the list of mechanical inventions he meant to introduce he added a couple of items. But for the present, should he . . .

A small gray thing with six legs, not much larger than a pinhead, emerged from the hair under her armpit. Pale against her olive-brown skin, it crept with glacial slowness . . .

Padway shot out of bed. Face writhing with revulsion,

he pulled his clothes on without taking time to wash. The room smelled. Rome must have blunted his sense of smell, or he'd have noticed it before.

Julia awoke as he was finishing. He threw a muttered good morning at her and tramped out.

He spent two hours in the public baths that day. The next night Julia's knock brought a harsh order to get away from his room and stay away. She began to wail. Padway snatched the door open. "One more squawk and you're fired!" he snapped, and slammed the door.

She was obedient but sulky. During the next few days he caught venomous glances from her; she was no actress.

The following Sunday he returned from the Ulpian Library to find a small crowd of men in front of his house. They were just standing and looking. Padway looked at the house and could see nothing out of order.

He asked a man: "What's funny about my house, stranger?"

The man looked at him silently. They all looked at him silently. They moved off in twos and threes. They began to walk fast, sometimes glancing back.

Monday morning two of the workmen failed to report. Nerva came to Padway and, after much clearing of the throat, said: "I thought you'd like to know, lordly Martinus. I went to mass at the Church of the Angel Gabriel yesterday as usual."

"Yes?" That Church was on Long Street four blocks from Padway's house.

"Father Narcissus preached a homily against sorcery. He talked about people who hired demons from Satanas and work strange devices. It was a very strong sermon. He sounded as if he might be thinking of you."

Padway worried. It might be coincidence, but he was pretty sure that Julia had gone to confessional and spilled the beans about fornicating with a magician. One sermon had sent the crowd to stare at the wizard's lair. A few more like that . . .

Padway feared a mob of religious enthusiasts more than anything on earth, no doubt because their mental processes were so utterly alien to his own.

He called Menandrus in and asked for information on Father Narcissus.

The information was discouraging from Padway's point of view. Father Narcissus was one of the most respected priests in Rome. He was upright, charitable, humane, and fearless. He was in deadly earnest twenty-four hours a day. And there was no breath of scandal about him, which fact by itself made him a distinguished cleric.

"George," said Padway, "didn't you once mention a bishop with concubines?"

Menandrus grinned slyly. "It's the Bishop of Bologna, sir. He's one of the Pope's cronies; spends more time at the Vatican than at his see. He has two women—at least, two that we know of. I have their names and everything. Everybody knows that a lot of bishops have one concubine, but two! I thought it would make a good story for the paper."

"It may yet. Write me up a story, George, about the Bishop of Bologna and his loves. Make it sensational, but accurate. Set it up and pull three or four galley proofs; then put the type away in a safe place."

It took Padway a week to gain an audience with the Bishop of Bologna, who was providentially in Rome. The bishop was a gorgeously dressed person with a beautiful, bloodless face. Padway suspected a highly convoluted brain behind that sweet, ascetic smile.

Padway kissed the bishop's hand, and they murmured pleasant nothings. Padway talked of the Church's wonderful work, and how he tried in his humble way to further it at every opportunity.

"For instance," he said, "—do you know of my weekly paper, reverend sir?"

"Yes, I read it with pleasure."

"Well, you know I have to keep a close watch on my boys, who are prone to err in their enthusiasm for news. I have tried to make the paper a clean sheet fit to enter any home, without scandal or libel. Though that sometimes meant I had to write most of an issue myself." He sighed. "Ah, sinful men! Would you believe it, reverend sir, that I have had to suppress stories of foul libel against members of the Holy Church? The most shocking of all came in recently." He took out one of the galley proofs. "I hardly dare show it to you, sir, lest your justified wrath at this filthy product of a disordered imagination should damn me to eternal flames."

The bishop squared his thin shoulders. "Let me see it, my son. A priest sees many dreadful things in his career. It takes a strong spirit to serve the Lord in these times."

Padway handed over the sheet. The bishop read it. A sad expression came over his angelic face. "Ah, poor weak mortals! They know not that they hurt themselves far more than the object of their calumny. It shows that we must have God's help at every turn lest we fall into sin. If you will tell me who wrote this, I will pray for him."

"A man named Marcus," said Padway. "I discharged him immediately, of course. I want nobody who is not prepared to co-operate with the Church to the full."

The bishop cleared his throat delicately. "I appreciate your righteous efforts," he said. "If there is some favor within my power—"

Padway told him about the good Father Narcissus, who was showing such a lamentable misunderstanding of Padway's enterprises . . .

Padway went to mass next Sunday. He sat well down in front, determined to face the thing out if Father Narcissus proved obdurate. He sang with the rest:

> "Imminet, imminet,
> Recta remuneret.
> Aethera donet,
> Ille supremus!"

He reflected that there was this good in Christianity: By its concepts of the Millennium and Judgment Day it accustomed people to looking forward in a way that the older religions did not, and so prepared their minds for the conceptions of organic evolution and scientific progress.

Father Narcisus began his sermon where he had left off a week before. Sorcery was the most damnable of crimes; they should not suffer a witch to live, etc. Padway stiffened.

But, continued the good priest with a sour glance at Padway, we should not in our holy enthusiasm confuse the practitioner of black arts and the familiar of devils with the honest artisan who by his ingenious devices ameliorates our journey through this vale of tears. After all, Adam invented the plow and Noah the ocean-going ship. And this new art of machine writing would make it possible to spread the word of God among the heathen more effectively . . .

When Padway got home, he called in Julia and told her he would not need her any more. Julia from Apulia began to weep, softly at first, then more and more violently. "What kind of man are you? I give you love. I give you everything. But no, you think I am just a little country girl you can do anythingyouwantandthenyougettired . . ." The patois came with such machine-gun rapidity that Padway could no longer follow. When she began to shriek and tear her dress, Padway ungallantly threatened to have Fritharik throw her out bodily forthwith. She quieted.

The day after she left, Padway gave his house a personal going over to see whether anything had been stolen or broken. Under his bed he found a curious object: a bundle of chicken feathers tied with horsehair around what appeared to be a long-defunct mouse; the whole thing stiff with dried blood. Fritharik did not know what it was. But George Menandrus did; he turned a little pale and muttered: "A curse!"

He reluctantly informed Padway that this was a bad-luck charm peddled by one of the local wizards; the discharged housekeeper had undoubtedly left it there to bring Padway to an early and gruesome death. Menandrus himself wasn't too sure he wanted to keep on with his job. "Not that I really believe in curses, excellent sir, but with my family to support I can't take chances . . ."

A raise in pay disposed of Menandrus' qualms. Menandrus was disappointed that Padway didn't use the occasion to have Julia arrested and hanged for witchcraft. "Just think," he said, "it would put us on the right side of the Church, and it would make a wonderful story for the paper!"

Padway hired another housekeeper. This one was gray-haired, rather frail-looking, and depressingly virginal. That was why Padway took her.

He learned that Julia had gone to work for Ebenezer the Jew. He hoped that Julia would not try any of her specialties on Ebenezer. The old banker did not look as if he could stand much of them.

Padway told Thomasus: "We ought to get the first message from Naples over the telegraph any time now."

Thomasus rubbed his hands together: "You are a wonder, Martinus. Only I'm worried that you'll overreach yourself. The messengers of the Italian civil service are complaining that this invention will destroy their livelihood. Unfair competition, they say."

Padway shrugged. "We'll see. Maybe there'll be some war news."

Thomasus frowned. "That's another thing that's worrying me. Thiudahad hasn't done a thing about the defense of Italy. I'd hate to see the war carried as far north as Rome."

"I'll make you a bet," said Padway. "The king's son-in-law, Evermuth the Vandal, will desert to the Imperialists. One solidus."

"Done!" Almost at that moment Junianus, who had been put in charge of operations, came in with a paper. It was the first message, and it carried the news that Belisarius had landed at Reggio; that Evermuth had gone over to him; that the Imperialists were marching on Naples.

Padway grinned at the banker, whose jaw was sagging. "Sorry, old man, but I need that solidus. I'm saving up for a new horse."

"Do You hear that, God? Martinus, the next time I lay a bet with a magician, you can have me declared incompetent and a guardian appointed."

Two days later a messenger came in and told Padway that the king was in Rome, staying at the Palace of Tiberius, and that Padway's presence was desired. Padway thought that perhaps Thiudahad had reconsidered the telescope proposal. But no.

"My good Martinus," said Thiudahad, "I must ask you to discontinue the operation of your telegraph. At once."

"What? Why, my lord king?"

"You know what happened? Eh? That thing of yours spread the news of my son-in-law's good fort—his treachery all over Rome a few hours after it happened. Bad for morale. Encourages the pro-Greek element, and brings criticism on me. *Me.* So you'll please not operate it any more, at least during the war."

"But, my lord, I thought that your army would find it useful for—"

"Not another word about it, Martinus. I forbid it. Now, let me see. Dear me, there was something else I wanted to see you about. Oh, yes, my man Cassiodorus would like to meet you. You'll stay for lunch, won't you? Great scholar, Cassiodorus."

So Padway presently found himself bowing to the pretorian prefect, an elderly, rather saintly Italian. They were immediately deep in a discussion of historiography, literature, and the hazards of the publishing business. Padway to his annoyance found that he was enjoying himself. He knew that he was abetting these spineless old dodderers in their criminal disregard of their country's defense. But— upsetting thought—he had enough of the unworldly intellectual in his own nature so that he couldn't help sympathizing with them. And he hadn't gone on an intellectual debauch of this kind since he'd arrived in old Rome.

"Illustrious Cassiodorus," he said, "perhaps you've noticed that in my paper I've been trying to teach the typesetter to distinguish between U and V, and also between I and J. That's a reform that's long been needed, don't you think?"

"Yes, yes, my excellent Martinus. The Emperor Claudius tried something of the sort. But which letter do you use for which sound in each case?"

Padway explained. He also told Cassiodorus of his plans for printing the paper, or at least part of it, in Vulgar Latin. At that Cassiodorus held up his hands in mild horror.

"Excellent Martinus! These wretched dialects that pass for Latin nowadays? What would Ovid say if he heard them? What would Virgil say? What would any of the ancient masters say?"

"As they were a bit before our time," grinned Padway, "I'm afraid we shall never know. But I will assert that even in their day the final s's and m's had been dropped from ordinary pronunciation. And in any event, the pronunciation and grammar have changed too far from the classical models ever to be changed back again. So if we want our new instrument for the dissemination of literature to be useful, we shall have to adopt a spelling that more or less agrees with the spoken language. Otherwise people won't bother to learn it. To begin with, we shall have to add a half dozen new letters to the alphabet. For instance—"

When Padway left, hours later, he had at least made an effort to bring the conversation around to measures for prosecuting the war. It had been useless, but his conscience was salved.

Padway was surprised, though he shouldn't have been, at the effect of the news of his acquaintance with the king and the prefect. Well-born Romans called on him, and he was even asked to a couple of very dull dinners that began at four P.M. and lasted most of the night.

As he listened to the windy conversation and the windier speeches, he thought that a twentieth-century after-dinner speaker could have taken lessons in high-flown, meaningless rhetoric from these people. From the slightly nervous way that his hosts introduced him around, he gathered that they still regarded him as something of a monster, but a well-behaved monster whom it might be useful to know.

Even Cornelius Anicius looked him up and issued the long-coveted invitation to his house. He did not apologize for the slight snub in the library, but his deferential manner suggested that he remembered it.

Padway swallowed his pride and accepted. He thought it foolish to judge Anicius by his own standards. And he wanted another look at the pretty brunette.

When the time came, he got up from his desk, washed his hands, and told Fritharik to come along.

Fritharik said, scandalized: "You are going to *walk* to this Roman gentleman's house?"

"Sure. It's only a couple of miles. Do us good."

"Oh, most respectable boss, you can't! It isn't done! I know; I worked for such a patrician once. You should have a sedan chair, or at least a horse."

"Nonsense. Anyway, we've got only one saddle-horse. You don't want to walk while I ride, do you?"

"N-no-not that I mind walking; but it would look funny for a gentleman's free retainer like me to go afoot like a slave on a formal occasion."

Damn this etiquette, thought Padway.

Fritharik said hopefully: "Of course there's the work-horse. He's a good-looking animal; one might almost mistake him for a heavy cavalry horse."

"But I don't want the boys in the shop to lose a couple of hours' production just because of some damned piece of face-saving—"

Padway rode the work-horse. Fritharik rode the remaining bony saddle-horse.

Padway was shown into a big room whose ornamentation reminded him of the late Victorian gewgaw culture. Through a closed door he could hear Anicius' voice coming through in rolling pentameters:

"Rome, the warrior-goddess, her seat had taken,
With breast uncovered, a mural crown on her head.
Behind, from under her spacious helmet escaping,
The hair of her plumed head flowed over her back.
Modest her mien, but sternness her beauty makes awesome.
Of purple hue is her robe, with fang-like clasp;
Under her bosom a jewel her mantle gathers.
A vast and glowing shield her side supports,
Whereon, in stout metal cast, the cave of Rhea—"

The servant had sneaked through the door and whispered. Anicius broke off his declamation and popped out with a book under his arm. He cried: "My dear Martinus! I crave your pardon; I was rehearsing a speech I am to give tomorrow." He tapped the book under his arm and smiled guiltily. "It will not be a strictly original speech; but you won't betray me, will you?"

"Of course not. I heard some of it through the door."

"You did? What did you think of it?"

"I thought your delivery was excellent." Padway resisted a temptation to add: "But what does it *mean?*" Such a question about a piece of post-Roman rhetoric would, he realized, be both futile and tactless.

"You did?" cried Anicius. "Splendid! I am greatly gratified! I shall be as nervous tomorrow as Cadmus when the dragon's teeth began to sprout, but the approval of one competent critic in advance will fortify me. And now I'll leave you to Dorothea's mercy while I finish this. You will not take offense, I hope? Splendid! Oh, daughter!"

Dorothea appeared and exchanged courtesies. She took Padway out in the garden while Anicius went back to his plagiarism of Sidonius.

Dorothea said: "You should hear father some time. He takes you back to the time when Rome really was the mistress of the world. If restoring the power of Rome could be done by fine talk, father and his friends would have restored it long ago."

It was hot in the garden, with the heat of an Italian June. Bees buzzed.

Padway said: "What kind of flower do you call that?"

She told him. He was hot. And he was tired of strain and responsibility and ruthless effort. He wanted to be young and foolish for a change.

He asked her more questions about flowers—trivial questions about unimportant matters.

She answered prettily, bending over the flowers to remove a bug now and then. She was hot too. There were little beads of sweat on her upper lip. Her thin dress stuck to her in places. Padway admired the places. She was standing close to him, talking with grave good humor about flowers and about the bugs and blights that beset them. To kiss her, all he had to do was reach and lean forward a bit. He could hear his blood in his ears. The way she smiled up at him might almost be considered an invitation.

But Padway made no move. While he hesitated his mind clicked off reasons: (a) He didn't know how she'd take it, and shouldn't presume on the strength of a mere friendly smile; (b) if she resented it, as she very likely would, there might be repercussions of incalculable scope; (c) if he made love to her, what would she think he was after? He didn't want a mistress—not that Dorothea Anicius would be willing to become such—and he was not, as far as he knew, in need of a wife; (d) he was in a sense already married . . .

So, he thought, you wanted to be young and foolish a few minutes ago, eh, Martin, my boy? You can't; it's too late; you'll always stop to figure things out rationally, as you've been doing just now. Might as well resign yourself to being a calculating adult, especially as you can't do anything about it.

But it made him a little sad that he would never be one of those impetuous fellows—usually described as tall and handsome—who take one look at a girl, know her to be their destined mate, and sweep her into their arms. He let Dorothea do most of the talking as they wandered back into the house to dinner with Cornelius Anicius and Anicius' oratory. Padway, watching Dorothea as she preceded him, felt slightly disgusted with himself for having let Julia invade his bed.

They sat down—or rather stretched themselves out on the couches, as Anicius insisted on eating in the good old Roman style, to Padway's acute discomfort. Anicius had a look in his eye that Padway found vaguely familiar.

Padway learned that the look was that of a man who is writing or is about to write a book. Anicius explained: "Ah, the degenerate times we live in, excellent Martinus! The lyre of Orpheus sounds but faintly; Calliope veils her face; blithe Thalia is mute; the hymns of our Holy Church have drowned Euterpe's sweet strains. Yet a few of us strive to hold high the torch of poetry while swimming the Hellespont of barbarism and hoeing the garden of culture."

"Quite a feat," said Padway, squirming in a vain effort to find a comfortable position.

"Yes, we persist despite Herculean discouragements. For instance, you will not consider me forward in submitting to your publisher's eagle-bright scrutiny a little book of verses." He produced a sheaf of papyrus. "Some of them are not really bad, though I their unworthy author say so."

"I should be very much interested," said Padway, smiling with effort. "As for publication, however, I should warn you that I'm contracted for three books by your excellent colleagues already. And between the paper and my schoolbook, it will be some weeks before I can print them."

"Oh," said Anicius with a drooping inflection.

"The Illustrious Trajanus Herodius, the Distinguished John Leontius, and the Respectable Felix Avitus. All epic poems. Because of market conditions these gentlemen have undertaken the financial responsibility of publication."

"Meaning—ah?"

"Meaning that they pay cash in advance, and get the whole price of their books when sold, subject to bookseller's discounts. Of course, distinguished sir, if the book is really good, the author doesn't have to worry about getting back his cost of publication."

"Yes, yes, excellent Martinus, I see. What chances do you think my little creation would have?"

"I'd have to see it first."

"So you would. I'll read some of it now, to give you the idea." Anicius sat up. He held the papyrus in one hand and made noble gestures with the other:

"Mars with his thunderous trumpet his lord acclaims,
The youthful Jupiter, new to his throne ascended,
Above the stars by all-wise Nature placed.
The lesser deities their sire worship,
To ancient sovereignty with pomp succeeding—"

"Father," interrupted Dorothea, "your food's getting cold."

"What? Oh, so it is, child."

"And," continued Dorothea, "I think you ought to write some good Christian sentiment some time, instead of all that pagan superstition."

Anicius sighed. "If you ever have a daughter, Martinus, marry her off early, before she develops the critical faculty."

In August Naples fell to General Belisarius. Thiudahad had done nothing to help the town except seize the families of the small Gothic garrison to insure their fidelity. The only vigorous defense of the city was made by the Neapolitan Jews. These, having heard of Justinian's religious complexes, knew what treatment to expect under Imperial rule.

Padway heard the news with a sick feeling. There was so much that he could do for them if they'd only let him alone. And it would take such a little accident to snuff him out—one of the normal accidents of warfare, like that which happened to Archimedes. In this age civilians who got in the way of belligerent armies would be given the good old rough and ruthless treatment to which the military of his own twentieth century, after a brief hundred and fifty years of relatively humane forbearance, had seemed to be returning.

Fritharik announced that a party of Goths wanted to look Padway's place over. He added in his sepulchral voice: "Thiudegiskel's with them. You know, the king's son. Watch out for him, excellent boss. He makes trouble."

There were six of them, all young, and they tramped into the house wearing swords, which was not good manners by the standards of the times. Thiudegiskel was a handsome, blond young man who had inherited his father's high-pitched voice.

He stared at Padway, like something in a zoo, and said: "I've wanted to see your place ever since I heard you and the old man were mumbling over manuscripts together. I'm a curious chap, you know, active-minded. What the devil are all these silly machines for?"

Padway did some explaining, while the prince's companions made remarks about his personal appearance in Gothic, under the mistaken impression that he couldn't understand them.

"Ah, yes," said Thiudegiskel, interrupting one of the explanations. "I think that's all I'm interested in here. Now, let's see that bookmaking machine."

Padway showed him the presses.

"Oh, yes, I understand. Really a simple thing, isn't it? I could have invented it myself. All very well for those who like it. Though I can read and write and all that. Better than most people, in fact. But I never cared for it. Dull business, not suited to a healthy man like me."

"No doubt, no doubt, my lord," said Padway. He hoped that the red rage he was feeling didn't show in his face.

"Say, Willimer," said Thiudegiskel, "you remember that tradesman we had fun with last winter? He looked something like this Martinus person. Same big nose."

Willimer roared with laughter. "Do I remember it! *Guths in himinam!* I'll never forget the way he looked when we told him we were going to baptize him in the Tiber, with rocks tied to him so the angels couldn't carry him off! But the funniest thing was when some soldiers from the garrison arrested us for assault!"

Thiudegiskel said to Padway, between guffaws: "You ought to have been there, Martinus. You should have seen old Liuderis' face when he found out who we were! We made him grovel, I can tell you. I've always regretted that I missed the flogging of those soldiers who pinched us. That's one thing about me; I can appreciate the humor of things like that."

"Would you like to see anything more, my lord?" asked Padway, his face wooden.

"Oh, I don't know—Say, what are all those packing cases for?"

"Some stuff just arrived for our machines, my lord, and we haven't gotten around to burning the cases," Padway lied.

Thiudegiskel grinned good-naturedly. "Trying to fool me, huh? I know what you're up to. You're going to sneak your stuff out of Rome before Belisarius gets here, aren't you? That's one thing about me; I can see through little tricks like that. Well, can't say I blame you. Though it sounds as though you had inside information on how the war will go." He examined a new brass telescope on a workbench. "This is an interesting little device. I'll take it along, if you don't mind."

That was too much even for Padway's monumental prudence. "No, my lord, I'm sorry, but I need that in my business."

Thiudegiskel's eyes were round with astonishment. "Huh? You mean I can't have it?"

"That, my lord, is it."

"Well . . . uh . . . uh . . . if you're going to take that attitude, I'll pay for it."

"It isn't for sale."

Thiudegiskel's neck turned slowly pink with embarrassment and anger. His five friends moved up behind him, their left hands resting on their sword hilts.

The one called Willimer said in a low tone: "I *think*, gentlemen, that our king's son has been insulted."

Thiudegiskel had laid the telescope on the bench. He

reached out for it; Padway snatched it up and smacked the end of the tube meaningfully against his left palm. He knew that, even if he got out of this situation in one piece, he'd curse himself for a double-dyed knight-erranting idiot. But at the moment he was too furious to care.

The uncomfortable silence was broken by the shuffle of feet behind Padway; he saw the Goths' eyes shift from him. He glanced around. In the doorway was Fritharik, with his sword belt hitched around so the scabbard was in front, and Nerva, holding a three-foot length of bronze bar-stock. Behind them came the other workmen with an assortment of blunt instruments.

"It seems," said Thiudegiskel, "that these people have no manners whatever. We should give them a lesson. But I promised my old man to lay off fighting. That's one thing about me; I always keep my promises. Come along boys." They went.

"*Whew!*" said Padway. "You boys certainly saved my bacon. Thanks."

"Oh, it was nothing," said George Menandrus airily. "I'm rather sorry they didn't stay to fight it out. I'd have enjoyed smacking their thick skulls."

"You? *Honh!*" snorted Fritharik. "Boss, the first thing I saw when I started to round the men up was this fellow sneaking out the back door. You know how I changed his mind? I said I'd hang him with a rope made of his own guts if he didn't stick! And the others, I threatened to cut their heads off and stick them on the fence palings in front of the house." He contemplated infinite calamities for a few seconds, then added: "But it won't do any good, excellent Martinus. Those fellows will have it in for us, and they're pretty influential, naturally. They can get away with anything. We'll all end in nameless graves yet."

Padway struggled mightily to get the movable parts of his equipment packed for shipment to Florence. As far as he could remember his Procopius, Florence had not been besieged or sacked in Justinian's Gothic War, at least in the early part.

But the job was not half done when eight soldiers from the garrison descended on him and told him he was under arrest. He was getting rather used to arrest by now, so he calmly gave his foremen and editor orders about getting the equipment moved and set up, and about seeing Thomasus and trying to get in touch with him. Then he went along.

On the way he offered to stand the Goths drinks. They accepted quickly. In the wineshop he got the commander aside to suggest a little bribe to let him go. The Goth seemed to accept, and pocketed a solidus. Then when Padway, his mind full of plans for shaving his beard, getting a horse, and galloping off to Florence, broached the subject of his release, the Goth looked at him with an air of pained surprise.

"Why, most distinguished Martinus, I couldn't think of letting you go! Our commander-in-chief, the noble Liuderis, is a man of stern and rigid principles. If my men talked, he'd hear about it, and he'd break me sure. Of course I appreciate your little *gift,* and I'll try to put in a good word for you."

Padway said nothing, but he made a resolve that it would be a long day before he put in a good word for this officer.

CHAPTER VIII

LIUDERIS BLEW OUT his snowy whiskers and explained: "I am sorry you deceived me, Martinus. I never thought a true Arian would stoop to . . . ah . . . conniving with these pro-Greek Italians to let a swarm of Orthodox fanatics into Italy."

"Who says so?" asked Padway, more annoyed than apprehensive.

"No less a person than the . . . ah . . . noble Thiude-giskel. He told how when he visited your house, you not only insulted and reviled him, but boasted of your connections with the Imperialists. His companions corroborated him. They said you had inside information about a plan for betraying Rome, and that you were planning to move your effects elsewhere to escape any disturbances. When my men arrested you, they found that you were in fact about to move."

"My dear sir!" said Padway in exasperation. "Don't you think I have *any* brains? If I were in on some plot of some sort, do you think I would go around telling the world about it?"

Liuderis shrugged. "I would not know. I am only doing my duty, which is to hold you for questioning about this secret plan. Take him away, Sigifrith."

Padway hid a shudder at the word "questioning." If this honest blockhead got set on an idea, he'd have a swell chance of talking him out of it.

The Goths had set up a prison camp at the north end of the city, between the Flaminian Way and the Tiber. Two sides of the camp were formed by a hastily erected fence, and the remaining two by the Wall of Aurelian. Padway found that two Roman patricians had preceded him in custody; both said they had been arrested on suspicion of complicity in an Imperialist plot. Several more Romans arrived within a few hours.

The camp was no escape-proof masterpiece, but the Goths made the best of it. They kept a heavy guard around the fence and along the wall. They even had a squad camped across the Tiber, in case a prisoner got over the wall and tried to swim the river.

For three days Padway rusticated. He walked from one end of the camp to the other, and back, and forward, and back. When he got tired of walking he sat. When he got tired of sitting he walked. He talked a little with his fellow prisoners, but in a moody and abstracted manner.

He'd been a fool—well, at least he'd been badly mistaken—in supposing that he could carry out his plans with as little difficulty as in Chicago. This was a harsh, convulsive world; you had to take it into account, or you'd get caught in the gears sooner or later. Even the experts at political intrigue and uniformed banditry often came to a bad end. What chance would such a hopelessly unwarlike and unpolitical alien as himself have?

Well, what chance did he have anyway? He'd kept out of

public affairs as much as possible, and here he was in a horrifying predicament as a result of a petty squabble over a brass telescope. He might just as well have gone adventuring up to the hilt. If he ever got out, he *would* go adventuring. He'd show 'em!

The fourth day failed to settle Padway's gnawing anxiety about his interrogation. The guards seemed excited about something. Padway tried to question them, but they rebuffed him. Listening to their muttering talk, he caught the word *folkmote*. That meant that the great meeting was about to be held near Terracina, at which the Goths would consider what to do about the loss of Naples.

Padway got into talk with one of the patrician prisoners.

"Bet you a solidus," he said, "that they depose Thiudahad and elect Wittigis king in his place."

The patrician, poor man, took him on.

Thomasus the Syrian arrived. He explained: "Nerva tried to get in to see you, but he couldn't afford a high enough bribe. How do they treat you?"

"Not badly. The food's not exactly good, but they give us plenty of it. What worries me is that Liuderis thinks I know all about some alleged conspiracy to betray Rome, and he may use drastic methods to try to get information out of me."

"Oh, that. There's a conspiracy afoot, all right. But I think you'll be safe for a few days anyway. Liuderis has gone off to a convention, and the Goths' affairs are all in confusion." He went on to report on the state of Padway's business. "We got the last case off this morning. Ebenezer the Jew is going up to Florence in a couple of weeks. He'll look in and see that your foremen haven't run off with all your property."

"You mean to see *whether* they've run off with it. Any war news?"

"None, except that Naples suffered pretty badly. Belisarius' Huns got out of hand when the town was captured. But I suppose you know that. You can't tell me that you haven't some magical knowledge of the future."

"Maybe. Which side do you favor, Thomasus?"

"Me? Why—I haven't thought about it much, but I suppose I favor the Goths. These Italians haven't any more fight than a lot of rabbits, so the country can't be really independent. And if we have to be ruled by outsiders, the Goths have been a lot easier on us than Justinian's tax gathers would be. Only my Orthodox friends can't be made to see it that way. Like my cousin, Antiochus, for instance. They become completely irrational when they get off on the subject of Arian heretics."

When Thomasus was ready to go, he asked Padway: "Is there anything I can bring you? I don't know what the guards will allow, but if there's something—"

Padway thought. "Yes," he said. "I'd like some painting equipment."

"Painting? You mean you're going to whitewash the Wall of Aurelian?"

"No; stuff for painting pictures. *You* know." Padway made motions.

"Oh, *that* kind of painting. Sure. It'll pass the time."

Padway wanted to get on top of the wall, to give the camp a proper looking-over for ways of escape. So when Thomasus brought his painting supplies he applied to the commander of the guards, a surly fellow named Hrotheigs, for permission. Hrotheigs took one look, and spoke one word: *"Ni!"*

Padway masked his annoyance and retired to ponder on How to Win Friends. He spent the better part of the day experimenting with his equipment, which was a bit puzzling to one unaccustomed to it. A fellow prisoner explained that you coated one of the thin boards with wax, painted in water color on this surface, and then warmed the board until the wax became soft enough to absorb the pigment. It was ticklish business; if you overheated the board, the wax melted and the colors ran.

Padway was not a professional artist by any means. But an archæologist has to know something about drawing and painting in the exercise of his profession. So the next day Padway felt confident enough to ask Hrotheigs if he would like his portrait painted.

The Goth for the first time looked almost pleased. *"Could* you make a picture of me? I mean, one for me to keep?"

"Try to, excellent captain. I don't know how good it'll be. You may end up looking like Satanas with a gutache."

"Huh? Like whom? Oh, I see! Haw! Haw! Haw! You *are* a funny fellow."

So Padway painted a picture. As far as he could see, it looked as much like any black-beared ruffian as it did like Hrotheigs. But the Goth was delighted, asserting that it was his spit and image. The second time he made no objections to Padway's climbing the wall to paint landscapes from the top, merely detailing a guard to keep close to him at all times.

Saying that he had to pick the best vantage point for painting, Padway walked up and down the wall the length of the camp. At the north end, where the wall turned east toward the Flaminian Gate, the ground outside sloped down for a few yards to a recess in the river bank—a small pool full of water lilies.

He was digesting this information when his attention was attracted to the camp. A couple of guards were bringing in a prisoner in rich Gothic clothes who was not co-operating. Padway recognized Thiudegiskel, the king's precious son. This was too interesting. Padway went down the ladder.

"*Hails,*" he said. "Hello."

Thiudegiskel was squatting disconsolately by himself. He was somewhat disheveled, and his face had been badly bruised. Both eyes would soon be swollen shut. The Roman patricians were grinning unsympathetically at him.

He looked up. "Oh, it's you," he said. Most of the arrogance seemed to have been let out of him, like air out of a punctured balloon.

"I didn't expect to run into you here," said Padway. "You look like you had a hard time of it."

"*Unh.*" Thiudegiskel moved his joints painfully. "A couple of those soldiers we had flogged for arresting us got hold of me." Surprisingly, he grinned, showing a broken front tooth. "Can't say I blame them much. That's one thing about me; I can always see the other fellow's point of view."

"What are you in for?"

"Hadn't you heard? I'm not the king's son any more. Or rather my old man isn't king. The convention deposed him and elected that fathead Wittigis. So Fathead has me locked up so I can't make trouble."

"*Tsk, tsk.* Too bad."

Thiudegiskel grinned painfully again. "Don't try to tell me *you're* sorry for me. I'm not that stupid. But say, maybe you can tell me what sort of treatment to expect, and whom to bribe, and so on."

Padway gave the young man a few pointers on getting on with the guards, then asked: "Where's Thiudahad now?"

"I don't know. The last I'd heard he'd gone up to Tivoli to get away from the heat. But he was supposed to come back down here this week. Some piece of literary research he's working on."

Between what Padway remembered of the history of the time and the information he had recently picked up, he had a good picture of the course of events. Thiudahad had been kicked out. The new king, Wittigis, would put up a loyal and determined resistance. The result would be worse than no resistance at all as far as Italy was concerned. He could not beat the Imperialists, having no brains to speak of. He would begin his campaign with the fatal mistake of marching off to Ravenna, leaving Rome with only its normal garrison.

Neither could the Imperialist beat him with their slender forces except by years of destructive campaigning. Anything, from Padway's point of view, was preferable to a long war. If the Imperialists did win, their conquest would prove ephemeral. Justinian should not be blamed too much; he would require supernatural foresight to foresee all this. That was the point: Padway *did* have such foresight. So wasn't it up to him to do something about it?

Padway had no violent prejudices in favor either of Gothic or of Imperial rule. Neither side had a political setup for which he could feel enthusiasm. Liberal capitalism and socialist democracy both had good points, but he did not think there was the remotest chance of establishing either one definitively in the sixth-century world.

If the Goths were lazy and ignorant, the Greeks were rapacious and venal. Yet these two were the best rulers available. The sixth-century Italian was too hopelessly unmilitary to stand on his own feet, and he was supinely aware of the fact.

On the whole the Gothic regime had not had an ill effect. The Goths enforced tolerance on a people whose idea of religious liberty was freedom to hang, drown, or burn all members of sects other than their own. And the Goths looked on the peninsula as a pleasant home to be protected and preserved. This was a more benign attitude than could be expected of a savage like the Meroving monarch, Theudebert of Austrasia, or an insatiable grafter like Justinian's quartermaster-general, John of Cappadocia.

Suppose, then, he decided to work for a quick victory by the Goths instead of a quick victory for the Imperialists. How could the Gothic regime be succored? It would do no good for him to try to persuade the Goths to get rid of Wittigis. If the Gothic king, whoever he was, could be induced to take Padway's advice, something might be done. But old Thiudahad, worthless as he was by himself, *might* be managed.

A plan began to form in Padway's mind. He wished he'd told Thomasus to hurry back sooner. To keep darkness from falling—

When Thomasus did appear, Padway told him: "I want a couple of pounds of sulphur, mixed with olive oil to form a paste, and some candles. And forty feet of light rope, strong enough to support a man. Believe it or not, I got the idea from the voluptuous Julia. Remember how she acted when I fumigated the house?"

"Look here, Martinus, you're perfectly safe for the time being, so why don't you stay here instead of trying some crazy scheme of escaping?"

"Oh, I have reasons. The convention should break up today or tomorrow, from what I hear, and I've got to get out before it does."

"Listen to him! Just listen! Here I am, the best friend he has in Rome, and does he pay attention to my advice? No! He wants to break out of the camp, and maybe get an arrow through the kidney for his pains, and then go get mixed up with Gothic politics. Did you ever hear the like? Martinus, you haven't some wild idea of getting yourself elected king of the Goths, have you? Because it won't work. You have to be——"

"I know," grinned Padway. "You have to be a Goth of the noble family of the Amalings. That's why I'm in such a hurry to get out. You want the business saved so you'll get your loans back, don't you?"

"But how on earth am I going to smuggle those things in? The guards watch pretty closely."

"Bring the sulphur paste in a container at the bottom of a food basket. If they open it, say it's something my physician ordered. Better coach Vekkos to corroborate. And for the rope—let's see—I know, go to my tailor and get a green cloak like mine. Have him fasten the rope inside around the edges, lightly, so it can be ripped out quickly. Then, when you come in, lay your cloak alongside mine, and pick mine up when you go."

"Martinus, that's a crazy plan. I'll get caught sure, and what will become of my family? No, you'd better do as I say. I can't risk innocent persons' futures. What time would you want me to come around with the rope and things?"

Padway sat on the Wall of Aurelian in the bright morning sunshine. He affected to be much interested in the Tomb of Hadrian down river on the other side. The guard who was detailed to him, one Aiulf, looked over his shoulder. Padway appreciated Aiulf's interest, but he sometimes wished the Goth's beard was less long and bristly. It was a disconcerting thing to have crawling over your shoulder and down your shirt front when you were trying to get the color just right.

"You see," he explained in halting Gothic, "I hold the brush out and look past it at the thing I am painting, and mark its apparent length and height off on the brush with my thumb. That is how I keep everything in proper proportion."

"I see," said Aiulf in equally bad Latin—both were having a little language practice. "But suppose you want to paint a small picture—how would you say—with a lot of things in it just the same? The measurements on the brush would all be too large, would they not?" Aiulf, for a camp guard, was not at all stupid.

Padway's attention was actually on things other than the Tomb. He was covertly watching all the guards, and his little pile of belongings. All the prisoners did that, for obvious reasons. But Padway's interest was special. He was wondering when the candle concealed in the food basket would burn down to the sulphur paste. He had apparently had a lot of trouble that morning getting his brazier going; actually he had been setting up his little infernal machine. He also couldn't help stealing an occasional nervous glance at the soldiers across the river, and at the lily-covered pool behind him.

Aiulf grew tired of watching and retired a few steps. The guard sat down on his little stool, took up his flutelike instrument and started to play faint moaning notes. The thing sounded like a banshee lost in a rain barrel, and never failed to give Padway the slithering creeps. But he valued Aiulf's good will too much to protest.

He worked and worked, and still his contraption showed no signs of life. The candle must have gone out; it would surely have burned down to the sulphur by now. Or the sulphur had failed to light. It would soon be time for lunch. If they called him down off the wall, it would arouse suspicion for him to say he wasn't hungry. Perhaps.

Aiulf stopped his moaning for an instant. "What is the matter with your ear, Martinus? You keep rubbing it."

"Just an itch," replied Padway. He didn't say that fingering his ear lobe was a symptom of shrieking nervousness. He kept on painting. One result of his attempt, he thought, would be the lousiest picture of a tomb ever painted by an amateur artist.

As he gave up hope, his nerves steadied. The sulphur hadn't lit, and that was that. He'd try again tomorrow . . .

Below, in the camp, a prisoner coughed; then another. Then they were all coughing. Fragments of talk floated up: "What the devil——" "Must be the tanneries——" "Can't be, they're two or three miles from here——" "That's burning sulphur, by all the saints——" "Maybe the Devil is paying us a call——" People moved around; the coughing increased; the guards trailed into the camp. Somebody located the source of the fumes and kicked Padway's pile. Instantly a square yard was covered with yellow mush over which little blue flames danced. There were strangled shouts. A thin wisp of blue smoke crawled up through the still air. The guards on the wall, including Aiulf, hurried to the ladder and down.

Padway had planned his course so carefully in his mind that he went through it almost unconscious of the invididual acts. Over his brazier were two little pots of molten wax, both already pigmented. He plunged his hands into the scalding stuff and smeared his face and beard with dark green wax. It hardened almost instantly. With his fingers he then smeared three large circles of yellow wax from the other pot over the green.

Then, as if he were just strolling, he walked up to the angle of the wall, squatted down out of sight of those in the camp, ripped the rope out of the lining of his cloak, and slipped a bight over a projection at the corner of the wall. A last glance across the river showed that the soldiers over there had not, apparently, noticed anything, though they could have heard the commotion inside the wall if they had listened. Padway lowered himself down the north face of the wall, hand over hand.

He flipped the rope down after him. As he did so, a flash of sunlight on his wrist made him curse silently. His watch would be ruined by prolonged soaking; he should have thought to give it to Thomasus. He saw a loose stone in the wall. He pulled it out, wrapped the watch in his handkerchief, put it in the hole, and replaced the stone. It took only a few seconds, but he knew he was being insanely foolish to risk the loss of time for the sake of the watch. On the other hand, being the kind of person he was, he just could not ruin the watch knowingly.

He trotted down the slope to the pond. He did not throw himself in, but walked carefully out to where it was a couple of feet deep. He sat down in the dark water, like a man getting into an over-hot tub bath, and stretched out on his back among the pond lilies until only his nose and eyes were above water. He moved the water plants around until they hid him pretty thoroughly. For the rest, he had to rely on the green of his cloak and his bizarre facial camouflage for concealment. He waited, listening to his own heart and the murmur from over the wall.

He did not have long to wait. There were shouts, the blowing of whistles, the pounding of large Gothic feet on the top of the wall. The guards waved to the soldiers across the river. Padway didn't dare turn his head far enough to see, but he could imagine a rowboat's being put out.

"*Ailôe*! The fiend seems to have vanished into thin air—"

"He's hiding somewhere, you idiot! Search, search! Get the horses out!"

Padway lay still while guards searched around the base of the wall and poked swords into bushes barely big enough to hide a Sealyham. He lay still while a small fish maddeningly investigated his left ear. He lay still, his eyes almost closed, while a couple of Goths walked around the pond and stared hard at it and him, hardly thirty feet from them. He lay still while a Goth on a horse rode splashing through the pond, actually passing within fifteen feet of him. He lay still through the whole long afternoon, while the sounds of search and pursuit rose and ebbed, and finally faded away completely.

Nevitta Gummund's son was justifiably startled when a man rose from the shadows of the bushes that lined the driveway to his house and called him by name. He had just ridden up to the farm. Hermann, in tow as usual, had his sword halfway out before Martin Padway identified himself.

He explained: "I got here a couple of hours ago, and wanted to borrow a horse. Your people said you were away at the convention, but that you'd be back sometime tonight. So I've been waiting." He went on to tell briefly of his imprisonment and escape.

The Goth bellowed. "Ha! Ha! You mean to say, ha! ha! that you lay in the pond all day, right under the noses of the guards, with your face painted up like a damned flower? Ha! ha! Christ, that's the best thing I ever heard!" He dismounted. "Come on in the house and tell me more about it. *Whew*, you certainly look like a frog pond, old *friend!*" Later, he said more seriously: "I'd like to trust you, Martinus. By all accounts, you're a pretty reliable young man, in spite of your funny foreign ways. But how do I *know* that Liuderis wasn't right? There *is* something queer about you, you know. People say you can foresee the future, but try to hide the fact. And, some of those machines of yours do smell a little bit of magic."

"I'll tell you," said Padway thoughtfully. "I can see a little bit in the future. Don't blame me; I just happen to have that power. Satanas has nothing to do with it. That is, I can sometimes see what will happen *if* people are allowed to do what they intend to. If I use my knowledge to intervene, that changes the future, so my vision isn't true any more.

"In this case, I know that Wittigis will lose the war. And will lose in the worst possible way—at the end of years of fighting which will completely devastate Italy. Not his fault. He's simply built that way. The last thing I want is to see the country ruined; it would spoil a lot of plans I have. So I propose to intervene and change the natural course of events. The results may be better; they could hardly be worse."

Nevitta frowned. "You mean you're going to try to defeat the Goths quickly. I don't think I could agree to such—"

"No. I propose to win your war for you. If I can."

CHAPTER IX

PADWAY WASN'T MISTAKEN, and if Procopius' history had not lied, Thiudahad ought to pass along the Flaminian Way within the next twenty-four hours in his panicky flight to Vienna. All the way, Padway had asked people whether the king had passed that way. All said no.

Now, on the outskirts of Narnia, he was as far north as he dared go. The Flaminian Way forked at this point, and he had no way of knowing whether Thiudahad would take the new road or the old. So he and Hermann made themselves easy by the side of the road and listened to their horses cropping grass. Padway looked at his companion with a bilious eye. Hermann had taken much too much beer aboard at Ocriculum.

To Padway's questions and his instructions about taking turns at watching the road, he merely grinned idiotically and said, *"Ja, ja!"* He had finally gone to sleep in the middle of a sentence, and no amount of shaking would arouse him.

Padway walked up and down in the shade, listening to Hermann's snores and trying to think. He had not slept since the previous day, and here that whiskery slob was taking the ease that he, Padway, needed badly. Maybe he should have grabbed a couple of hours at Nevitta's—but if he'd once gotten to sleep nothing short of an earthquake would have gotten him up. His stomach was jumpy; he had no appetitie; and this accursed sixth-century world didn't even have coffee to lighten the weights that dragged down the eyelids.

Suppose Thiudahad didn't show up? Or suppose he went roundabout, by the Salarian Way? Or suppose he'd already passed? Time after time he'd tensed himself as dust appeared down the road, only to have it materialize as a farmer driving an oxcart, or a trader slouching along on a mule, or a small half-naked boy driving goats.

Could his, Padway's, influence have changed Thiudahad's plans so that his course of action would be different from what it should have been? Padway saw his influence as a set of ripples spreading over a pool. By the mere fact of having known him, the lives of people like Thomasus and Fritharik had already been changed radically from what they would have been if he'd never appeared in Rome.

But Thiudahad had only seen him twice, and nothing very drastic had happened either time. Thiudahad's course in time and space might have been altered, but only very slightly. The other higher-up Goths, such as King Wittigis, ought not to have been affected at all. Some of them might have read his paper. But few of them were literary and many were plain illiterate.

Tancredi had been right about the fact that this was an entirely new branch of the tree of time, as he called it. The things that Padway had done so far, while only a fraction of what he hoped to do, couldn't help but change history somewhat. Yet he had not vanished into thin air, as he should have if this was the same history that had produced him in the year 1908 A.D.

He glanced at his wrist, and remembered that his watch was cached in the Wall of Aurelian. He hoped he'd get a chance to recover it some day, and that it would be in running order when he did.

That new bit of dust down the road was probably another damned cow or flock of sheep. No, it was a man on a horse. Probably some fat Narnian burgher. He was in a hurry, whoever he was. Padway's ears caught the blowing of a hard-ridden mount; then he recognized Thiudahad.

"Hermann!" he yelled.

"*Akhkhkhkhkhkhg,*" snored Hermann. Padway ran over and hit the Goth with his boot. Hermann said: "*Akhkhkhkhg. Akhkhkhkhg. Meina luibs—guhhg. Akhkhkhg.*"

Padway gave up; the ex-king would be up to them in an instant. He swung aboard his horse and trotted out into the road with his arm up. "*Hai,* Thiudahad! My lord!"

Thiudahad kicked his horse and hauled on the reins at the same time, apparently undecided whether to stop, try to run with Padway, or turn around the way he had come. The exausted animal thereupon put his head down and bucked.

Waters of the Nar showed blue between Thiudahad and his horse for a second; he came down on the saddle with a thump and clutched it frantically. His face was white with terror and covered with dust.

Padway leaned over and gathered up the reins. "Calm yourself, my lord," he said.

"Who . . . who . . . what—Oh, it's the publisher. What's your name? Don't tell me; I know it. Why are you stopping—We've got to get to Ravenna . . . Ravenna—"

"Calm yourself. You'd never reach Ravenna alive."

"What do you mean? Are you out to murder me, too?"

"Not at all. But, as you may have heard, I have some small talent reading the future."

"Oh, dear, yes, I've heard. What's . . . what's my future? Don't tell me I'm going to be killed! *Please* don't tell me that, excellent Martinus. I don't want to die. If they'll just let me live I won't bother anybody again, ever." The little gray-bearded man fairly gibbered with fright.

"If you'll keep still for a few minutes, I'll tell you what I can. Do you remember when, for a consideration, you swindled a noble Goth out of a beautiful heiress who had been promised to him in marriage?"

"Oh, dear me. That would be Optaris Winithar's son, wouldn't it? Only don't say 'swindled,' excellent Martinus. Merely . . . ah . . . exerted my influence on the side of the man. But why?"

"Wittigis gave Optaris a commission to hunt you down and kill you. He's following you now, riding day and night. If you continue toward Ravenna, this Optaris will catch up with you before you get there, pull you off your horse, and cut your throat—like this, *khh!*" Padway clutched his own throat with one hand, tilted up his chin, and drew a finger across his Adam's apple.

Thiudahad covered his face with his hands. "What'll I do? What'll I do? If I could get to Ravenna, I have friends there—"

"That's what *you* think. I know better."

"But isn't there anything? I mean, is Optaris fated to kill me no matter what I do? Can't we hide?"

"Perhaps. My prophecy is good only if you try to carry out your original plan."

"Well, we'll hide, then."

"All right, just as soon as I get this fellow awake." Padway indicated Hermann.

"Why wait for him? Why not just leave him?"

"He works for a friend of mine. He was supposed to take care of me, but it's turned out the other way around." They dismounted, and Padway resumed his efforts to arouse Hermann.

Thiudahad sat down on the grass and moaned: "Such ingratitude! And I was such a good king—"

"Sure," said Padway acidly, "except for breaking your oath to Amalaswentha not to interfere in public affairs, and then having her murdered—"

"But you don't understand, excellent Martinus. She had our noblest patriot, Count Tulum, murdered, along with those other two friends of her son Athalarik—"

"—and intervening—for a consideration, again—in the last Papal election; offering to sell Italy to Justinian in return for an estate near Constantinople and an annuity—"

"*What?* How did you know—I mean it's a lie!"

"I know lots of things. To continue: neglecting the defense of Italy; failing to relieve Naples—"

"Oh, dear me. You don't understand, I tell you. I hate all this military business. I admit I'm no soldier; I'm a scholar. So I leave it to my generals. That's only sensible, isn't it?"

"As events have proved—no."

"Oh, dear. Nobody understands me," moaned Thiudahad. "I'll tell you, Martinus, why I did nothing about Naples. I knew it was no use. I had gone to a Jewish magician, Jeconias of Naples, who has a great reputation for successful prophecy. Everybody knows the Jews are good at that. This man took thirty hogs, and put ten in each of three pens. One pen was labeled 'Goths,' one 'Italians,' and one 'Imperialists.' He starved them for some weeks. We found that all the 'Goths' had died; that the 'Italians' were some of them dead, and the rest had lost their hair; but the 'Imperialists' were doing fine. So we knew the Goths were bound to lose. In that case, why sacrifice a lot of brave boys' lives to no effect?"

"Bunk," said Padway. "My prophecies are as good as that fat faker's any day. Ask my friends. But any prophecy is good only as long as you follow your original plans. If you follow yours, you'll get your throat cut like one of your magical hogs. If you want to live, you'll do as I say and like it."

"What? Now, look here, Martinus, even if I'm not king anymore, I'm of noble birth, and I won't be dictated to—"

"Suit yourself." Padway rose and walked toward his horse. "I'll ride down the road a way. When I meet Optaris, I'll tell him where to find you."

"*Eek!* Don't do that! I'll do what you say! I'll do anything, only don't let that awful man catch me!"

"All right. If you obey orders, I may even be able to get you back your kingship. But it'll be purely nominal this time, understand." Padway didn't miss the crafty gleam in Thiudahad's eyes. Then the eyes shifted past Padway.

"Here he comes! It's the murderer, Optaris!" he squealed.

Padway spun around. Sure enough, a burly Goth was poking up the road toward them. This was a fine state of affairs, thought Padway. He'd wasted so much time talking that the pursuer had caught up with them. He should have had a few hours' leeway still; but there the man was. What to do; what to do?

He had no weapon but a knife designed for cutting steaks rather than human throats. Thiudahad had no sword, either.

Padway, brought up in a world of Thompson submachine-guns, swords seemed silly weapons, always catching you between the knees. So it had never occurred to him to form the habit of toting one. He realized his error as his eye caught one flash of Optaris' blade. The Goth leaned forward and kicked his horse straight at them.

Thiudahad stood rooted to the spot, trembling violently and making little meowing sounds of terror. He wet his dry lips and squealed one word over and over: "*Armaio!* Mercy!" Optaris grinned through his beard and swung his right arm up.

At the last instant Padway dived at the ex-king and tackled him, rolling him out of the way of Optaris' horse. He scrambled up as Optaris reined in furiously, the animal's hoofs kicking dust forward as they braked. Thiudahad got up, too, and bolted for the shelter of the trees. With a yell of rage Optaris jumped to the ground and took after him. Meantime, Padway had had a rush of brains to the head. He bent over Hermann, who was beginning to revive, tore Hermann's sword out of the scabbard, and sprinted to cut off Optaris. It wasn't necessary. Optaris saw him coming and started for him, evidently preferring to settle with Padway before the latter could take him in flank.

Now Padway cursed himself for all kinds of a fool. He

had only the crudest theoretical knowledge of fencing, and
no tactical experience whatever. The heavy Gothic broadsword was unfamiliar and uncomfortable in his sweaty
hand. He could see the whites of Optaris' eyes as the Goth
trotted up to him, took his measure, shifted his weight, and
whipped his sword arm up for a back-hand slash.

Padway's parry was more instinctive than designed. The
blades met with a great clang, and Padway's borrowed
sword went sailing away, end over end, into the woods.
Quick as a flash Optaris struck again, but met only air and
swung himself halfway around. If Padway was an incompetent fencer, there was nothing the matter with his legs. He
sprinted after his sword, found it, and kept right on running with Optaris panting heavily after him. He'd been a
minor quarter-mile star in college; if he could run the legs
off Optaris maybe the odds would be nearer even when they
finally—*umph!* He tripped over a root and sprawled on his
face.

Somehow he rolled over and got to his feet before Optaris came up to him. And, somehow, he got himself between Optaris and a pair of big oaks that grew too close together to be squeezed between. So there was nothing for
him to do but stand and take it. As the Goth chumped forward and swung his sword over his head, Padway, in a last
despairing gesture, thrust as far as he could at Optaris' exposed chest, more with the idea of keeping the man off
than of hurting him.

Now, Optaris was an able fighter. But the sword-play of
his age was entirely with the edge. Nobody had ever
worked a simple stop thrust on him. So it was no fault of
his that in his effort to get within cutting distance of Padway he spitted himself neatly on the outthrust blade. His
own slash faltered and ended against one of the oaks, The
Goth gasped, tried to breathe, and his thick legs slowly
sagged. He fell, pulling the sword out of his body. His
hands clawed at the dirt, and a great river of blood ran
from his mouth.

When Thiudahad and Hermann came up they found
Padway vomiting quietly against a tree trunk. He barely
heard their congratulations.

He was reacting to his first homicide with a combination

of humane revulsion and buck fever. He was too sensible to blame himself much, but he was still no mere thoughtless adventurer to take a killing lightly. To save Thiudahad's worthless neck, he had killed one who was probably a better man, who had a legitimate grudge against the ex-king, and who had never harmed Padway. If he could only have talked to Optaris, or have wounded him slightly . . . But that was water over the dam; the man was as dead as one of John the Egyptian's customers. The living presented a more immediate problem.

He said to Thiudahad: "We'd better disguise you. If you're recognized, Wittigis will send another of your friends around to call. Better take that beard off first. It's too bad you already have your hair cut short, Roman style."

"Maybe," said Hermann, "could cut him off nose. Then nobody recognize."

"Oh!" cried Thiudahad, clutching the member indicated. "Oh, dear me! You wouldn't *really* disfigure me that way, most excellent, most noble Martinus?"

"Not if you behave yourself, my lord. And your clothes are entirely too fancy. Hermann, could I trust you to go into Narnia and buy an Italian peasant's Sunday-go-to-church outfit?"

"*Ja, ja,* you give me *silubr.* I go."

"What?" squeaked Thiudahad. "I will not get myself up in such an absurd costume! A prince of the Amalings has his dignity—"

Padway looked at him narrowly and felt the edge of Hermann's sword. He said silkily: "Then, my lord, you *do* prefer the loss of your nose? No? I thought not. Give Hermann a couple of solidi. We'll make a prosperous farmer of you. How are you on Umbrian dialect?"

CHAPTER X

LIUDERIS OSKAR'S SON, commander of the garrison of the city of Rome, looked out of his office window gloomily at the gray September skies. The world had been turning upside down too often for this simple, loyal soul. First Thiudahad is deposed and Wittigis elected king. Then Wittigis, by some mysterious process, convinces himself and the other Gothic leaders that the way to deal with the redoubtable Belisarius is to run off to Ravenna, leaving an inadequate garrison in Rome. And now it transpires that the citizens are becoming dissatisfied; worse, that his troops are afraid to try to hold the city against the Greeks; worse yet, that Pope Silverius, blandly violating his oaths to Wittigis on the ground that the king is a heretic, has been corresponding with Belisarius with the object of arranging a bloodless surrender of the city.

But all these shocks were mild compared to that which he got when the two callers announced by his orderly turned out to be Martin Padway and ex-King Thiudahad, whom he recognized immediately despite his clean-shaven state. He simply sat, stared, and blew out his whiskers. "You!" he said. "You!"

"Yes, us," said Padway mildly. "You know Thiudahad, King of the Ostrogoths and Italians, I believe. And you know me. I'm the king's new quæstor, by the way." (That meant he was a combination of secretary, legal draftsman, and ghost writer.)

"But . . . but we have another king! You two are supposed to have prices on your heads or something."

"Oh, that," smiled Padway negligently. "The Royal Council was a little hasty in its action as we hope to show them in time. We'll explain—"

"But where have you been? And how did you escape from my camp? And what are you doing here?"

"One thing at a time, please, excellent Liuderis. First, we've been up at Florence collecting a few supplies for the campaign. Second—"

"What campaign?"

"—second, I have ways of getting out of camps denied to ordinary men. Third, we're here to lead your troops against the Greeks and destroy them."

"You are mad, both of you! I shall have you locked up until—"

"Now, now, wait until you hear us. Do you know of my . . . ah . . . little gifts for seeing the future results of men's actions?"

"Unh, I *have* heard things. But if you think you can seduce me away from my duty by some wild tale—"

"Exactly, my dear sir. The king will tell you how I foresaw Optaris' unfortunate attempt on his life, and how I used my knowledge to thwart Optaris' plans. If you insist, I can produce more evidence.

"For instance, I can tell you that you'll get no help from Ravenna. That Belisarius will march up the Latin Way in November. That the Pope will persuade your garrison to march away before they arrive. And that *you* will remain at your post, and be captured and sent to Constantinople."

Liuderis gasped. "Are you in league with Satanas? Or perhaps you are the Devil himself? I have not told a soul of my determination to stay if my garrison leaves, and yet you know of it."

Padway smiled. "No such luck, excellent Liuderis. Just an ordinary flesh-and-blood man who happens to have a few special gifts. Moreover, Wittigis will eventually lose his war, though only after years of destructive fighting. That is, all these things will happen unless you change your plans."

It took an hour of talk to wear Liuderis down to the point where he asked: "Well, what plans for operations against the Greeks did you have in mind?"

Padway replied: "We know they'll come by the Latin Way, so there's no point in leaving Terracina garrisoned. And we know about when they'll come. Counting the Terracina garrison, about how many men could you collect by the end of next month?"

Liuderis blew out his whiskers and thought. "If I called in the men from Formia—six thousand, perhaps seven. About half and half archers and lancers. That is, assuming that King Wittigis did not hear of it and interfere. But news travels slowly."

"If I could show you how you'd have a pretty good chance against the Greeks, would you lead them out?"

"I do not know. I should have to think. Perhaps. If as you say our king—excuse me, noble Thiudahad, I mean the *other* king—is bound to be defeated, it might be worth taking a chance on. What would you do?"

"Belisarius has about ten thousand men," replied Padway. "He'll leave two thousand to garrison Naples and other southern towns. He'll still out-number us a little. I notice that your brave Wittigis ran off when he had twenty thousand available."

Liuderis shrugged and looked embarrassed. "It is true, that was not a wise move. But he expects many thousands more from Gaul and Dalmatia."

"Have your men had any practice at night attacks?" asked Padway.

"Night attacks? You mean to assault the enemy at *night*? No. I never heard of such a proceeding. Battles are always fought in the daytime. A night attack does not sound very practical to me. How would you keep control of your men?"

"That's just the point. Nobody ever heard of the Goths making a night attack, so it ought to have some chance of success. But it'll require special training. First, you'll have to throw out patrols on the roads leading north, to turn back people who might carry the news to Ravenna. And I need a couple of good catapult engineers. I don't want to depend entirely on the books in the libraries for my artillery. If none of your troops knows anything about catapults, we ought to be able to dredge up a Roman or two who does. And you might appoint me to your staff—you don't have staffs? Then it's time you started—at a reasonable salary—"

Padway lay on a hilltop near Fregellae and watched the Imperialists through a telescope. He was surprised that Belisarius, as the foremost soldier in his age, hadn't thrown scouts out farther, but, then this was 536. His advance party consisted of a few hundred mounted Huns and Moors, who galloped about, pushing up side roads a few hundred yards and racing back. Then came two thousand of the famous *cataphracti* or cuirassiers, trotting in orderly formation. The low, cold sun glittered on the scales of their armor. Their standard was a blown-up leather serpent writhing from the top of a long pole, like a balloon from Macy's Thanksgiving Day parade.

These were the best and certainly the most versatile soldiers in the world, and everybody was afraid of them. Padway, watching their cloaks and scarves flutter behind them, didn't feel too confident himself. Then came three thousand Isaurian archers marching afoot, and finally two thousand more cuirassiers.

Liuderis, at Padway's elbow, said: "That is some sort of signal. *Ja,* I believe they are going to camp there. How did you know they would pick that spot, Martinus?"

"Simple. You remember that little device I had on the wheel of that wagon? That measures distance. I measured the distances along the road. Knowing their normal day's march and the point they started from, the rest was easy."

"*Tsk, tsk,* wonderful. How do you think of all those things?" Liuderis' big, trustful eyes reminded Padway of those of a St. Bernard. "Shall I have the engineers set up Brunhilde now?"

"Not yet. When the sun sets we'll measure the distance to the camp."

"How will you do that without being seen?"

"I'll show you when the time comes. Meanwhile make sure that the boys keep quiet and out of sight."

Liuderis frowned. "They will not like having to eat a cold supper. If we do not watch them, somebody will surely start a fire."

Padway sighed. He'd had plenty of sad experience with the temperamental and undisciplined Goths. One minute they were as excited as small boys over the plans of Myste-

rious Martinus, as they called him; the next day they were
growling on the edge of mutiny about the enforcement of
some petty regulation. Since Padway felt that it wouldn't
do for him to order them around directly, poor Liuderis
had to take it.

The Byzantines set up their camp with orderly prompti-
tude. Those, Padway thought, were real soldiers. You
could accomplish something with men like that to command. It would be a long time before the Goths attained
such a smooth perfection of movement. The Goths were
still obsessed with childish, slam-bang ideas of warfare.

Witness the grumbling that had greeted Padway's requi-
sition of a squad for engineers. Running catapults was a
sassy job, inconsistent with knightly honor. And well-born
lancers fight on foot like a lot or serfs? Perish the thought!
Padway had seduced them away from their beloved horses
by an ingenious method: He, or rather Liuderis at his
suggestion, formed a company of pikemen, loudly an-
nouncing that only that the best men would be admitted,
and that furthermore candidates would be made to *pay* for
admission. Padway explained that there was no type of
troop wherein morale and discipline were as vital as in
heavy infantry, because one man flinching from a cavalry
charge might break the line of spears and let the enemy in.

It was getting too dark for his telescope to be useful. He
could make out the general's standard in front of a big tent.
Perhaps Belisarius was one of those little figures around
it. If he had a machine-gun—but he didn't have, and never
would. You needed machines to make a machne-gun, and
machines to make those machines, and so on. If he ever
got a workable muzzle-loading musket he'd be doing well.

The standard no doubt bore the letters S. P. Q. R.—the
Senate and the People of Rome. An army of Hunnish,
Moorish, and Anatolian mercenaries, commanded by a
Thracian Slav who worked for a Dalmatian autocrat who
reigned in Constantinople and didn't even rule the city of
Rome, called himself the Army of the Roman Republic
and saw nothing funny in the act.

Padway got up, grunting at the weight of his shirt of
scale mail. He wished a lot of things, such as that he'd had
time to train some mounted archers. They were the only

troops who could really deal on even terms with the deadly Byzantine cuirassiers. But he'd have to hope that darkness would nullify the Imperialists' advantage in missile fire.

He superintended the driving of a stake into the ground and paced off the base of a triangle. With a little geometry he figured the quarter-mile distance that was Brunhilde's range, and ordered the big catapult set up. The thing required eleven wagon-loads of lumber, even though it was not of record size. Padway hovered around his engineers nervously, jumping and hissing reprimands when somebody dropped a piece of wood.

Snatches of song came from the camp. Apparently Padway's scheme of leaving a wagon-load of brandy where foragers would be sure to find it had had results, despite Belisarius' well-known strictness with drunken soldiers.

The bags of sulphur paste were brought out. Padway looked at his watch, which he had recovered from the hole in the wall. It was nearly midnight, though he'd have sworn the job hadn't taken over an hour.

"All ready?" he asked. "Light the first bag." The oil-soaked rags were lit. The bag was placed in the sling. Padway himself pulled the lanyard. *Wht-bam!* said Brunhilde. The bag did a fiery parabola. Padway raced up the little knoll that masked his position. He missed seeing the bag land in the camp. But the drunken songs ended, instead there was a growing buzz as of a nest of irritated hornets. Behind him whips cracked and ropes creaked in the dark, as the horses heaved on the block-and-tackle he'd rigged up for quick recocking. *Wht-bam!* The fuse came out of the second bag in midair, so that it continued its course to the camp unseen and harmless. Never mind, another would follow in a few seconds. Another did. The buzz was louder, and broken by clear, high-pitched commands. *Wht-bam!*

"Liuderis!" Padway called. "Give your signal!"

Over in the camp the horse lines began to scream. The horses didn't like the sulphur dioxide. Good; maybe the Imperialist cavalry would be immobilized. Under the other noises Padway heard the clank and shuffle of the Goths, getting under way. Something in the camp was burning brightly. Its light showed a company of Goths on Padway's right picking their way over the broken, weed-covered ground. Their big round shields were painted white for recognition, and every man had a wet rag tied over his nose. Padway thought they ought to be able to frighten the Imperialists if they couldn't do anything else. On all sides the night was alive with the little orange twinkle of firelight on helmets, scale skirts, and sword blades.

As the Goths closed in, the noise increased tenfold, with the addition of organized battle yells, the flat snap of bowstrings, and finally the blacksmith's symphony of metal on metal. Padway could see "his" men, black against the fires, grow smaller and then drop out of sight into the camp ditch. Then there was only a confused blur of movement and a great din as the attackers scrambled up the other side —invisible until they popped up into the firelight again— and mixed it with the defenders.

One of the engineers called to say that that was all the sulphur bags, and what should they do now? "Stand by for further orders," repled Padway.

"But, captain, can't we go fight? We're missing all the fun!"

"Ni, you can't! You're the only engineer corps west of the Adriatic that's worth a damn, and I won't have you getting yourselves killed off!"

"Huh!" said a voice in the dark. "This is a cowardly way of doing, standing back here. Let's go, boys. To hell with Mysterious Martinus!" And before Padway could do anything, the twenty-odd catapult men trotted off toward the fires.

Padway angrily called for his horse and rode off to find Liuderis. The commander was sitting his horse in front of a solid mass of lancers. The firelight picked out their helms and faces and shoulders, and the forest of vertical lances. They looked like something out of a Wagnerian opera.

Padway asked: "Has there been any sign of a sortie yet?"

"No."

"There will be, if I know Belisarius. Who's going to lead this troop?"

"I am."

"Oh, lord! I thought I explained why the commander should—"

"I know, Martinus," said Liuderis firmly. "You have lots of ideas. But you're young. I'm an old soldier, you know. Honor requires that I lead my men. Look, isn't something doing in the camp?"

True enough, the Imperial cavalry was coming out. Belisarius had, despite his difficulties, managed to collect a body of manageable horses and cuirassiers to ride them. As they watched, this group thundered out the main gate, the Gothic infantry scattering in all directions before them. Liuderis shouted, and the mass of Gothic knights clattered off, picking up speed as they went. Padway saw the Imperalists swing widely to take the attacking foe in the rear, and then Liuderis' men hid them. He heard the crash as the forces met, and then everything was dark confusion for a few minutes.

Little by little the noise died. Padway wondered just what had happened. He felt silly, sitting alone on his horse a quarter mile from all the action. Theoretically, he was where the staff, the reserves, and the artillery ought to be. But there were no reserves, their one catapult stood deserted off in the dark somewhere, and the artillerists and staff were exchanging sword strokes with the Imperialists up front.

With a few mental disparagements of sixth-century ideas of warfare, Padway trotted toward the camp. He came across a Goth quite peacefully tying up his shin with a piece torn from his tunic, another who clutched his stomach and moaned, and a corpse. Then he found a considerable body of dismounted Imperial cuirassiers standing weaponless.

"What are you doing?" he asked.

One replied: "We're prisoners. There were some Goths supposed to be guarding us, but they were angry at missing the looting, so they went off to the camp."

"What became of Belisarius?"

"Here he is." The prisoner indicated a man sitting on the ground with his head in his hands. "A Goth hit him on the head and stunned him. He's just coming to. Do you know what will be done with us, noble sir?"

"Nothing very drastic, I imagine. You fellows wait here

until I send somebody for you." Padway rode on toward the camp. Soldiers were strange people, he thought. With Belisarius to lead them and a fair chance to use their famous bow-plus-lance tactics, the *cataphracti* could lick thrice their number of any other troops. Now, because their leader had been conked on the head, they were as meek as lambs.

There were more corpses and wounded near the camp, and a few riderless horses calmly grazing. In the camp itself were Imperial soldiers, Isaurians and Moors and Huns, standing around in little clumps, holding bits of clothing to their noses against the reek of sulphur fumes. Goths ran hither and thither among them looking for movable property worth stealing.

Padway dismounted and asked a couple of the looters where Liuderis was. They said they didn't know, and went on about their business. He found an officer he knew, Gaina by name. Gaina was squatting by a corpse and weeping. He turned a streaked, bearded face up to Padway.

"Liuderis is dead," he said between sobs. "He was killed in the mêlée when we struck the Greek cavalry."

"Who's that?" Padway indicated the corpse.

"My younger brother."

"I'm sorry. But won't you come with me and get things organized? There are a hundred cuirassiers out there with nobody guarding them. If they come to their senses they'll make a break—"

"No, I will stay with my little brother. You go on, Martinus. You can take care of things." Gaina dissolved in fresh tears.

Padway hunted until he found another officer, Gudareths, who seemed to have some sort of wits about him. At least, he was making frantic efforts to round up a few troopers to guard the surrendered Imperialists. The minute he turned his back on his men, they melted off into the general confusion of the camp.

Padway grabbed him. "Forget them," he snapped. "Liuderis is dead, I hear, but Belisarius is alive. If we don't nab him—"

So they took a handful of Goths in tow and walked back

to where the Imperial general still sat among his men. They moved the lesser prisoners away, and set several men to guard Belisarius. Then they put a solid hour rounding up troopers and prisoners and getting them into some sort of order.

Gudareths, a small, cheerful man, talked continually: "That was some charge, some charge. Never saw a better, even in the battle against the Gepids on the Danube. We took them in flank, neatest thing you ever saw. The Greek general fought like a wild man, until I hit him over the head. Broke my sword, it did. Best stroke I ever made, by God. Even harder than the time I cut off that Bulgarian Hun's head, five years ago. Oh, yes, I've killed hundreds of enemies in my time. Thousands, even. I'm sorry for the poor devils. I'm not really a bloodthirsty fellow, but they will try to stand up against me. Say, where were you during the charge?" He looked sharply at Padway, like an accusatory chipmunk.

"I was supposed to be running the artillery. But my men ran off to join the fight. And by the time I arrived it was all over."

"*Aiw*, no doubt, no doubt. Like one time when I was in a battle with the Burgunds. My orders kept me out of the thick until it was nearly over. Of course, when I arrived I must have killed at least twenty—"

The train of troops and prisoners headed north on the Latin Way. Padway, still a little bewildered to find himself in command of the Gothic army, simply by virtue of having taken over Liuderis' responsibilities on the night of confusion, rode near the front. The best are always the first to go, he thought sadly, remembering the simple, honest old Santa Claus who lay dead in one of the wagons in the rear, and thinking of the mean and treacherous little king whom he had to manage when he got back to Rome.

Belisarius, jogging along beside him, was even less cheerful. The Imperial general was a surprisingly young man, in his middle thirties, tall and a bit stout, with gray eyes and curly brown beard. His Slavic ancestry showed in his wide cheek bones.

He said gravely: "Excellent Martinus, I ought to thank

you for the consideration you showed my wife. You went out of your way to make her comfortable on this sad journey."

"Quite all right, illustrious Belisarius. Maybe you'll capture me some day."

"That seems hardly likely, after this fiasco. By the way, if I may ask, just what are you? I hear you called Mysterious Martinus! You're no Goth, nor yet an Italian, by your speech."

Padway gave his impressively vague formula about America.

"Really? They must be a people skilled in war, these Americans. I knew when the fight started that I wasn't dealing with any barbarian commander. The timing was much too good, especially on that cavalry charge. *Phew!* I can still smell that damnable sulphur!"

Padway saw no point in explaining that his previous military experience consisted of one year of R.O.T.C. in a Chicago high school. He asked: "How would you like the idea of coming over to our side? We need a good general, and as Thiudahad's quæstor I'll have my hands full otherwise."

Belisarius frowned. "No, I swore an oath to Justinian."

"So you did. But as you'll probably hear, I can sometimes see a little into the future. And I can tell you that the more faithful you are to Justinian, the meaner and more ungrateful he'll be to you. He'll—"

"I said no!" said Belisarius sternly. "You can do what you like with me. But the word of Belisarius is not to be questioned."

Padway argued some more. But, remembering his Procopius, he had little hope of shaking the Thracian's stern rectitude. Belisarius was a fine fellow, but his rigid virtue made him a slightly uncomfortable companion. He asked: "Where's your secretary, Procopius of Cæsarea?"

"I don't know. He was in southern Italy, and supposedly on his way to join us."

"Good. We'll gather him in. We shall need a competent historian."

Belisarius' eyes widened. "How do you know about the

histories he's collecting notes for? I thought he'd told nobody but me."

"Oh, I have ways. That's why they call me Mysterious Martinus."

They marched into Rome by the Latin Gate, north past the Circus Maximus and the Colosseum, and up the Quirinal Valley to the Old Viminal Gate and the Pretorian Camp.

Here Padway gave orders to encamp the prisoners, and told Gudareths to set a guard over them. That was obvious enough. Then he found himself in the midst of a crowd of officers looking at him expectantly. He could not think what orders to give next.

He rubbed his ear lobe for a few seconds, then took the captive Belisarius aside, "Say, illustrious general," he said in a low voice, "what in hell do I do next? This military business isn't my proper trade."

There was a hint of amusement in Belisarius' broad and usually solemn face. He answered: "Call out your paymaster and have him pay the men's wages. Better give them a little bonus for winning the battle. Detail an officer to round up some physicians to tend the wounded; at least I don't suppose a barbarian army like this has its own medical corps. There ought to be a man whose duty it is to check the rolls. Find out about it. I hear the commander of the Rome garrison was killed. Appoint a man in his place, and have the garrison returned to barracks. Tell the commanders of the other contingents to find what lodging they can for their men. If they are to board at private houses, say the owners will be compensated at standard rates. You can find those out later. But you ought to make a speech."

Me make a speech?" hissed Padway in horror. "My Gothic is lousy——"

"That's part of the business, you know. Tell them what good soldiers they are. Make it short. They won't listen very closely anyway."

CHAPTER XI

AFTER SOME SEARCHING Padway located Thiudahad in the Arian Library. The little man was barricaded behind a huge load of books. Four bodyguards sprawled on a table, a bench, and the floor, snoring thunderously. The librarian was glaring at them with a look compounded of hydrofluoric acid and cobra venom, but did not dare protest.

Thiudahad looked up blearily. "Oh, yes, it's the publisher fellow. Martinus, isn't it?"

"That's right, my lord. I might add that I'm your new quæstor."

"What? What? Who told you so"

"You did. You appointed me."

"Oh, dear me, so I did. Silly of me. When I get engrossed in books I really don't know what's going on. Let's see, you and Liuderis were going to fight the Imperialists, weren't you?"

"Hoc ille, my lord. It's all over."

"Really? I suppose you sold out to Belisarius, didn't you? I hope you arranged for an estate and an annuity from Justinian for me."

"It wasn't necessary, my lord. We won."

"What?"

Padway gave a résumé of the last three days' events. "And you'd better get to bed early tonight, my lord. We're leaving in the morning for Florence."

"Florence? Why, in heaven's name?"

"We're on our way to intercept your generals, Asinar and Grippas. They're coming back from Dalmatia, having been ordered out by the Imperial general, Constantianus. If we can catch them before they get to Ravenna and learn about Wittigis, we might be able to get your crown back."

Thiudahad sighed. "Yes, I suppose we ought to. But how did you know that Asinar and Gippas were coming home?"

"Trade secret, my lord. I've also sent a force of two thousand to reoccupy Naples. It's held by General Herodianus with a mere three hundred, so there shouldn't be much trouble."

Thiudahad narrowed his watery eyes. "You do get things done, Martinus. If you can deliver that vile usurper Wittigis into my hands—*aaah!* I'll send clear to Constantinople for a torturer, if I can't find one ingenious enough in Italy!"

Padway did not answer that one, having his own plans for Wittigis. He said instead: "I have a pleasant surpise for you. The pay chests of the Imperial army—"

"Yes?" Thiudahad's eyes gleamed. "They're mine, of course, Very considerate of you, excellent Martinus."

"Well, I did have to dip into them a little to pay our troops and clear up the army's bills. But you'll find the rest an agreeable addition to the royal purse. I'll be waiting for you at home."

Padway neglected to state that he had sequestered over half the remainder and deposited the money with Thomasus. Who owns the pay chests of a captured army, especially when the captor is a volunteer theoretically serving one of two rival kings, was a question that the legal science of the time was hardly equipped to decide. In any event Padway was sure he could make better use of the money than Thiudahad. I'm becoming quite a hardened criminal, he thought with pride.

Padway rode up to Cornelius Anicius' home. Its rhetorical owner was out at the baths, but Dorothea came out. Padway had to admit that it made him feel pretty good to sit on a powerful horse in a (to him) romantic get-up, with cloak and boots and all, and report to one of the prettier girls of Rome on his success.

She said: "You know, Martinus, father was silly at first about your social standing. But after all you've done he's forgotten about that. Of course he is not enthusiatic about Gothic rule. But he much prefers Thiudahad, who *is* a scholar, to that savage Wittigis."

"I'm glad of that. I like your old man."

"Everybody's talking about you now. They call you 'Mysterious Martinus.' "

"I know. Absurd, isn't it?"

"Yes. You never seemed very mysterious to me, in spite of your foreign background."

"That's great. You're not afraid of me, are you?"

"Not in the least. If you made a deal with Satanas as some people hint, I'm sure the Devil got the worst of it." They laughed. She added: "It's nearly dinner time. Won't you stay? Father will be back any time."

"I'm sorry, but I can't possibly. We're off to the wars again tomorrow."

As he rode off, he thought: If I *should change* my mind about the expediency of marriage, I'd know where to begin. She's attractive and pleasant, and has what passes for a good education here . . .

Padway made one more attempt to shake Belisarius, but without success. He did, however, enlist five hundred of the Imperial cuirassiers as a personal guard. His share of the Imperialist loot would suffice to pay them for some weeks. After that he'd see.

The trip to Florence was anything but pleasant. It rained most of the way, with intermittent snow squalls as they climbed toward the City of Flowers. Being in a hurry, Padway took only cavalry.

In Florence he sent his officers around to buy warmer clothes for the troops, and looked in on his business. It seemed to be surviving, though Fritharik said: "I don't trust any of them, excellent boss. I'm sure the foreman and this George Menandrus have been stealing, though I can't prove it. I don't understand all this writing and figuring. If you leave them alone long enough they'll steal everything, and then where'll we be? Out in the cold, headed for a pair of nameless graves."

"We'll see," said Padway. He called in the treasurer, Proclus Proclus, and asked to see the books. Proclus Proclus instantly looked apprehensive, but he got the books. Padway waded into the figures. They were all nice and neat, since he himself had taught the treasurer double-entry bookkeeping. All his employees were astounded to hear Padway burst into a shout of laughter.

"What . . . what is it, noble sir?" asked Proclus Proclus.

"Why, you poor fool, didn't you realize that with my system of bookkeeping, your little thefts would stick up in the accounts like a sore toe? Look here: thirty solidi last month, and nine solidi and some sesterces only last week. You might just as well have left a signed receipt every time you stole something!"

"What . . . what are you going to do to me?"

"Well—I *ought* to have you jailed and flogged." Padway was silent for a while and watched Proclus Proclus squirm. "But I hate to have your family suffer. And I certainly oughtn't to keep you on, after this. But I'm pretty busy, and I can't take the time to train a new treasurer to keep books in a civilized manner. So I'll just take a third of your salary until these little *borrowings* of yours are paid back."

"Thank you, thank you kindly, sir. But just to be fair—George Menandrus ought to pay a share of it, too. He—"

"Liar!" shouted the editor.

"Liar yourself! Look, I can prove it. Here's an item for one solidus, November 10th. And on November 11th George shows up with a pair of new shoes and a bracelet. I know where he bought them. On the 15th—"

"How about it, George?" asked Padway.

Menandrus finally confessed, though he insisted that the thefts were merely temporary borrowings to tide him over until pay day.

Padway divided the total liability between the two of them. He warned them sternly against recidivism. Then he left a set of plans with the foreman for new machines and metal-working processes, including plans for a machine for spinning copper plate into bowls. The intelligent Nerva caught on immediately.

As Padway was leaving, Fritharik asked him: "Can't I go with you, excellent Martinus? It's very dull here in Florence. And you need somebody to take care of you. I've saved up almost enough to get my jeweled sword back, and if you'll let—"

"No, old man. I'm sorry, but I've got to have *one* person

I can trust here. When this damned war and politics is over, we'll see."

Fritharik sighed gustily. "Oh, very well, if you insist. But I hate to think of your going around unprotected with all these treacherous Greeks and Italians and Goths. You'll end in an unmarked grave yet, I fear."

They shivered and skidded over the icy Apennines to Bologna. Padway resolved to have his men's horses shod if he could ever get a few days to spare—stirrups had been invented but not horseshoes. From Bologna to Padua—still largely in ruins from its destruction by Attila's Huns—the road was no longer the splendid stone-paved affair they had been traveling on, but a track in the mud. However, the weather turned almost springlike, which was something.

At Padua they found they had missed the Dalmatian force by one day. Thiudahad wanted to halt. "Martinus," he whined, "you've dragged my old bones all over northern Italy, and nearly frozen me to death. That's not considerate. You do owe your king some consideration, don't you?"

Padway repressed his irritation with some effort. "My lord, *do* you or *don't* you want your crown back?"

So poor Thiudahad had to go along. By hard riding they caught up with the Dalmatian army halfway to Atria. They heaved past thousands and thousands of Goths, afoot and horsemen. There must have been well over fifty thousand of them. All these big, tough-looking men had skedaddled at the mere thought that Count Constantianus was approaching.

The count had had only a small force, but Padway was the only one present who knew that, and his source of information was not strictly kosher. The Goths cheered Thiudahad and Padway's Gothic lancers, and stared and muttered at the five hundred cuirassiers. Padway had made his guard don Gothic helmets and Italian military cloaks in lieu of the spiked steel helmets and burnoose-like mantels they had worn. But still their leen chins, tight pants, and high yellow boots made them sufficiently different to arouse suspicion.

Padway found the two commanders up near the head of the column. Asinar was tall and Grippas was short, but otherwise both were just a couple of middle-aged and be-whiskered barbarians. They respectfully saluted Thiudahad, who seemed to move slightly from so much latent force. Thiudahad introduced Padway as his new prefect—no, he meant his new quæstor.

Asinar said to Padway: "In Padua we heard a rumor that war and usurpation had been going on in Italy. Just what is the news, anyway?"

Padway was for once thankful that his telegraph hadn't been operating that far north. He laughed scornfully. "Oh, our lord General Wittigis got a brainstorm a couple of weeks ago. He put himself up in Ravenna, where the Greeks couldn't kill him, and had himself proclaimed king. We've cleaned up the Greeks, and are on our way to settle with Wittigis now. These boys will be a help." All of which was rather unjust to Wittigis.

Padway wondered whether there'd be anything left of his character after a few years in this mendacious atmosphere. The two Gothic generals accepted his statement without comment. Padway decided quickly that neither of them could be called very bright.

They marched into Ravenna at noon the day after next. The mists were so thick about the northern causeway that a man had to precede the leading horsemen on foot to keep them from spattering off into the marsh.

There was some alarm in Ravenna when the force appeared in the fog. Padway and Thiudahad prudently kept quiet as Asinar and Grippas identified themselves. As a result, most of the huge force was in the city before somebody noticed the little gray man with Padway. Immediately there were shouts and runnings to and fro.

Presently a Goth in a rich red cloak ran out to the head of the column. He shouted: "What the devil's going on here? Have you captured Thiudahad, or is it the other way around?"

Asinar and Grippas sat on their horses and said: "Uh . . . well . . . that is—"

Padway spurred up front and asked: "Who are you, my dear sir?"

"If it's any of your business, I'm Unilas Wiljarith's son,

general of our lord Wittigis, King of the Goths and Italians. Now who are *you?*"

Padway grinned and replied smoothly: "I'm delighted to know you, General Unilas. I'm Martin Paduei, quæstor to old lord Thiudahad, King of the Goths and Italians. Now that we know each other—"

"But, you fool, there isn't any King Thiudahad! He was deposed! We've got a new king! Or hadn't you heard about it?"

"Oh, I've heard lots of things. But, my excellent Unilas, before you make any more rude remarks, consider that we —that is to say King Thiudahad—have over sixty thousand troops in Ravenna, whereas you have about twelve thousand. You don't want any unnecessary unpleasantness, do you?"

"Why, you impudent . . . you . . . uh . . . did you say *sixty* thousand?"

"Maybe seventy; I haven't counted them."

"Oh. That's different."

"I thought you'd see it that way."

"What are you going to do?"

"Well, if you can tell where *General* Wittigis is, I thought we might pay him a call."

"He's getting married today. I think he ought to be on his way to St. Vitalis' Church about now."

"You mean he hasn't married Mathaswentha yet?"

"No. There was some delay in getting his divorce."

"Quick, how do you get to St. Vitalis' Church?"

Padway hadn't hoped to be in time to interfere with Wittigis' attempt to engraft himself on the Amal family tree by his forcible marriage of the late Queen Amalaswentha's daughter. But this was too good an opportunity to let slip.

Unilas pointed out a dome flanked by two towers. Padway shouted to his guard and kicked his horse into a canter. The five hundred men galloped after, spattering unfortunate pedestrians with mud. They thundered across a bridge over one of Ravenna's canals, the stench from which fully lived up to its reputation, and up to the door of St. Vitalis' Church.

There were a score of guards at the door, through which organ music wafted faintly. The guards brought their spears up to "poise."

Padway reined in and turned to the commander of his guard, a Macedonian named Achilleus. "Cover them," he snapped.

There was a quick, concerted movement among the cuirassiers, who had been sorting themselves into a semicircle in front of the church door. The next instant the guards were looking at a hundred stiff Byzantine bows drawn to the cheek. "*Nu*," said Padway in Gothic, "if you boys will put your stickers down and your hands up, we have an appointment—oh, that's better. Much better." He slid off his horse. "Achilleus, give me a troop. Then surround the church, and keep those in in and those out out until I finish with Wittigis."

He marched into St. Vitalis' Church with a hundred cuirassiers at his heels. The organ music died with a wail, and people turned to look at him. It took his eyes a few seconds to become accustomed to the gloom.

In the center of the huge octagon was a pickle-faced Arian bishop, and three people stood before him. One was a big man in a long, rich robe, with a crown on his dark graying hair: King Wittigis. Another was a tallish girl with a strawberries-and-cream complexion and her hair in thick golden braids: the princess Mathaswentha. The third was an ordinary Gothic soldier, somewhat cleaned up, who stood beside the bride and held her arm behind her back. The audience was a handful of Gothic nobles and their ladies.

Padway walked very purposefully down the aisle, *thump, thump, thump*. People squirmed and rustled in their seats and murmured: "The Greeks! The Greeks are in Ravenna!"

The bishop spoke up: "Young man, what is the meaning of this intrusion?"

"You'll soon learn, my lord bishop. Since when has the Arian faith countenanced the taking of a woman to wife against her will?"

"What's that? Who is being taken against her will? What

business is this wedding of yours? Who are you, who dares interrupt—"

Padway laughed his most irritating laugh. "One question at a time, please. I'm Martinus Paduei, quæstor to King Thiudahad. Ravenna is in our hands, and prudent persons will comport themselves accordingly. As for the wedding, it isn't normally necessary to assign a man to twist the bride's arm to make sure she gives the right answers. You don't want to marry this man, do you, my lady?"

Mathaswentha jerked her arm away from the soldier, who had been relaxing his grip. She made a fist and punched him in the nose with enough force to rock his head back on its hinges. Then she swung at Wittigis, who dodged back. "You beast!" she cried. "I'll claw your eyes—"

The bishop grabbed her arm. "Calm yourself, my daughter! Please! In the house of God—"

King Wittigis had been blinking at Padway, gradually soaking in the news. Mathaswentha's attack shocked him out of his lethargy. He growled: "You're trying to tell me that the miserable pen pusher, Thiudahad, has taken the town? *My* town?"

"That, my lord, is the general idea. I fear you'll have to give up your idea of becoming an Amaling and ruling the Goths. But we'll—"

Wittigis' face had been turning darker and darker red. Now he burst into a shocking roar. "You swine!" he yelled. "You think I'll hand over my crown and bride peaceably? By Jesus, I'll see you in the hottest hell first!" As he spoke he whipped out his sword and ran heavily at Padway, his gold-embroidered robe flapping.

Padway was not entirely taken by surprise. He got his own sword out and parried Wittigis' terrific downward cut easily enough, though the force of the blow almost disarmed him. Then he found himself chest to chest with the Goth, hugging the barrel torso and chewing Wittigis' pepper-and-salt beard. He tried to shout to his men, but it was like trying to talk with a mouth full of shredded wheat.

He spat out, it seemed, half a bale of the stuff. "Grab

. . . *gffth* . . . *pffth* . . . grab him, boys! Don't hurt him!"

That was easier said than done. Wittigis struggled like a captive gorilla, even when five men were hanging onto him, and he bellowed and foamed all the while. The Gothic gentlemen were standing up, some with hands on their sword hilts, but in a hopeless minority, none seemed anxious to die for his king just then. Wittigis began to sob between roars.

"Tie him up until he cools off," said Padway unfeelingly. "My lord bishop, may I trouble you for pen and paper?"

The bishop looked bleakly at Padway, and called a sexton, who led Padway to a room off the vestibule. Here he sat down and wrote:

Martinus Paduei to Thomasus the Syrian. Greetings:
My dear Thomasus: I am sending you with this letter the person of Wittigis, former King of the Goths and Italians. His escort has orders to deliver him to your house secretly, so forgive me for any alarm they cause you if they get you out of bed.

As I remember, we have a telegraph tower under construction on the Flaminian Way near Helvillum. Please arrange to have a chamber constructed in the earth underneath this tower and fitted up as an apartment forthwith. Incarcerate Wittigis therein with an adequate guard. Have him made as comfortable as possible, as I judge him a man of moody temperament, and I do not wish him to harm himself.

The utmost secrecy is to be observed at all times. That should not be too difficult, as this tower is in a wild stretch of country. It would be advisable to have Wittigis delivered to the tower by guards other than those who take him to Rome, and to have him guarded by men who speak neither Latin nor Gothic. They shall release their prisoner only on my order, delivered either in person or via the telegraph, or without orders in the event of my imprisonment or death.

With best regards,
MARTINUS PADUEI.

Padway said to Wittigis: "I'm sorry to have to treat you so roughly, my lord. I would not have interfered if I hadn't known it was necessary to save Italy."

Wittigis had relapsed into morose taciturnity. He glared silently.

Padway continued: "I'm really doing you a favor, you know. If Thiudahad got hold of you, you would die—slowly."

There was still no reply.

"Oh, well, take him away boys. Wrap him up so the people won't recognize him, and use the back streets."

Thiudahad peered moistly at Padway. "Marvelous, marvelous, my dear Martinus. The Royal Council accepted the inevitable. The only trouble is that the evil usurper had my crown altered to fit his big head; I'll have to alter it back. Now I can devote my time to some real scholarly research. Let's see—there was something else I wanted to ask you. Oh, yes, what did you do with Wittigis?"

Padway put on a benign smile. "He's out of your reach, my lord king."

"You mean you killed him? Now, that's too bad! Most inconsiderate of you, Martinus. I told you I'd promised myself a nice long session with him in the torture chambers—"

"No, he's alive. Very much so."

"What? What? Then produce him, at once!"

Padway shook his head. "He's where you'll never find him. You see, I figured it would be foolish to waste a good spare king. If anything happened to you, I might need one in a hurry."

"You're insubordinate, young man! I won't stand for it! You'll do as your king orders you, or else—"

Padway grinned, shaking his head. "No, my lord. Nobody shall hurt Wittigis. And you'd better not get rough with me, either. His guards have orders to release him if anything happens to me. He doesn't like you any better than you like him. You can figure the rest out for yourself."

"You devil!" spat the king venomously. "Why, oh, why

did I ever let you save my life? I haven't had a moment's peace since. You might have a little consideration for an old man," he whined. "Let's see, what was I talking about?"

"Perhaps," said Padway, "about the new book we're going to get out in our joint names. It has a perfectly splendid theory, about the mutual attraction of masses. Accounts for the movements of the heavenly bodies, and all sorts of things. It's called the law of gravitation."

"Really? Now, that's most interesting, Martinus, most interesting. It would spread my fame as a philosopher to the ends of the earth, wouldn't it?"

Padway asked Unilas if Wittigis' nephew Urias was in Ravenna. Unilas said yes, and sent a man to hunt him up.

Urias was big and dark like his uncle. He arrived scowling defiance. "Well, Mysterious Martinus, now that you've overthrown my uncle by trickery, what are you going to do with me?"

"Not a thing," said Padway. "Unless you force me to."

"Aren't you having a purge of my uncle's family?"

"No. I'm not even purging your uncle. In strict confidence, I'm hiding Wittigis to keep Thiudahad from harming him."

"Really? Can I believe that?"

"Sure. I'll even get a letter from him, testifying to the good treatment he's getting."

"Letters can be produced by torture."

"Not with Wittigis. For all your uncle's faults, I think you will agree that he's a stubborn chap."

Urias relaxed visibly. "That's something. Yes, if that's true, perhaps you have some decency, after all."

"Now to get down to business. How do you feel about working for us—that is, nominally for Thiudahad but actually for me?"

Urias stiffened. "Out of the question. I'm resigning my commission, of course. I won't take any action disloyal to my uncle."

"I'm sorry to hear that. I need a good man to command the reoccupation of Dalmatia."

Urias shook his head stubbornly. "It's a question of loyalty. I've never gone back on my plighted word yet."

Padway sighed. "You're as bad as Belisarius. The few trustworthy and able men in the world won't work with me because of previous obligations. So I have to struggle along with crooks and dimwits."

Darkness seemed to want to fall by mere inertia—

CHAPTER XII

LITTLE BY LITTLE Ravenna's nonce population flowed away, like trickles of water from a wet sponge on a tile floor. A big trickle flowed north, as fifty thousand Goths marched back toward Dalmatia. Padway prayed that Asinar, who seemed to have little more glimmering of intelligence than Grippas, would not have another brainstorm and come rushing back to Italy before he'd accomplished anything.

Padway did not dare leave Italy long enough to take command of the campaign himself. He did what he could by sending some of his personal guard along to teach the Goths horse-archery tactics. Asinar might decide to ignore this newfangled nonsense as soon as he was out of sight. Or the cuirassiers might desert to Count Constantianus. Or—but there was no point in anticipating calamities.

Padway finally found time to pay his respects to Mathaswentha. He told himself that he was merely being polite and making a useful contact. But he knew that actually he didn't want to leave Ravenna without another look at the luscious wench.

The Gothic princess received him graciously. She spoke excellent Latin, in a rich contralto vibrant with good health. "I thank you, excellent Martinus, for saving me from that beast. I shall never be able to repay you properly."

They walked into her living room. Padway found that it

was no effort at all to keep in step with her. But then; she was almost as tall as he was.

"It was very little, my lady," he said. "We just happened to arrive at an opportune time."

"Don't deprecate yourself, Martinus. I know a lot about you. It takes a real man to accomplish all you have. Especially when one considers that you arrived in Italy, a stranger, only a little over a year ago."

"I do what I must, princess. It may seem impressive to others, but to me it's more as if I had been forced into each action by circumstances, regardless of my intentions."

"A fatalistic doctrine, Martinus. I could almost believe that you're a pagan. Not that I'd mind."

Padway laughed. "Hardly. I understand that you can still find pagans if you hunt around the Italian hills."

"No doubt. I should like to visit some of the little villages some day. With a good guide, of course."

"I ought to be a pretty good guide, after the amount of running around I've done in the last couple of months."

"Would you take me? Be careful; I'll hold you to it, you know."

"That doesn't worry me any, princess. But it would have to be some day. At the present rate, God knows when I'll get time for anything but war and politics, neither of which is my proper trade."

"What is, then?"

"I was a gatherer of facts; a kind of historian of periods that had no history. I suppose you could call me a historical philosopher."

"You're a fascinating person, Martinus. I can see why they call you Mysterious. But if you don't like war and politics, why do you engage in them?"

"That would be hard to explain, my lady. In the course of my work in my own country, I had occasion to study the rise and fall of many civilizations. In looking around me here, I see many symptoms of a fall."

"Really? That's a strange thing to say. Of course, my own people, and barbarians like the Franks, have occupied most of the Western Empire. But they're not a danger to civilization. They protect it from the real wild men like the

Bulgarian Huns and the Slavs. I can't think of a time when our western culture was more secure."

"You're entitled to your opinion, my lady," said Padway. "I merely put together such facts as I have, and draw what conclusions I can. Facts such as the decline in the population of Italy, despite the Gothic immigrations. And such things as the volume of shipping."

"Shipping? I never thought of measuring civilization *that* way. But in any event, that doesn't answer my question."

"*Triggws*, to use one of your own Gothic words. Well, I want to prevent the darkness of barbarism from falling over western Europe. It sounds conceited, the idea that one man could do anything like that. But I can trý. One of the weaknesses of our present set-up is slow communication. So I promote the telegraph company. And because my backers are Roman patricians suspected of Græcophile leanings, I find myself in politics up to my neck. One thing leads to another, until todaÿ I'm practically running Italy."

Mathaswentha looked thoughtful. "I suppose the trouble with slow communication is that a general can revolt or an invader overrun the border weeks before the central government hears about it."

"Right. I can see you're your mother's daughter. If I wanted to patronize you, I should say that you had a man's mind."

She smiled. "On the contrary, I should be very much pleased. At least, if you mean a man like yourself. Most of the men around here—*bah!* Squalling infants, without one idea among them. When I marry, it must be to a man— shall we say both of thought and action?"

Padway met her eyes, and was aware that his heart had stepped up several beats per minute. "I hope you find him, princess."

"I may yet." She sat up straight and looked at him directly, almost defiantly, quite unconcerned with the inner confusion she was causing him. He noticed that sitting up straight didn't make her look any less desirable. On the contrary.

She continued: "That's one reason I'm so grateful to you for saving me from the beast. Of all these thick-headed ninnies he had the thickest head. What became of him, by the way? Don't pretend innocence, Martinus. Everybody knows your guards took him into the vestibule of the church, and then he apparently vanished."

"He's safe, I hope, both from our point of view and his."

"You mean you hid him? Death would have been safer yet."

"I had reasons for not wanting him killed."

"You did? I give you fair warning that if he ever falls into my hands, I shall not have such reasons."

"Aren't you a bit hard on poor old Wittigis? He was merely trying, in his own muddle-headed way, to defend the kingdom."

"Perhaps. But after that performance in the church I hate him." The gray eyes were cold as ice. "And when I hate, I don't do it halfway."

"So I see," said Padway dryly, jarred out of the pink fog for the moment. But then Mathaswentha smiled again, all curvesome and desirable woman. "You'll stay to dinner, of course? There will only be a few people, and they'll leave early."

"Why—" There were piles of work to be done that evening. And he needed to catch up on his sleep—a chronic condition with him. "Thank you, my lady, I shall be delighted."

By the third visit to Mathaswentha, Padway was saying to himself: There's a real woman. Ravishing good looks, forceful character, keen brain. The man who gets her will have one in a million. Why shouldn't I be the one? She seems to like me. With her to back me up, there's nothing I couldn't accomplish. Of course, she *is* a bit bloodthirsty. You wouldn't exactly describe her as a "sweet" girl. But that's the fault of the times, not of her. She'll settle down when she has a man of her own to do her fighting for her.

In other words, Padway was as thoroughly in love as such a rational and prudent man can ever be.

But how did one go about marrying a Gothic princess? You certainly didn't take her out in an automobile and kiss her lipstick off by way of a starter. Nor did you begin by knowing her in high school, the way he had known Betty. She was an orphan, so you couldn't approach her old man.

He supposed that the only thing to do was to bring the subject up a little at a time and see how she reacted.

He asked: "Mathaswentha, my dear, when you spoke of the kind of man you'd like to marry, did you have any other specifications in mind?"

She smiled at him, whereat the room swam slightly. "Curious, Martinus? I didn't have many, aside from those I mentioned. Of course he shouldn't be *too* much older than I, as Wittigis was."

"You wouldn't mind if he wasn't much taller than you?"

"No, unless he were a mere shrimp."

"You haven't any objections to large noses?"

She laughed a rich, throaty laugh. "Martinus, you *are* the funniest man. I suppose it's that you and I are different. I go directly for what I want, whether it's love, or revenge, or anything else."

"What do I do?"

"You walk all around it, and peer at it from every angle, and spend a week figuring out whether you want it badly enough to risk taking it." She added quickly. "Don't think I mind. I like you for it."

"I'm glad of that. But about noses—"

"Of *course* I don't mind! I think yours, for instance, is aristocratic-looking. Nor do I mind little red beards or wavy brown hair or any of the other features of an amazing young man named Martinus Paduei. That's what you were getting at, wasn't it?"

Padway knew a great relief. This marvelous woman went out of her way to ease your difficulties! "As a matter of fact it was, princess."

"You needn't be so frightfully respectful, Martinus. Anybody would know you are a foreigner, the way you meticulously use all the proper titles and epithets."

Padway grinned. "I don't like to take chances, as you know. Well, you see, now, it's this way. I—uh—was wondering—uh—if you don't dislike these—uh—characteristics, whether you couldn't learn to —uh—uh—"

"You don't by any chance mean love, do you?"

"Yes!" said Padway loudly.

With practice I might."

"Whew!" said Padway mopping his forehead.

"I'd need teaching," said Mathaswentha. "I've lived a sheltered life, and know little of the world."

"I looked up the law," said Padway quickly, "and while there's an ordinance against marriage of Goths to Italians, there's nothing about Americans. So——"

Mathaswentha interrupted: "I could hear you better, dear Martinus, if you came closer."

Padway went over and sat down beside her. He began again: The Edicts of Theoderik——"

She said softly: "I know the laws, Martinus. That is not what I need instruction in."

Padway suppressed his tendency to talk frantically of impersonal matters to cover emotional turmoil. He said, "My love, your first lesson will be this." He kissed her hand.

Her eyes were half closed, her mouth slightly open, and her breath was quick and shallow. She whispered: "Do the Americans, then, practice the art of kissing as we do?"

He gathered her in and applied the second lesson.

Mathaswentha opened her eyes, blinked, and shook her head. "That was a foolish question, my dear Martinus. The Americans are way ahead of us. What ideas you put in an innocent girl's head!" She laughed joyfully. Padway laughed too.

Padway said: "You've made me very happy, princess."

"You've made me happy, too, my prince. I thought I should never find anyone like you." She swayed into his arms again.

Mathaswentha sat up and straightened her hair. She said in a brisk, businesslike manner: "There are a lot of questions to settle before we decide anything finally. Wittigis, for instance."

"What about him?" Padway's happiness suddenly wasn't quite so complete.

"He'll have to be killed, naturally."

"Oh?"

"Don't 'oh' me, my dear. I warned you that I am no halfhearted hater. And Thiudahad, too."

"Why him?"

She straightened up, frowning. "He murdered my mother, didn't he? What more reason do you want? And eventually you will want to become king yourself——"

"No, I won't," said Padway.

"Not want to be king? Why, Martinus!"

"Not for me, my dear. Anyhow, I'm not an Amaling."

"As my husband you will be considered one."

"I still don't want—"

"Now, darling, you just *think* you don't. You will change your mind. While we are about it, there is that former serving-wench of yours, Julia I think her name is—"

"What about—what do you know about her?"

"Enough. We women hear everything sooner or later."

The little cold spot in Padway's stomach spread and spread. "But—but—"

"Now, Martinus, it's a small favor that your betrothed is asking. And don't think that a person like me would be jealous of a mere house-servant. But it would be a humiliation to me if she were living after our marriage. It needn't be a painful death—some quick poison . . ."

Padway's face was as blank as that of a renting agent at the mention of cockroaches. His mind was whirling. There seemed to be no end to Mathaswentha's lethal little plans. His underwear was damp with cold sweat.

He knew now that he was not in the least in love with Mathaswentha. Let some roaring Goth have this fierce blond Valkyr! He preferred a girl with less direct ideas of getting what she wanted. And no insurance man would give a policy on a member of the Amal clan, considering their dark and bloody past.

"Well?" said Mathaswentha.

"I was thinking," replied Padway. He did not say that he was thinking, frantically, how to get out of this fix.

"I just remembered," he said slowly, "I have a wife back in America."

"Oh. This is a fine time to think of *that*," she answered coldly.

"I haven't seen her for a long time."

"Well, then, there's a divorce, isn't there?"

"Not in my religion. We congregationalists believe there's a special compartment in hell for frying divorced persons."

"Martinus!" Her eyes were a pair of gray blow-torches. "You're afraid. You're trying to back out. No man shall ever do that to me and live to tell——"

"No, no, not at all!" cried Padway. "Nothing of the sort, my dear! I'd wade through rivers of blood to reach your side."

"*Hmmm.* A very pretty speech, Martinus Paduei. Do you use it on all the girls?"

"I mean it. I'm mad about you."

"Then why don't you act as if——"

"I'm devoted to you. It was stupid of me not to think of this obstacle sooner."

"Do you really love me?" She softened a little.

"Of course I do! I've never known anyone like you." The last sentence was truthful. "But facts are facts."

Mathaswentha rubbed her forehead, obviously struggling with conflicting emotions. She asked: "If you haven't seen her for so long, how do you know she's alive?"

"I don't. But I don't know that she isn't. You know how strict your laws are about bigamy. Edicts of Athalarik, Paragraph Six. I looked it up."

"You would," she said with some bitterness. "Does anyone else in Italy know about this American bitch of yours?"

"N-no—but——"

"Then aren't you being a bit silly, Martinus? What difference does it make, if she's on the other side of the earth?"

"Religion."

"Oh, the devil fly away with the priests! I'll handle the Arians when we're in power. For the Catholics, you have influence with the Bishop of Bologna, I hear, and that means with the Pope."

"I don't mean the churches. I mean my personal convictions."

"A practical fellow like you? Nonsense. You're using them as an excuse——"

Padway, seeing the fires about to flare up again, interrupted: "Now, Mathaswentha, you don't want to start a religious argument, do you? You let my creed alone and I'll say nothing against yours. Oh, I just thought of a solution."

"What?"

"I'll send a messenger to America to find out whether my wife is still alive."

"How long will that take?"

"Weeks. Months, perhaps. If you really love me you won't mind waiting."

"I'd wait," she said without enthusiasm. She looked up sharply. "Suppose your messenger finds the woman alive?"

"We'll worry about that when the time comes."

"Oh, no, we won't. We'll settle this now."

"Look, darling, don't you trust your future husband? Then—"

"Don't evade, Martinus. You're as slippery as a Byzantine lawyer."

"In that case, I suppose I'd take a chance on my immortal—"

"Oh, but, Martinus!" she cried cheerfully. "How stupid of me not to see the answer before! You shall instruct your messenger, if he finds her alive, to poison her! Such things can always be managed discreetly."

"That *is* an idea."

"It's the obvious idea! I'd prefer it to a mere divorce anyway, for the sake of my good name. Now all our worries are over." She hugged him with disconcerting violence.

"I suppose they are," said Padway with an utter lack of conviction. "Let's continue our lessons, dearest." He kissed her again, trying for a record this time.

She smiled up at him and sighed happily. "You shall never kiss anyone else, my love."

"I wouldn't think of it, princess."

"You'd better not," she said. "You will forgive me, dear boy, for getting a little upset just now. I am but an innocent young girl, with no knowledge of the world and no will of her own."

At least, thought Padway, he was not the only liar present. He stood up and pulled her to her feet. "I must go now. I'll send the messenger off the first thing. And tomorrow I leave for Rome."

"Oh, Martinus! You surely don't have to go. You just *think* you do—"

"No, really. State business, you know. I'll think of you all the way." He kissed her again. "Be brave, my dear. Smile, now."

She smiled a trifle tearfully and squeezed the breath out of him.

When Padway got back to his quarters, he hauled his orderly, an Armenian cuirassier, out of bed. "Put on your right boot," he ordered.

The man rubbed his eyes. "My *right* boot? Do I understand you, noble sir?"

"You do. Quickly, now." When the yellow rawhide boot was on, Padway turned his back to the orderly and bent over. He said over his shoulder, "You will give me a swift kick in the fundament, my good Tirdat."

Tirdat's mouth fell open. *"Kick my commander?"*

"You heard me the first time. Go ahead. Now."

Tirdat shuffled uneasily, but at Padway's glare he finally hauled off and let fly. The kick almost sent Padway sprawling. He straightened up, rubbing the spot. "Thank you, Tirdat. You may go back to bed." He started for the wash bowl to brush his teeth with a willow twig. (Must start the manufacture of real toothbrushes one of these days, he thought.) He felt much better.

But Padway did not get off to Rome the next day, or even the day after that. He began to learn that the position of king's quæstor was not just a nice well-paying job that let you order people around and do as you pleased. First Wakkis Thurumund's son, a Gothic noble of the Royal Council, came around with a rough draft of a proposed amendment to the law against horse stealing.

He explained: "Wittigis agreed to this revision of the law, but the counter-revolution took place before he had a chance to change it. So, excellent Martinus, it's up to you to discuss the matter with Thiudahad, put the amendment in proper legal language, and *try* to hold the king's attention long enough to get his signature." Wakkis grinned. "And may the saints help you if he's in a stubborn mood, my lad!"

Padway wondered what the devil to do; then he dug up Cassiodorus, who as head of the Italian Civil Service ought to know the ropes. The old scholar proved a great help, though Padway saw fit to edit some of the unnecessarily flowery phrases of the prefect's draft.

He asked Urias around for lunch. Urias came and was friendly enough, though still somewhat bitter about the treatment of his uncle Wittigis. Padway liked him. He thought, I can't hold out on Mathaswentha indefinitely. And I shan't dare take up with another girl while she looks on me as a suitor. But this fellow is big and good-looking, and he seems intelligent. If I could engineer a match—

He asked Urias whether he was married. Urias raised eyebrows. "No. Why?"

"I just wondered. What do you intend to do with yourself now?"

"I don't know. Go rusticate on my land in Picenum, I suppose. It'll be a dull life, after the soldiering I've been doing the past few years."

Padway asked casually: "Have you ever met the Princess Mathaswentha?"

"Not formally. I arrived in Ravenna only a few days ago for the wedding. I saw her in the church, of course, when you barged in. She's attractive, isn't she?"

"Quite so. She's a person worth knowing. If you like, I'll try to arrange a meeting."

Padway, as soon as Urias had gone, rushed around to Mathaswentha's house. He contrived to make his arrival look as unpremeditated as possible. He started to explain: "I've been delayed, my dear. I may not get off to Rome *ubb*—" Mathaswentha had slid her arms around his neck and stopped his little speech in the most effective manner. Padway didn't dare seem tepid, but that wasn't at all difficult. The only trouble was that it made coherent thought impossible at a time when he wanted all his craft. And the passionate wench seemed satisfied to stand in the vestibule and kiss him all afternoon.

She finally said: "Now, what were you saying, my dearest?"

Padway finished his statement. "So I thought I'd drop in for a moment." He laughed. "It's just as well I'm going to Rome; I shall never get any work done as long as I'm in the city with you. Do you know Wittigis' nephew Urias by the way?"

"No. And I'm not sure I want to. When we kill Wittigis, we shall naturally have to consider killing his nephews, too.

I have a silly prejudice against murdering people I know socially."

"Oh, my dear, I think that's a mistake. He's a splendid young man; you'd really like him. He's one Goth with both brains and character; probably the only one."

"Well, I don't know——"

"And I need him in my business, only he's got scruples against working for me. I thought maybe you could work your flashing smile on him, to soften him up a bit."

"If you think I could really help you, perhaps——"

Thus the Gothic princess had Padway and Urias for company at dinner that night. Mathaswentha was pretty cool to Urias at first. But they drank a good deal of wine, and she unbent. Urias was good company. Presently they were all laughing uproariously at his imitation of a drunken Hun, and at Padway's hastily translated off-color stories. Padway taught the other two a Greek popular song that Tirdat, his orderly, had brought from Constantinople. If Padway hadn't been conscious of a small gnawing anxiety for the success of his various plots, he'd have said he was having the best time of his life.

CHAPTER XIII

BACK IN ROME, Padway went to see his captive Imperial generals. They were comfortably housed and seemed well enough pleased with their situation, though Belisarius was moody and abstracted. Enforced inactivity didn't sit well with the former commander-in-chief.

Padway asked him: "As you can learn easily enough, we shall soon have a powerful state here. Have you changed your mind about joining us?"

"No, my lord quæstor, I have not. An oath is an oath."

"Have you ever broken an oath in your life?"

"Not to my knowledge."

"If for any reason you should swear an oath to me, I suppose, you'd consider yourself as firmly bound by it as by the others, wouldn't you?"

"Naturally. But that's a ridiculous supposition."

"Perhaps. How would it be if I offered you parole and transportation back to Constantinople, on condition that you would never again bear arms against the kingdom of the Goths and Italians?"

"You're a crafty and resourceful man, Martinus. I thank you for the offer, but I couldn't square it with my oath to Justinian. Therefore I must decline."

Padway repeated his offer to the other generals. Constantianus, Perianus, and Bessas accepted at once. Padway's reasoning was as follows: These three were just fair-to-middling commanders. Justinian could get plenty more of this kind, so there was not much point in keeping them. Of course they'd violate their oaths as soon as they were out of his reach. But Belisarius was a real military genius; he mustn't be allowed to fight against the kingdom again. Either he'd have to come over, or give his parole—which he alone would keep—or be kept in detention.

On the other hand, Justinian's clever but slightly warped mind was unreasonably jealous of Belisarius' success and his somewhat stuffy virtue. When he learned that Belisarius had stayed behind in Rome rather than give a parole that he'd be expected to break, the emperor *might* be sufficiently annoyed to do something interesting.

Padway wrote:

King Thiudahad to the Emperor Justinian, Greetings.

Your serene highness: We send you with this letter the persons of your generals Constantianus, Perianus, and Bessas, under parole not to bear arms against us again. A similar parole was offered your general Belisarius, but he declined to accept it on grounds of his personal honor.

As continuation of this war seems unlikely to achieve any constructive result, we take the opportunity of stating the terms that we should consider reasonable for the establishment of enduring peace between us.

1. Imperial troops shall evacuate Sicily and Dalmatia forthwith.

2. An indemnity of one hundred thousand solidi in gold shall be paid us for damages done by your invading armies.

3. We shall agree never again to make war, one upon the other, without mutual consultation in advance. Details can be settled in due course.

4. We shall agree not to assist any third parties, by men, money, or munitions, which hereafter shall make war upon either of us.

5. We shall agree upon a commercial treaty to facilitate the exchange of goods between our respective realms.

This is of course a very rough outline, details of which would have to be settled by conference between our representatives. We think you will agree that these terms, or others very similar in intent, are the least that we could reasonably ask under the circumstances.

We shall anticipate the gracious favor of a reply at your serenity's earliest convenience.

by MARTINUS PADUEI, Quæstor.

When he saw who his visitor was, Thomasus got up with a grunt and waddled toward him, good eye sparkling and hand outstretched. "Martinus! It's good to see you again. How does it feel to be important?"

"Wearisome," said Padway, shaking hands vigorously. "What's the news?"

"News? News? Listen to that! He's been making most of the news in Italy for the past two months, and he wants to know what the news is!"

"I mean about our little bird in a cage."

"Huh? Oh, you mean"—Thomasus looked around cautiously—"ex-King Wittigis? He was doing fine at last reports, though nobody's been able to get a civil word out of him. Listen, Martinus, of all the lousy tricks I ever heard of, springing the job of hiding him on me without warning was the worst. I'm sure God agrees with me, too. Those soldiers dragged me out of bed, and then I had them and their prisoner around the house for several days."

"I'm sorry, Thomasus. But you were the only man in Rome I felt I could trust absolutely."

"Oh, well, if you put it that way. But Wittigis was the worst grouch I ever saw. Nothing suited him."

"How's the telegraph company coming?"

"That's another thing. The Naples line is working regularly. But the lines to Ravenna and Florence won't be finished for a month, and until they are there's no chance of a profit. *And* the minority stockholders have discovered that they're a minority. You should have heard them howl! They're after your blood. At first Count Honorius was with them. He threatened to jail Vardan and Ebenezer and me if we didn't sell him—give him, practically—a controlling interest. But we learned he needed money worse than he needed the stock, and bought his from him. So the other patricians have to be satisfied with snubbing us when they pass us in the street."

"I'm going to start another paper as soon as I get time," said Padway. "There'll be two, one in Rome and one in Florence."

"Why one in Florence?"

"That's where our new capital's going to be."

"*What?*"

"Yes. It's better located than Rome with regard to roads and such, and it has a much better climate than Ravenna. In fact I can't think of a place that *hasn't* a better climate than Ravenna, hell included. I sold the idea to Cassiodorus, and between us we got Thiudahad to agree to move the administrative offices thither. If Thiudahad wants to hold court in the City of Fogs, Bogs and Frogs, that's his lookout. I'll be just as glad not to have him in my hair."

"In your hair? Oh, ho-ho-ho, you *are the* funniest fellow, Martinus. I wish I could say things the way you do. But all this activity takes my breath away. What else of revolutionary nature are you planning?"

"I'm going to try to start a school. We have a flock of teachers on the public payroll now, but all they know is grammar and rhetoric. I'm going to have things taught that really matter: mathematics, and the sciences, and medicine. I see where I shall have to write all the textbooks myself."

"Just one question, Martinus. When do you find time to sleep?"

Padway grinned wanly. "Mostly I don't. But if I can ever get out of all this political and military activity I hope to catch up. I don't really like it, but it's a necessary means to an end. The end is things like the telegraph and the presses. My politicking and soldiering may not make any difference a hundred years from now, but the other things will, I hope."

Padway started to go, then said: "Is Julia from Apulia still working for Ebenezer the Jew?"

"The last I heard she was. Why? Do you want her back?"

"God forbid. She's got to disappear from Rome."

"Why?"

"For her own safety. I can't tell you about it yet."

"But I thought you disliked her—"

"That doesn't mean I want her murdered. And my own hide may be in danger, too, unless we get her out of town."

"Oh, God, why didst Thou let me get involved with a politician? I don't know, Martinus; she's a free citizen . . ."

"How about your cousin in Naples, Antiochus? I'd made it worth his while to hire her at higher wages."

"Well, I—"

"Have her go to work for Antiochus under another name. Fix it up quietly, old man. If the news leaks out, we'll all be in the soup."

"Soup? Ha, ha. Very funny. I'll do what I can. Now, about that old six-month note of yours . . ."

Oh, dear, thought Padway, now it would begin again. Thomasus was easy enough to get on with most of the time. But he could not or would not conduct the simplest financial transactions without three hours of frantic haggling. Perhaps he enjoyed it. Padway did not.

Jogging along the road to Florence again, Padway regretted that he had not seen Dorothea while he was in Rome. He had not dared. That was one more reason for getting Mathaswentha married off quickly. Dorothea would be a much more suitable if less spectacular girl for *him*. Not that he was in love with her. But he probably would be if he saw enough of her, he thought somewhat cold-bloodedly.

But he had too much else to do now. If he could only get time to relax, to catch up on his sleep, to investigate the

things that really interested him, to have a little fun! He
liked fun as much as the next man, even if the next man
would consider his ideas of fun peculiar.

But his sharp, conscientious mind goaded him on. He
knew that his job rested on the unstable foundation of his
influence over a senile, unpopular king. As long as Padway
pleased them the Goths would not interfere, as they were
accustomed to leaving civil administration in the hands of
non-Goths. But when Thiudahad went? Padway had lots of
hay to gather, and there were plenty of thunderheads sticking up over the barn.

In Florence Padway leased office space in the name of
the government, and looked in on his own business. This
time there were no irregularities in the accounts. Either
there had been no more stealing, or the boys were getting
cleverer at concealing it.

Fritharik renewed his plea to be allowed to come along,
showing with much pride his jeweled sword, which he had
redeemed and had sent up from Rome. The sword disappointed Padway, though he did not say so. The gems were
merely polished, not cut; faceting had not been invented.
But wearing it seemed to add inches to Fritharik's already
imposing stature. Padway, somewhat against his better
judgment, gave in. He appointed the competent and apparently honest Nerva his general manager.

They were snowed in by a late storm for two days crossing the mountains, and arrived in Ravenna still shivering.
The town with its clammy atmosphere and its currents of
intrigue depressed him, and the Mathaswentha problem
made him nervous. He called on her and made some insin-
cere love to her, which made him all the more anxious to
get away. But there was lots of public business to be handled.

Urias announced that he was ready and willing to enter
Padway's service. "Mathaswentha talked me into it," he
said. "She's a wonderful woman, isn't she?"

"Certainly is," replied Padway. He thought he detected a
faintly guilty and furtive air about the straightforward
Urias when he spoke of the princess. He smiled to himself.
"What I had in mind was setting up a regular military

school for the Gothic officers, somewhat on the Byzantine model, with you in charge."

"What? Oh, my word, I hoped you'd have a command on the frontiers for me."

So, thought Padway, he wasn't the only one who disliked Ravenna. "No, my dear sir. This job has to be done for the sake of the kingdom. And I can't do it myself, because the Goths don't think any non-Goth knows anything about soldiering. On the other hand I need a literate and intelligent man to run the thing, and you're the only one in sight."

"But, most excellent Martinus, have you ever tried to teach a Gothic officer anything? I admit that an academy is needed, but—"

"I know. I know. Most of them can't read or write and look down on those who do. That's why I picked *you* for the job. You're respected, and if anybody can put sense into their heads you can." He grinned sympathetically. "I wouldn't have tried so hard to enlist your services if I'd had just an easy, everyday job in mind."

"Thanks. I see you know how to get people to do things for you."

Padway went on to tell Urias some of his ideas. How the Goths' great weakness was the lack of co-ordination between their mounted lancers and their foot archers; how they needed both reliable foot spearmen and mounted archers to have a well-rounded force. He also described the crossbow, the calthorp, and other military devices.

He said: "It takes five years to make a good long-bowman, whereas a recruit can learn to handle a crossbow in a few weeks.

"And if I can get some good steel workers, I'll show you a suit of plate armor that weighs only half as much as one of those scale-mail shirts, but gives better protection and allows fully as much freedom of action." He grinned. "You may expect grumbling at all these newfangled ideas from the more conservative Goths. So you'd better introduce them gradually. And remember, they're your ideas; I won't try to deprive you of the credit for them."

"I understand," grinned Urias. "So if anybody gets hanged for them, it'll be me and not you. Like that book on astronomy that came out in Thiudahad's name. It has every churchman from here to Persia sizzling. Poor old Thiudahad gets the blame, but I know you furnished the ideas and put him up to it. Very well, my mysterious friend, I'm game."

Padway himself was surprised when Urias appeared with a very respectable crossbow a few days later. Although the device was simple enough, and he'd furnished an adequate set of drawings for it, he knew from sad experience that to get a sixth-century artisan to make something he'd never seen before, you had to stand over him while he botched six attempts, and then make it yourself.

They spent an afternoon in the great pine wood east of the city shooting at marks. Fritharik proved uncannily accurate, though he affected to despise missile weapons as unworthy of a noble Vandal knight. "But," he said, "it is a remarkably easy thing to aim."

"Yes," replied Padway. "Among my people there's a legend about a crossbowman who offended a government official, and was compelled as punishment to shoot an apple off his son's head. He did so, without harming the boy."

When he got back, Padway learned that he had an appointment the next day with an envoy from the Franks. The envoy, one Count Hlodovik, was a tall, lantern-jawed man. Like most Franks he was clean-shaven except for the mustache. He was quite gorgeous in a red silk tunic, gold chains and bracelets, and a jeweled baldric. Padway privately thought that the knobby bare legs below his short pants detracted from his impressiveness. Moreover, Hlodovik was rather obviously suffering from a hangover.

"Mother of God, I'm thirsty," he said. "Will you please do something about that, friend quæstor, before we discuss business?" So Padway had some wine sent in. Hlodovik drank in deep gulps. "Ah! That's better. Now, friend quæstor, I may say that I don't think I've been very well treated here. The king would only see me for a wink of the eye; said you handle the business. Is that the proper reception for the envoy of King Theudebert, King Hildebert, and King Hlotokar? Not just *one* king, mind you; *three*."

"That's a lot of kings," said Padway, smiling pleasantly. "I am greatly impressed. But you mustn't take offense, my lord count. Our king is an old man, and he finds the press of public business hard to bear."

"So, *hrrmp*. We'll forget about it, then. But we shall not find the reason for my coming hither so easy to forget. Briefly, what became of that hundred and fifty thousand solidi that Wittigis promised my masters, King Theudebert, King Hildebert, and King Hlotokar if they wouldn't attack him while he was involved with the Greeks? Moreover, he ceded Provence to my masters, King Theudebert, King Hildebert, and King Hlotokar. Yet your general Sisigis has not evacuated Provence. When my masters sent a force to occupy it a few weeks ago, they were driven back and several were killed. You should know that the Franks, who are the bravest and proudest people on earth, will never submit to such treatment. What are you going to do about it?"

Padway answered: *"You,* my lord Hlodovik, should know that the acts of an unsuccessful usurper cannot bind the legitimate government. We intend to hold what we have. So you may inform your masters, King Theudebert, King Hildebert, and King Hlotokar, that there will be no payment and no evacuation."

"Do you really mean that?" Hlodovik seemed astonished. "Don't you know, young man, that the armies of the Franks could sweep the length of Italy, burning and ravaging, any time they wished? My masters, King Theudebert, King Hildebert, and King Hlotokar, are showing great forbearance and humanity by offering you a way out. Think carefully before you invite disaster."

"I have thought, my lord," replied Padway. "And I respectfully suggest that you and your masters do the same. Especially about a little military device that we are introducing. Would you like to see it demonstrated? The parade ground is only a step from here."

Padway had made the proper preparations in advance. When they arrived at the parade ground, Hlodovik weaving slightly all the way, they found Urias, Fritharik, the crossbow, and a supply of bolts. Padway's idea was to have Fritharik take a few demonstration shots at a target. But Fritharik and Urias had other ideas. The latter walked off fifty feet, turned, and placed an apple on his head. Fritharik cocked the crossbow, put a bolt in the groove, and raised the bow to his shoulder.

Padway was frozen speechless with horror. He didn't dare shout at the two idiots to desist for fear of losing face before the Frank. And if Urias was killed, he hated to think of the damage that would be done to his plans.

The crossbow snapped. There was a short *splash*, and fragments of apple flew about. Urias, grinning, picked pieces of apple out of his hair and walked back.

"Do you find the demonstration impressive, my lord?" Padway asked.

"Yes, quite," said Hlodovik. "Let's see that device. Hm-m-m. Of course, the brave Franks don't believe that any battle was ever won by a lot of silly arrows. But for hunting, now, this mightn't be bad. How does it work? I see; you pull the string back to here—"

While Fritharik was demonstrating the crossbow, Padway took Urias aside and told him, in a low tone, just what he thought of such a fool stunt. Urias tried to look serious, but couldn't help a faint, small-boy grin. Then there was another snap, and something whizzed between them not a foot from Padway's face. They jumped and spun around. Hlodovik was holding the crossbow, a foolish look on his long face. "I didn't know it went off so easily," he said.

Fritharik lost his temper. "What are you trying to do, you drunken fool? Kill somebody—"

"What's that? *You* call me a fool? Why—" and the Frank's sword came halfway out of the scabbard.

Fritharik jumped back and grabbed his own sword hilt. Padway and Urias pounced on the two and grabbed their elbows.

"Calm yourself, my lord!" cried Padway. "It's nothing to start a fight over. I'll apologize personally."

The Frank merely got madder and tried to shake off Padway. "I'll teach that low-born bastard! My honor is insulted!" he shouted. Several Gothic soldiers loafing around the field looked up and trotted over. Hlodovik saw them coming and put his sword back, growling: "This is fine treatment for the representative of King Theudebert, King

Hildebert, and King Hlotokar. Just wait till they hear of this."

Padway tried to mollify him, but Hlodovik merely grumped, and soon left Ravenna. Padway dispatched a warning to Sisigis to be on the lookout for a Frankish attack. His conscience bothered him a good deal. In a way he thought he ought to have tried to appease the Franks, as he hated the idea of being responsible for war. But he knew that that fierce and treacherous tribe would only take each concession as a sign of weakness. The time to stop the Franks was the first time.

Then another envoy arrived, this time from the Kutrigurs or Bulgarian Huns. The usher told Padway: "He's very dignified; doesn't speak any Latin or Gothic, so he uses an interpreter. Says he's a boyar, whatever that is."

"Show him in."

The Bulgarian envoy was a stocky, bowlegged man with high cheek bones, a fiercely upswept mustache, and a nose even bigger than Padway's. He wore a handsome furlined coat, baggy trousers, and a silk turban wound about his shaven skull, from the rear of which two black pigtails jutted absurdly. Despite the finery, Padway found reason to suspect that the man had never had a bath in his life. The interpreter was a small, nervous Thracian who hovered a pace to the Bulgar's left and rear.

The Bulgar clumped in, bowed stiffly, and did not offer to shake hands. Probably not done among the Huns, thought Padway. He bowed back and indicated a chair. He regretted having done so a moment later, when the Bulgar hiked his boots up on the upholstery and sat cross-legged. Then he began to speak, in a strangely musical tongue which Padway surmised was related to Turkish. He stopped every three or four words for the interpreter to translate. It ran something like this:

Envoy: (Twitter, twitter.)
Interpreter: I am the Boyar Karojan—
Envoy: (Twitter, twitter.)
Interpreter: The son of Chakir—

Envoy: (Twitter, twitter.)

Interpreter. Who was the son of Tardu—

Envoy: (Twitter, twitter.)

Interpreter: Envoy of Kardam—

Envoy: (Twitter, twitter.)

Interpreter: The son of Kapagan—

Envoy: (Twitter, twitter.)

Interpreter: And Great Khan of the Kutrigurs.

It was distracting to listen to, but not without a certain poetic grandeur. The Bulgar paused impassively at that point. Padway identified himself, and the duo began again:

"My master, the Great Khan—"

"Has received an offer from Justinian, Emperor of the Romans—"

"Of fifty thousand solidi—"

"To refrain from invading his dominions."

"If Thiudahad, King of the Goths—"

"Will make us a better offer—"

"We will ravage Thrace—"

"And leave the Gothic realm alone."

"If he does not—"

"We will take Justinian's gold—"

"And invade the Gothic territories—"

"Of Pannonia and Noricum."

Padway cleared this throat and began his reply, pausing for translation. This method had its advantages, he found. It gave him time to think.

"My master, Thiudahad, King of the Goths and Italians—"

"Authorizes me to say—"

"That he has better use for his money—"

"Than to bribe people not to attack him—"

"And that if the Kutrigurs think—"

"That they can invade our territory—"

"They are welcome to try—"

"But that we cannot guarantee them—"

"A very hospitable reception."

The envoy replied:

"Think man, on what you say."

"For the armies of the Kutrigurs—"

"Cover the Sarmatian steppe like locusts."

"The hoofbeats of their horses—"

"Are a mighty thunder."

"The flight of their arrows—"

"Darkens the sun."

"Where they have passed—"

"Not even grass will grow."

Padway replied:

"Most excellent Karojan—"

"What you say may be true."

"But in spite of their thundering and sun-darkening—"

"The last time the Kutrigurs—"

"Assailed our land, a few years ago—"

"They got the pants beat off them."

As this was translated, the Bulgar looked puzzled for a moment. Then he turned red. Padway thought he was angry, but it soon appeared that he was trying to keep from laughing. He said between sputters:

"This time, man, it will be different."

"If any pants are lost—"

"They will be yours."

"How would this be?"

"You pay us sixty thousand—"

"In three installments—"

"Of twenty thousand each?"

But Padway was immovable. The Bulgar finished:

"I shall inform my master—"

"Kardam, the Great Khan of the Kutrigurs—"

"Of your obduracy."

"For a reasonable bribe—"

"I am prepared to tell him—"

"Of the might of the Gothic arms—"

"In terms that shall dissuade him—"

"From his projected invasion."

Padway beat the Bulgar down to half the bribe he originally asked, and they parted on the best of terms. When he went around to his quarters he found Fritharik trying to wind a towel around his head.

The Vandal looked up with guilty embarrassment. "I was trying, excellent boss, to make a headgear like that of the Hunnish gentleman. It has style."

Padway had long since decided that Thiudahad was a pathological case. But lately the little king was showing more definite signs of mental failure. For instance, when Padway went to see about a new inheritance law, Thiudahad gravely listened to him explain the reasons that the Royal Council and Cassiodorus had agreed upon bringing the Gothic law more into line with the Roman.

Then he said: "When are you going to put out another book in my name, Martinus? Your name *is* Martinus, isn't it? Martinus Paduei, Martinus Paduei. Didn't I appoint you prefect or something? Dear me, I can't seem to remember anything. Now, what's this you want to see me about? Always business, business, business. I hate business. Scholarship is more important. Silly state papers. What is it, an order for an execution? I hope you're going to torture the rascal as he deserves. I can't understand this absurd prejudice of yours against torture. The people aren't happy unless they're terrified of their government. Let's see, what was I talking about?"

It was convenient in one way, as Thiudahad didn't bother him much. But it was awkward when the king simply refused to listen to him or to sign anything for a day at a time.

Then he found himself in a hot dispute with the paymaster-general of the Gothic army. The latter refused to put the Imperialist mercenaries whom Padway had captured on the rolls. Padway argued that the men were first-rate soldiers who seemed glad enough to serve the Italo-Gothic state, and that it would cost little more to enlist them than to continue to feed them as prisoners. The paymaster-general replied that national defense had been a prerogative of the Goths since the time of Theoderik, and the men in question were not, with some few exceptions, Goths. Q. E. D.

Each stubbornly maintained his point, so the dispute was carried to Thiudahad. The king listened to the argument with a specious air of wisdom.

Then he sent the paymaster-general away and told Padway: "Lots to be said on both sides, dear sir, lots to be said on both sides. Now, if I decide in your favor, I shall expect a suitable command for my son, Thiudegiskel."

Padway was horrified, though he tried not to show it.

"But, my lord king, what military experience has Thiudegiskel had?"

"None; that's just the trouble. Spends all his time drinking and wenching with his wild young friends. He needs a bit of responsibility. Something good, consistent with the dignity of his birth."

Padway argued some more. But he didn't say that he couldn't imagine a worse commander than this self-conceited and arrogant puppy. Thiudahad was obstinate. "After all, Martinus, I'm king, am I not? You can't browbeat me and you can't frighten me with your Wittigis. Heh, heh I'll have a surprise for you one of these days. What was I talking about? Oh, yes. You do, I think, owe Thiudegiskel something for putting him in that horrid prison camp——"

"But *I* didn't put him in jail——"

"Don't interrupt, Martinus. It isn't considerate. Either you give him a command, or I decide in favor of the other man, what's-his-name. That is my final royal word."

So Padway gave in. Thiudegiskel was put in command of the Gothic forces in Calabria, where, Padway hoped, he wouldn't be able to do much harm. Later he had occasion to remember that hope.

Padway may seem rash to have incorporated such an alien element as the ex-Imperialists in the Italo-Gothic army. But in this age there was no such thing as nationalism in the modern sense. The ties that counted were those of religion and personal loyalty to a commander. Many of the Imperialists were Thracian Goths who had remained in the Balkans at that time of the migration under Theoderik. And some Itailan Goths had served the Empire as mercenaries. They mixed with little prejudice on either side.

Then three things happened. General Sisigis sent word of suspicious activity among the Franks.

Padway got a letter from Thomasus, which told of an attempt on the life of ex-King Wittigis. The assassin had inexplicably sneaked into the dugout, where Wittigis, though slightly wounded in the process, had killed him with his bare hands. Nobody knew who the assassin was until Wittigis had declared, with many a bloodcurdling curse, that he recognized the man as an old-time secret agent of Thiudahad. Padway knew what that meant. Thiudahad had discovered Wittigis' whereabouts, and meant to put his rival out of the way. If he succeeded, he'd be prepared to defy Padway's management, or even to heave him out of his office. Or worse.

Finally Padway got a letter from Justinian. It read:

Flavius Anicius Justinian, Emperor of the Romans, to King Thiudahad, Greetings.

Our serenity's attention has been called to the terms which you propose for termination of the war between us.

We find these terms so absurd and unreasonable that our deigning to reply at all is an act of great condescension on our part. Our holy endeavor to recover for the Empire the provinces of western Europe, which belonged to our forebears and rightfully belong to us, will be carried through to a victorious conclusion.

As for our former general, Flavius Belisarius, his refusal of parole is an act of gross disloyalty, which we shall fittingly punish in due course. Meanwhile the illustrious Belisarius may consider himself free of all obligations to us. Nay more, we order him to place himself unreservedly under the orders of that infamous heretic and agent of the Evil One who calls himself Martinus of Padua, of whom we have heard.

We are confident that, between the incompetence and cowardice of Belisarius and the heavenly wrath that will attach to those who submit to the unclean touch of the diabolical Martinus, the doom of the Gothic kingdom will not be long delayed.

Padway realized, with a slightly sick feeling, that he had a lot to learn about diplomacy. His defiance of Justinian, and of the Frankish kings, and of the Bulgars, had each been justified, considered by itself. But he shouldn't have committed himself to taking them on all at once.

The thunderheads were piling up fast.

CHAPTER XIV

PADWAY DASHED BACK to Rome and showed Justinian's letter to Belisarius. He thought he had seldom seen a more unhappy man than the stalwart Thracian.

"I don't know," was all Belisarius would say in answer to his questions. "I shall have to think."

Padway got an interview with Belisarius' wife, Antonina. He got along fine with this slim, vigorous redhead.

She said: "I told him repeatedly that he'd get nothing but ingratitude from Justinian. But you know how he is—reasonable about everything except what concerns his honor. The only thing that would make me hesitate is my friendship with the Empress Theodora. That's not a connection to be thrown over lightly. But after this letter —I'll do what I can, excellent Martinus."

Belisarius, to Padway's unconcealed delight, finally capitulated.

The immediate danger point seemed to be Provence. Padway's runner-collecting service had gathered a story of another bribe paid by Justinian to the Franks to attack the Goths. So Padway did some shuffling. Asinar, who had sat at Senia for months without the gumption to move against the Imperialists in Spalato, was ordered home. Sisigis, who if no genius was not obviously incompetent, was transferred to command of Asinar's Dalmatian army. And Belisarius was given command of Sisigis' forces in Gaul. Belisarius, before leaving for the North, asked Padway for all the information available about the Franks.

Padway explained: "Brave, treacherous, and stupid. They have nothing but unarmored infantry, who fight in a single deep column. They come whooping along, hurl a volley of throwing-axes and javelins, and close with the sword. If you can stop them by a line of reliable pikemen, or by cavalry charges, they're suckers for mounted archers. They're very numerous, but such a huge mass of infantry can't forage enough territory to keep themselves fed. So they have to keep moving or starve.

"Moreover, they're so primitive that their soldiers are not paid at all. They're expected to make their living by looting. If you can hold them in one spot long enough, they melt away by desertion. But don't underestimate their numbers and ferocity.

"Try to send agents into Burgundy to rouse the Burgunds against the Franks, who conquered them only a few years ago." He explained that the Burgunds were of East-German origin, like the Goths and Lombards, spoke a language much like theirs, and like them were primarily stock-raisers. Hence they did not get on with the West-German Franks, who were agriculturists when they were not devastating their neighbors' territory.

If there was going to be more war, Padway knew one invention that would settle it definitely in the Italo-Goths' favor. Gunpowder was made of sulphur, charcoal, and saltpeter. Padway had learned that in the sixth grade. The first two were available without question.

He supposed that potassium nitrate could be obtained somewhere as a mineral. But he did not know where, or what it would look like. He could not synthesize it with the equipment at hand, even had he known enough chemistry. But he remembered reading that it occurred at the bottom of manure-piles. And he remembered an enormous pile in Nevitta's yard.

He called on Nevitta and asked for permission to dig. He whooped with joy when, sure enough, there were the crystals, looking like maple sugar. Nevitta asked him if he was crazy.

"Sure," grinned Padway. Didn't you know? I've been that way for years."

His old house on Long Street was a full of activity as ever, despite the move to Florence. It was used as Rome headquarters by the Telegraph Company. Padway was having another press set up. And now the remaining space downstairs became a chemical laboratory. Padway did not know what proportions of the three ingredients made good gunpowder, and the only way to find out was by experiment.

He gave orders, in the government's name, for casting and boring a cannon. The brass foundry that took the job was not co-operative. They had never seen such a contraption and were not sure they could make it. What did he want this tube for, a flower pot?

It took them an interminable time to get the pattern and core made, despite the simplicity of the thing. The first one they delivered looked all right, until Padway examined the breach end closely. The metal here was spongy and pitted. The gun would have blown up the first time it was fired.

The trouble was that it had been cast muzzle down. The solution was to add a foot to the length of the barrel, cast it muzzle up, and saw off the last foot of flawed brass.

His efforts to produce gunpowder got nowhere. Lots of proportions of the ingredients would burn beautifully when ignited. But they did not explode. He tried all proportions; he varied his method of mixing. Still all he got was a lively sizzle, a big yellow flame, and a stench. He tried packing the stuff into improvised firecrackers. They went *fuff*. They would not go *bang*.

Perhaps he had to touch off a large quantity at once, more tightly compressed yet. He pestered the foundary daily until the second cannon appeared.

Early next morning he and Fritharik and a couple of helpers mounted the cannon on a crude carriage of planks in a vacant space near the Viminal Gate. The helpers had previously piled up a sandhill for a target, thirty feet from the gun.

Padway rammed several pounds of powder down the barrel, and a cast-iron ball after it. He filled the touch-hole.

He said in a low voice: "Fritharik, give me that candle. Now get back everybody. Way over there, and lie down. You too, Fritharik."

"Never!" said Fritharik indignantly. "Desert my lord in the hour of danger? I should say not!"

"All right, if you want to chance being blown to bits. Here goes."

Padway touched the candle flame to the touch-hole.

The powder sizzled and sparkled.

The gun went *pfoomp!* The cannon-ball hopped from the muzzle, thumped to earth a yard away, rolled another yard, and stopped.

Back went the beautiful shiny new gun to Padway's house, to be put in the cellar with the clock.

In the early spring, Urias appeared in Rome. He explained that he'd left the military academy in the hands of subordinates, and was coming down to see about raising a militia force of Romans, which had been another of Padway's ideas. But he had an unhappy, hangdog air that made Padway suspect that that wasn't the real reason.

To Padway's leading questions he finally burst out: "Excellent Martinus, you'll simply have to give me a command somewhere away from Ravenna. I can't stand it any longer."

Padway put his arm around Urias' shoulders. "Come on, old man, tell me what is bothering you. Maybe I can help."

Urias looked at the gound. "Uh . . . well . . . that is— Look here, just what *is* the arrangement between you and Mathaswentha?"

"I thought that was it. You've been seeing her, haven't you?"

"Yes, I have. And if you send me back there, I shall see her some more in spite of myself. Are you and she betrothed, or what?"

"I did have some such idea once." Padway put on the air of one about to make a great sacrifice. "But, my friend, I wouldn't stand in the way of anybody's happiness. I'm sure you're much better suited to her than I. My work keeps me too busy to make a good husband. So if you want to sue for her hand, go to it, with my blessing."

"You *mean* that?" Urias jumped up and began pacing the floor, fairly beaming. "I . . . I don't know how to thank you . . . it's the greatest thing you could do for me . . . I'm your friend for life—"

"Don't mention it; I'm glad to help you out. But now that you're down here, you might as well finish the job you came to do."

"Oh," said Urias soberly. "I suppose I ought to, at that. But how shall I press my suit, then?"

"Write her."

"But how can I? I don't know the pretty phrases. In fact, I've never written a love letter in my life."

"I'll help you out with that, too. Here, we can start right now." Padway got out writing materials, and they were presently concocting a letter to the princess. "Let's see," said Padway reflectively, "we ought to tell her what her eyes are like."

"They're just like eyes, aren't they?"

"Of course, but in this business you compare them to the stars and things."

Urias thought. "They're about the color of a glacier I once saw in the Alps."

"No, that wouldn't do. It would imply that they were as cold as ice."

"They also remind you of a polished sword blade."

"Similar objection. How about the northern seas?"

"*Hm-m-m.* Yes, I think that would do, Martinus. Gray as the northern seas."

"It has a fine poetic ring to it."

"So it has. Northern seas it shall be, then." Urias wrote slowly and awkwardly.

Padway said: "Hey, don't bear down so hard with that pen. You'll poke a hole in that paper."

As Urias was finishing the letter, Padway clapped on his hat and made for the door.

"*Hai,*" said Urias, "what's your hurry?"

Padway grinned. "I'm just going to see some friends; a family named Anicius. Nice people. I'll introduce you to them some day when you're safely sewed up."

Padway's original idea had been to introduce a mild form of selective conscription, beginning with the city of Rome and requiring the draftees to report for weekly drill. The Senate, which at this time was a mere municipal council, balked. Some of them disliked or distrusted Padway. Some wanted to be bribed.

Padway did not want to give into them until he had tried everything else. He had Urias announce drills on a voluntary basis, at current wages. Results were disappointing.

Padway's thoughts were abruptly snatched from the re-militarization of the Italians when Junianus came in with a telegraph message. It read simply:

WITTIGIS ESCAPED FROM DETENTION LAST NIGHT. NO TRACE OF HIM HAS BEEN FOUND.

(SIGNED)
ATURPAD THE PERSIAN,
COMMANDING.

For a minute Padway simply stared at the message. Then he jumped up and yelled: "Fritharik! Get our horses!"

They clattered over to Urias' headquarters. Urias looked grave. "This puts me in an awkward position, Martinus. My uncle will undoubtedly try to regain his crown. He's a stubborn man, you know."

"I know. But you know how important it is to keep things going the way they are."

"*Ja.* I won't go back on you. But you couldn't expect me to try to harm my uncle. I like him, even if he is a thick-headed old grouch."

"You stick with me and I promise you I'll do my best to see that he isn't harmed. But just now I'm concerned with keeping him from harming *us.*"

"How do you suppose he got out? Bribery?"

"I know as much as you do. I doubt the bribery; at least Aturpad is considered an honorable man. What do you think Wittigis will do?"

"If it were me, I'd hide out for a while and gather my partisans. That would be logical. But my uncle never was very logical. And he hates Thiudahad worse than anything on earth. Especially after Thiudahad's attempt to have him murdered. My guess is that he'll head straight for Ravenna and try to do Thiudahad in personally."

"All right, then, we'll collect some fast cavalry and head that way ourselves."

Padway thought he was pretty well hardened to long-distance riding. But it was all he could do to stand the pace that Urias set. When they reached Ravenna in the early morning he was reeling, red-eyed, in the saddle.

They asked no questions, but galloped straight for the palace. The town seemed normal enough. Most of the citizens were at breakfast. But at the palace the normal guard was not to be seen.

"That looks bad," said Urias. They and their men dismounted, drew their swords, and marched in six abreast. A guard appeared at the head of the stairs. He grabbed at his sword, then recognized Urias and Padway.

"Oh, it's you," he said noncommittally.

"Yes, it's us," replied Padway. "What's up?"

"Well . . . uh . . . you'd better go see for yourselves, noble sirs. Excuse me." And the Goth whisked out of sight.

They tramped on through the empty halls. Doors shut before they came to them, and there was whispering behind them. Padway wondered if they were walking into a trap. He sent back a squad to hold the front door.

At the entrance to the royal apartments they found a clump of guards. A couple of these brought their spears up, but the rest simply stood uncertainly. Padway said calmly, "Stand back, boys," and went in.

"Oh, merciful Christ!" said Urias softly.

There were several people standing around a body on the floor. Padway asked them to stand aside, which they did meekly. The body was that of Wittigis. His tunic was ripped by a dozen sword and spear wounds. The rug under him was sopping.

The chief usher looked amazedly at Padway. "This just happened, my lord. Yet you have come all the way from Rome because of it. How did you know?"

"I have ways," said Padway. "How did it happen?"

"Wittigis was let into the palace by a guard friendly to him. He would have killed our noble king, but he was seen, and other guards hurried to the rescue. The guards killed him," he added unnecessarily. Anybody could see that.

A sound from the corner made Padway look up. There crouched Thiudahad, half dressed. Nobody seemed to be paying much attention. Thiudahad's ashy face peered at Padway.

"Dear me, it's my new perfect, isn't it? Your name is Cassiodorus. But how much younger you look, my dear sir. Ah, me, we all grow old sometime. Heh-heh. Let's publish a

book, my dear Cassiodorus. Heigh-ho, yes, indeed, a lovely
new book with purple covers. Heh-heh. We'll serve it for
dinner, with pepper and gravy. That's the way to eat a
fowl. Yes, three hundred pages at least. By the way, have
you seen that rascally general of mine, Wittigis? I heard he
was coming to call. Dreadful bore; no scholar at all.
Heigh-ho, dear me, I feel like dancing. Do you dance, my
dear Wittigis? La-la-la, la-la-la, dum de-um de-um."

Padway told the king's house physician: "Take care of
him, and don't let him out. The rest of you, go back to
work as if nothing has happened. Somebody take charge of
the body. Replace this rug, and make the preparations for
a dignified but modest funeral. Urias, maybe you'd better
tend to that." Urias was weeping. "Come on, old man, you
can do your grieving later. I sympathize, but we've got
things to do." He whispered something to him, whereat
Urias cheered up.

CHAPTER XV

THE MEMBERS OF the Gothic Royal Council appeared at
Padway's office with a variety of scowls. They were men of
substance and leisure, and did not like being dragged practically away from their breakfast tables, especially by a
mere civil functionary.

Padway acquainted them with the circumstances. His
news shocked them to temporary silence. He continued:
"As you know, my lords, under the unwritten constitution
of the Gothic nation, an insane king must be replaced as
soon as possible. Permit me to suggest that present circumstances make the replacement of the unfortunate Thiudahad an urgent matter."

Wakkis growled: "That's partly *your* doing, young man.
We could have bought off the Franks—"

"Yes, my lord. I know all that. The trouble is that the

Franks won't stay bought, as you very well know. In any event, what's done is done. Neither the Franks nor Justinian have moved against us yet. If we can run the election of a new king off quickly, we shall not be any worse off than we are."

Wakkis replied: "We shall have to call another convention of the electors, I suppose."

Another councilor, Mannfrith, spoke up: "Apparently our young friend is right, much as I hate to take advice from outsiders. When and where shall the convention be?"

There were a lot of uncertain throaty noises from the Goths. Padway said: "If my lords please, I have a suggestion. Our new civil capital is to be at Florence, and what more fitting way of inaugurating it is there than holding our election there?"

There was more growling, but nobody produced a better idea. Padway knew perfectly well that they didn't like following his directions, but that, on the other hand, they were glad to shirk thought and responsibility themselves.

Wakkis said: "We shall have to give time for the messages to go out, and for the electors to reach Florence—"

Just then Urias came in. Padway took him aside and whispered: "What did she say?"

"She says she will."

"When?"

"Oh, in about ten days, I think. It don't look very nice so soon after my uncle's death."

"Never mind that. It's now or never."

Mannfrith asked. "Who shall the candidates be? I'd like to run myself, only my rheumatism has been bothering me so."

Somebody said: "Thiudegiskel will be one. He's Thiudahad's logical successor."

Padway said: "I think you'll be pleased to hear that our esteemed General Urias will be a candidate."

"What?" cried Wakkis. "He's a fine young man, I admit, but he's ineligible. He's not an Amaling."

Padway broke into a triumphant grin. "Not now, my lords, but he will be by the time the election is called." The Goths looked startled. "And, my lords, I hope you'll all give us the pleasure of your company at the wedding."

During the wedding rehearsal, Mathaswentha got Padway aside. She said: "Really, Martinus, you've been most noble about this. I hope you won't grieve too much."

Padway tried his best to look noble. "My dear, your happiness is mine. And if you love this young man, I think you're doing just the right thing."

"I *do* love him," replied Mathaswentha. "Promise me you won't sit around and mope, but will go out and find some nice girl who is suited to you."

Padway sighed convincingly. "It'll be hard to forget, my dear. But since you ask it, I'll promise. Now, now, don't cry. What will Urias think? You want to make *him* happy, don't you? There, that's a sensible girl."

The wedding itself was quite a gorgeous affair in a semi-barbaric way. Padway discovered an unsuspected taste for stage management, and introduced a wrinkle he'd seen in pictures of United States Military Academy weddings: that of having Urias' friends make an arch of swords under which the bride and groom walked on their way down the church steps. Padway himself looked as dignified as his moderate stature and nondescript features permitted. Inwardly he was holding on tight to repress a snicker. It had just occurred to him that Urias' long robe looked amazingly like a bathrobe he, Padway, had once owned, except that Padway's robe hadn't had pictures of saints embroidered on it in gold thread.

As the happy couple departed, Padway ducked out of sight around a pillar. Mathaswentha, if she saw him out of the tail of her eye, may have thought that he was shedding a final tear. But actually he was allowing himself the luxury of a longdrawn *"Whew!"* of relief.

Before he reappeared, he heard a couple of Goths talking on the other side of the pillar:

"He'd made a good king, eh, Albehrts?"

"Maybe. *He* would, by himself. But I fear he'll be under the influence of this Martinus person. Not that I have anything specifically against Mysterious Martin, you understand. But—you know how it is."

"*Ja, ja.* Oh, well, one can always flip a sesterce to decide which to vote for."

Padway had every intention of keeping Urias under his influence. It seemed possible. Urias disliked and was impatient with matters of civil administration. He was a competent soldier, and at the same time was receptive to Padway's ideas. Padway thought somberly that if anything happened to *this* king he'd hunt a long time before finding another as satisfactory.

Padway had the news of the impending election sent out over the telegraph, thereby saving the week that would normally be necessary for messengers to travel the length and breadth of Italy, and incidentally convincing some of the Goths of the value of his contraptions. Padway also sent our another message, ordering all the higher military commanders to remain at their posts. He sold Urias the idea by arguing military necessity. His real reason was a determination to keep Thiudegiskel in Calabria during the election. Knowing Urias, he didn't dare explain this plan to him, for fear Urias would have an attack of knightly honor and, as ranking general, countermand the order.

The Goths had never seen an election conducted on time-honored American principles. Padway showed them. The electors arrived in Florence to find the town covered with enormous banners and posters reading:

VOTE FOR URIAS THE PEOPLE'S CHOICE!

Lower taxes! Bigger public works! Security for the aged! Efficient government!

And so forth. They also found a complete system of ward-heelers to take them in tow, show them the town—not that Florence was much to see in those days—and butter them up generally.

Three days before the election was due, Padway held a barbecue. He threw himself into debt for the fixings. Well, not exactly; he threw poor Urias into debt, being much too prudent to acquire any more liabilities in his own name than he could help.

While he kept modestly in the background, Urias made

a speech. Padway later heard comments to the effect that nobody had known Urias could make such good speeches. He grinned to himself. He had written the speech and had spent all his evenings for a week teaching Urias to deliver it. Privately Padway thought that his candidate's delivery still stank. But if the electors didn't mind, there was no reason why he should.

Padway and Urias relaxed afterward over a bottle of brandy. Padway said that the election looked like a pushover, and then had to explain what a pushover was. Of the two opposing candidates, one had withdrawn, and the other, Harjis Austrowald's son, was an elderly man with only the remotest connection with the Amal family.

Then one of the ward-heelers came in breathless. It seemed to Padway that people were always coming to see him breathless.

The man barked: "Thiudegiskel's here."

Padway wasted no time. He found where Thiudegiskel was staying, rounded up a few Gothic soldiers, and set out to arrest the young man. He found that Thiudegiskel had, with a gang of his own friends, taken over one of the better inns in town, pitching the previous guests and their belongings out in the street.

The gang were gorging themselves downstairs in plain sight. They hadn't yet changed their traveling clothes, and they looked tired but tough. Padway marched in. Thiudegiskel looked up. "Oh, it's *you* again. What do you want?"

Padway announced: "I have a warrant for your arrest on grounds of insubordination and deserting your post, signed by Ur—"

The high-pitched voice interrupted: *"Ja, ja,* I know all about that, my dear *Sineigs.* Maybe you thought I'd stay away from Florence while you ran off an election without me, eh? *But* I'm not like that, Martinus. Not one little bit. I'm here, I'm a candidate, and anything you try now I'll remember when I'm king. That's one thing about me; I've got an infernally long memory."

Padway turned to his soldiers: "Arrest him!"

There was a great scraping of chairs as the gang rose to its feet and grasped its collective sword hilts. Padway looked for his soldiers; they hadn't moved.

"Well?" he snapped.

The oldest of them, a kind of sergeant, cleared his throat. "Well, sir, it's this way. Now we know you're our superior and all that. But things are kind of uncertain, with this election and all, and we don't know whom we'll be taking orders from in a couple of days. Suppose we arrest this young man, and then he gets elected king? That wouldn't be so good for us, now would it, sir?"

"Why—you—" raged Padway.

But the only effect was that the soldiers began to slide out the door. The young Gothic noble named Willimer was whispering to Thiudegiskel, sliding his sword a few inches out of the scabbard and back.

Thiudegiskel shook his head and said to Padway: "My friend here doesn't seem to like you, Martinus. He swears he'll pay you a visit as soon as the election is over. So it might be healthier if you left Italy for a little trip. In fact, it's all I can do to keep him from paying his visit right now."

The soldiers were mostly gone now. Padway realized that he'd better go too, if he didn't want these well-born thugs to make hamburger of him.

He mustered what dignity he could. "You know the law against duelling."

Thiudegiskel's invincibly good-natured arrogance wasn't even dented. "Sure, I know it. But remember. *I'll* be the one enforcing it. I'm just giving you fair warning, Martinus. That's one thing about—"

But Padway didn't wait to hear Thiudegiskel's next contribution to the inexhaustible subject of himself. He went, full of rage and humiliation. By the time he finished cursing his own stupidity and thought to round up his eastern troops—the few who weren't up north with Belisarius—and make a second attempt, it was too late. Thiudegiskel had collected a large crowd of partisans in and around the hotel, and it would take a battle to dislodge them. The ex-Imperialists seemed far from enthusiastic over the prospect, and Urias muttered something about its being only honorable to let the late king's son have a fair try for the crown.

The next day Thomasus the Syrian arrived. He came in wheezing. "How are you, Martinus? I didn't want to miss all the excitement, so I came up from Rome. Brought my family along."

That meant something, Padway knew, for Thomasus' family consisted not only of his wife and four children, but an aged uncle, a nephew, two nieces, and his black house slave Ajax and *his* wife and children.

He answered: "I'm fine, thanks. Or I shall be when I catch up on my sleep. How are you?"

"Fine, thanks. Business has been good for a change."

"And how is your friend God?" Padway asked with a straight face.

"He's fine too—why, you blasphemous young scoundrel! That will cost you an extra interest on your next loan. How's the election?"

Padway told him. "It won't be as easy as I thought. Thiudegiskel has developed a lot of support among the conservative Goths, who don't care for self-made men like Wittigis and Urias. The upper crust prefer an Amaling by birth—"

"Upper crust? Oh, I see! Ha, ha, ha! I hope God listens to you. It might put Him in a good humor the next time He considers sending a plague or a quake."

Padway continued: "And Thiudegiskel is not as stupid as one might expect. He'd hardly arrived before he'd sent out friends to tear down my posters and put up some of his own. His weren't much to look at, but I was surprised that he thought of using any. There were fist-fights and one stabbing, not fatal, fortunately. So—you know Dagalaif Nevitta's son?"

"The marshal? By name only."

"He's not eligible to vote. Well, the town watch is too scared of the Goths to keep order, and I don't dare use my own guards for fear of rousing all the Goths against the 'foreigners.' I blackmailed the city fathers into hiring Dagalaif to deputize the other marshals who are not electors as election police. As Nevitta is on our side, I don't know how impartial my friend Dagalaif will be. But it'll save us from a pitched battle, I hope."

"Wonderful, wonderful, Martinus. Don't over-reach yourself; some of the Goths call your electioneering methods newfangled and undignified. I'll ask God to keep a special watch over you and your candidate."

The day before the election, Thiudegiskel showed his political astuteness by throwing a barbecue even bigger than Padway's. Padway, having some mercy on Urias' modest purse, had limited his party to the electors. Thiudegiskel, with the wealth of Thiudahad's immense Tuscan estates to draw upon, shot the works. He invited all the electors and their families and friends also.

Padway and Urias and Thomasus, with the former's ward-heelers, the latter's family, and a sizable guard, arrived at the field outside Florence after the festivities had begun. The field was covered with thousands of Goths of all ages, sizes, and sexes, and was noisy with East-German gutturals, the clank of scabbards, and the *flop-flop* of leather pants.

A Goth bustled up to them with beer suds in his whiskers. "Here, here, what are you people doing? You weren't invited."

"Ni ogs, frijond," said Padway.

"What? You're telling *me* not to be afraid?" The Goth bristled.

"We aren't even trying to come to your party. We're just having a little picnic of our own. There's no law against picnics, is there?"

"Well—then why all the armament? Looks to me as though you were planning a kidnapping."

"There, there," soothed Padway. "You're wearing a sword, aren't you?"

"But I'm official. I'm one of Willimer's men."

"So are these people our men. Don't worry about us. We'll stay on the other side of the road, if it'll make you happy. Now run along and enjoy your beer."

"Well, don't try anything. We'll be ready for you if you do." The Goth departed, muttering over Padway's logic.

Padway's party made themselves comfortable across the road, ignoring the hostile glares from Thiudegiskel's partisans. Padway himself sprawled on the grass, eating little and watching the barbecue through narrowed eyes.

Thomasus said: "Most excellent General Urias, that look tells me our friend Martinus is planning something particularly hellish."

Thiudegiskel and some of his gang mounted the speakers' stand. Willimer introduced the candidate with commendable brevity. Then Thiudegiskel began to speak. Padway hushed his own party and strained his ears. Even so, with so many people, few of them completely silent, between him and the speaker, he missed a lot of Thiudegiskel's shrill Gothic. Thiudegiskel appeared to be bragging as usual about his own wonderful character. But, to Padway's consternation, his audience ate it up. And they howled with laughter at the speaker's rough and ready humor.

"—and did you know, friends, that General Urias was twelve years old before his poor mother could train him not to wet his bed? It's a fact. That's one thing about me; I never exaggerate. Of course you *couldn't* exaggerate Urias' peculiarities. For instance, the first time he called on a girl—"

Urias was seldom angry, but Padway could see the young general was rapidly approaching incandescence. He'd have to think of something quickly, or there *would* be a battle.

His eye fell on Ajax and Ajax's family. The slave's eldest child was a chocolate-colored, frizzy-haired boy of ten.

Padway asked: "Does anybody know whether Thiudegiskel's married?"

"Yes," replied Urias. "The swine was married just before he left for Calabria. Nice girl, too; a cousin of Willimer."

"*Hm-m-m.* Say, Ajax, does that oldest boy of yours speak any Gothic?"

"Why no, my lord, why should he?"

"What's his name?"

"Priam."

"Priam, would you like to earn a couple of sesterces, all your own?"

The boy jumped up and bowed. Padway found such a servile gesture in a child vaguely repulsive. Must do something about slavery some day, he thought. "Yes, my lord," squeaked the boy.

"Can you say the word '*atta*'? That's Gothic for 'father.' "

Priam dutifully said: "*Atta*. Now where are my sesterces, my lord?"

"Not so fast, Priam. That's just the beginning of the job. You practice saying '*atta*' for a while."

Padway stood up and peered at the field. He called softly: "*Hai*, Dagalaif!"

The marshal detached himself from the crowd and came over. "*Hails*, Martinus! What can I do for you?"

Padway whispered his instructions.

Then he said to Priam: "You see the man in the red cloak on the stand, the one who is talking? Well, you're to go over there and climb up on the stand, and say '*atta*' to him. Loudly, so everybody can hear. Say it a lot of times, until something happens. Then you run back here."

Priam frowned in concentration. "But the man isn't my father! This is my father!" He pointed to Ajax.

"I know. But you do as I say if you want your money. Can you remember your instructions?"

So Priam trailed off through the crowd of Goths with Dagalaif at his heels. They were lost to Padway's sight for a few minutes, while Thiudegiskel shrilled on. Then the little Negro's form appeared on the stand, boosted up by Dagalaif's strong arms. Padway clearly heard the childish cry of "*Atta!*"

Thiudegiskel stopped in the middle of a sentence. Priam repeated: "*Atta! Atta!*"

"He seems to know you!" shouted a voice down front.

Thiudegiskel stood silent, scowling and turning red. A low mutter of laughter ran through the Goths and swelled to a roar.

Priam called "*Atta!*" once more, louder.

Thiudegiskel grabbed his sword hilt and started for the boy. Padway's heart missed a beat.

But Priam leaped off the stand into Dagalaif's arms, leaving Thiudegiskel to shout and wave his sword. He was apparently yelling, "It's a lie!" over and over. Padway could see his mouth move, but his words were lost in the thunder of the Gothic nation's Wagnerian laughter.

Dagalaif and Priam appeared, running toward them. The Goth was staggering slightly and holding his midriff. Padway was alarmed until he saw Dagalaif was suffering from a laughing and coughing spell.

He slapped him on the back until the coughs and gasps moderated. Then he said: "If we hang around here, Thiudegiskel will recover his wits, and he'll be angry enough to set his partisans on us with cold steel. In my country we had a word 'scram' that is, I think, applicable. Let's go."

"Hey, my lord," squealed Priam, "where's my two sesterces? Oh, thank you, my lord. Do you want me to call anybody else 'father,' my lord?"

CHAPTER XVI

PADWAY TOLD URIAS: "It looks like a sure thing now. Thiudegiskel will never live this afternoon's episode down. We Americans have some methods for making elections come out the right way, such as stuffing ballot boxes, and the use of floaters. But I don't think it'll be necessary to use any of them."

"What on earth is a floater, Martinus? You mean a float such as one uses in fishing?"

"No; I'll explain sometime. I don't want to corrupt the Gothic electoral system more than is absolutely necessary."

"Look here, if anybody investigates, they'll learn that Thiudegiskel was the innocent victim of a joke this afternoon. Then won't the effect be lost?"

"No, my dear Urias, that's not how the minds of electors work. Even if he's proved innocent, he's been made such an utter fool of that nobody will take him seriously, regardless of his personal merits, if any."

Just then a ward-heeler came in breathless. He gasped: "Thiu-Thiudegiskel—"

Padway complained: "I am going to make it a rule that

people who want to see me have to wait outside until they get their breath. What is it, Roderik?"

Roderik finally got it out. "Thiudegiskel has left Florence, distinguished Martinus. Nobody knows whither. Willimer and some of his other friends went with him."

Padway immediately sent out over the telegraph Urias' order depriving Thiudegiskel of his colonel's rank—or its rough equivalent in the vague and amorphous Gothic system of command. Then he sat and stewed and waited for news.

It came the next morning during the voting. But it did not concern Thiudegiskel. It was that a large Imperialist army had crossed over from Sicily and landed, not at Scylla on the toe of the Italian boot where one would expect, but up the coast of Bruttium at Vibo.

Padway told Urias immediately, and urged: "Don't say anything for a few hours. This election is in the bag—I mean it's certain—and we don't want to disturb it."

But rumors began to circulate. Telegraph systems are run by human beings, and few groups of more than a dozen human beings have kept a secret for long. By the time Urias' election by a two-to-one majority was announced, the Goths were staging an impromptu demonstration in the streets of Florence, demanding to be led against the invader.

Then more details came in. The Imperialists' army was commanded by Bloody John, and numbered a good fifty thousand men. Evidently Justinian, furious about Padway's letter, had been shipping adequate force into Sicily in relays.

Padway and Urias figured that they could, without recalling troops from Provence and Dalmatia, assemble perhaps half again as many troops as Bloody John had. But further news soon reduced this estimate. That able, ferocious, and unprincipled soldier sent a detachment across the Sila Mountains by a secondary road from Vibo to Scyllacium, while he advanced with his main body down the Popilian Way to Reggio. The Reggio garrison of fifteen thousand men, trapped at the end of the toe of the boot, struck a few blows for the sake of their honor and surrendered. Bloody John reunited his forces and started north toward the ankle.

Padway saw Urias off in Rome with many misgivings. The army looked impressive, surely, with its new corps of horse archers and its batteries of mobile catapults. But Padway knew that the new units were inexperienced in their novel ways of fighting, and that the organization was likely to prove brittle in practice.

Once Urias and the army had left, there was no more point in worrying. Padway resumed his experiments with gunpowder. Perhaps he should try charcoal from different woods. But this meant time, a commodity of which Padway had precious little. He soon learned that he had none at all.

By piecing together the contradictory information that came in by telegraph, Padway figured out that this had happened: Thiudegiskel had reached his force in Calabria without interference. He had refused to recognize the telegraphic order depriving him of his command, and had talked his men into doing likewise. Padway guessed that the words of an able and self-confident speaker like Thiudegiskel would carry more weight with the mostly illiterate Goths than a brief, cold message arriving over the mysterious contraption.

Bloody John had moved cautiously; he had only reached Consentia when Urias arrived to face him. That might have been arranged beforehand with Thiudegiskel, to draw Urias far enough south to trap him.

But, while Urias and Bloody John sparred for openings along the river Crathis, Thiudegiskel arrived in Urias' rear —on the Imperialist side. Though he had only five thousand lancers, their unexpected charge broke the main Gothic army's morale. In fifteen minutes the Crathis Valley was full of thousands of Goths—lancers, horse archers, foot archers, and pikemen—streaming off in every direction. Thousands were ridden down by Bloody John's cuirassiers and the large force of Gepid and Lombard horse he had with him. Other thousands surrendered. The rest ran off into the hills, where the rapidly gathering dusk hid them.

Urias managed to hold his lifeguard regiment together, and attacked Thiudegiskel's force of deserters. The story was that Urias had personally killed Thiudegiskel. Padway, knowing the fondness of soldiers for myths of this sort, had his doubts. But it was agreed that Thiudegiskel had been killed, and that Urias and his men had disappeared into the Imperial host in one final, desperate charge, and had been seen no more by those on the Gothic side who escaped from the field.

For hours Padway sat at his desk, staring at the pile of telegraph messages and at a large and painfully inaccurate map of Italy.

"Can I get you anything, excellent boss?" asked Fritharik.

Padway shook his head.

Junianus shook his head. "I fear that our Martinus' mind has become unhinged by disaster."

Fritharik snorted. "That just shows you don't know him. He gets that way when he's planning something. Just wait. He'll have a devilish clever scheme for upsetting the Greeks yet."

Junianus put his head in the door. "Some more messages, my lord."

"What are they?"

"Bloody John is halfway to Salerno. The natives are welcoming him. Belisarius reports he has defeated a large force of Franks."

"Come here, Junianus. Would you two boys mind stepping out for a minute? Now, Junianus, you're a native of Lucania, aren't you?"

"Yes, my lord."

"You were a serf, weren't you?"

"Well . . . uh . . . my lord . . . you see—" The husky young man suddenly looked fearful.

"Don't worry; I wouldn't let you be dragged back to your landlord's estate for anything."

"Well—yes, my lord."

"When the messages speak of the 'natives' welcoming the Imperialists, doesn't that mean the Italian landlords more than anybody else?"

"Yes, my lord. The serfs don't care one way or the other. One landlord is as oppressive as the next, so why should they get themselves killed fighting for any set of masters, Greek or Italian or Gothic as the case may be?"

"If they were offered their holdings as free proprietors, with no landlords to worry about, do you think they'd fight for that?"

"Why"— Junianus took a deep breath—"I think they would. Yes. Only it's such an extraordinary idea, if you don't mind my saying so."

"Even on the side of Arian heretics?"

"I don't think that would matter. The curials and the city folk may take their Orthodoxy seriously. But a lot of the peasants are half pagan anyway. And they worship their land more than any alleged heavenly powers."

"That's about what I thought," said Padway. "Here are some messages to send out. The first is an edict, issued by me in Urias' name, emancipating the serfs of Bruttium, Lucania, Calabria, Apulia, Campania, and Samnium. The second is an order to General Belisarius to leave screening force in Provence to fight a delaying action in case the Franks attack again and return south with his main body at once. Oh, Fritharik! Will you get Gudareths for me? And I want to see the foreman of the printshop."

When Gudareths arrived, Padway explained his plans to him. The little Gothic officer whistled. "My, my, that *is* a desperate measure, respectable Martinus. I'm not sure the Royal Council will approve. If you free all these low-born peasants, how shall we get them back into serfdom again?"

"We won't," snapped Padway. "As for the Royal Council, most of them were with Urias."

"But, Martinus, you can't make a fighting force out of them in a week or two. Take the word of an old soldier who has killed hundreds of foes with his own right arm. Yes, thousands, by God!"

"I know all that," said Padway wearily.

"What then? These Italians are no good for fighting. No spirit. You'd better rely on what Gothic forces we can scrape together. Real fighters, like me."

Padway said: "I don't expect to lick Bloody John with raw recruits. But we can give him a hostile country to advance through. You tend to those pikes, and dig up some more retired officers."

Padway got his army together and set out from Rome on a bright spring morning. It was not much of an army to look at: elderly Goths who had supposed themselves retired from active service, and young sprigs whose voices had not finished changing.

As they cluttered down Patrician Street from the Pretorian Camp, Padway had an idea. He told his staff to keep on; he'd catch up with them. And off he cantered, *poddle-op, poddle-op,* up the Suburban Slope toward the Esquiline.

Dorothea came out of Anicius' house. "Martinus!" she cried. "Are you off somewhere again?"

"That's right."

"You haven't paid us a real call in months! Every time I see you, you have only a minute before you must jump on your horse and gallop off somewhere."

Padway made a helpless gesture. "It'll be different when I've retired from all this damned war and politics. Is your excellent father in?"

"No; he's at the library. He'll be disappointed not to have seen you."

"Give him my best."

"Is there going to be more war? I've heard Bloody John is in Italy."

"It looks that way."

"Will you be in the fighting?"

"Probably."

"Oh, Martinus. Wait just a moment." She ran into the house.

She returned with a little leather bag on a loop of string. "This will keep you safe if anything will."

"What is it?"

"A fragment of St. Polycarp's skull."

Padway's eyebrows went up. "Do you believe in its effectiveness?"

"Oh, certainly. My mother paid enough for it, there's no doubt that it's genuine." She slipped the loop over his head and tucked the bag through the neck opening in his cloak.

It had not occurred to Padway that a well-educated girl would accept the superstitions of her age. At the same time he was touched. He said: "Thank you, Dorothea, from the bottom of my heart. But there's something that I think will be a more effective charm yet."

"What?"

"This." He kissed her mouth lightly, and threw himself aboard his horse. Dorothea stood with a surprised but not displeased look. Padway swung the animal around and sent it back down the avenue, *poddle-op, poddle-op*. He turned in the saddle to wave back—and was almost pitched off. The horse plunged and skidded into the nigh ox of a team that had just pulled a wagon out of a side street.

The driver shouted: *"Carus-dominus, Jesus-Christus, Maria-mater-Dei,* why don't you look where you're going? *San'tus-Petrus-Paulusque-Joannesque-Lucasque . . ."*

By the time the driver had run out of apostles Padway had ascertained that there was no damage. Dorothea was not in sight. He hoped that she had not witnessed the ruin of his pretty gesture.

CHAPTER XVII

IT WAS THE LATTER part of May, 537, when Padway entered Benevento with his army. Little by little the force had grown as the remnants of Urias' army trickled north. Only that morning a forage-cutting party had found three of these Goths who had settled down comfortably in a local farmhouse over the owner's protests, and prepared to sit out the rest of the war in comfort. These joined up, too, though not willingly.

Instead of coming straight down the Tyrrhenian or western coast to Naples, Padway had marched across Italy to the Adriatic, and had come down that coast to Teate. Then he had cut inland to Lucera and Benevento. As there was no telegraph line yet on the east coast, Padway kept in touch with Bloody John's movements by sending messengers across the Apennines to the telegraph stations that were still out of the enemy's hands. He timed his movements to reach Benevento after John had captured Salerno on the other side of the peninsula, had left a detachment masking Naples, and had started for Rome by the Latin Way.

Padway hoped to come down on his rear in the neighborhood of Capua, while Belisarius, if he got his orders sraight, would come directly from Rome and attack the Imperialists in front.

Somewhere between Padway and the Adriatic was Gudareths, profanely shepherding a train of wagons full of pikes and of handbills bearing Padway's emancipation proclamation. The pikes had been dug out of attics and improvised out of fence palings and such things. The Gothic arsenals at Pavia, Verona, and other northern cities had been too far away to be of help in time.

The news of the emancipation had spread like a gasoline fire. The peasants had risen all over southern Italy. But they seemed more interested in sacking and burning their landlords' villas than in joining the army.

A small fraction of them had joined up; this meant several thousand men. Padway, when he rode back to the rear of his column and watched this great disorderly rabble swarming along the road, chattering like magpies and taking time out to snooze when they felt like it, wondered how much of an asset they would be. Here and there one wore great-grandfather's legionary helmet and loricated cuirass, which had been hanging on the wall of his cottage for most of a century.

Benevento is on a small hill at the confluence of the Calore and Sabbato Rivers. As they plodded into the town, Padway saw several Goths sitting against one of the houses. One of these looked familiar. Padway rode up to him, and cried: "Dagalaif!"

The marshal looked up. *"Hails,"* he said in a toneless, weary voice. There was a bandage around his head, stained with black blood where his left ear should have been. "We heard you were coming this way, so we waited."

"Where's Nevitta?"

"My father is dead."

"What? Oh." Padway was silent for seconds. Then he

said: "Oh, hell. He was one of the few real friends I had."

"I know. He died like a true Goth."

Padway sighed and went about his business of getting his force settled. Dagalaif continued sitting against the wall, looking at nothing in particular.

. They lay in Benevento for a day. Padway learned that Bloody John had almost passed the road junction at Calatia on his way north. There was no news from Belisarius, so that the best Padway could hope for was to fight a delaying action, and hold John in southern Italy until more forces arrived.

Padway left his infantry in Benevento and rode down to Calatia with his cavalry. But this time he had a fairly respectable force of mounted arches. They were not as good as the Imperialist cuirassiers, but they would have to do.

Fritharik, riding beside him, said: "Aren't the flowers pretty, excellent boss? They remind me of the gardens in my beautiful estate in Carthage. Ah, that was something to see—"

Padway turned a haggard face. He could still grin, though it hurt. "Getting poetical, Fritharik?"

"*Me* a poet? *Honh!* Just because I like to have some pleasant memories for my last earthly ride—"

"What do you mean, your last?"

"I mean my last, and you can't tell me anything different. Bloody John outnumbers us three to one, they say. It won't be a nameless grave for us, because they won't bother to bury us. Last night I had a prophetic dream . . ."

As they approached Calatia, where Trajan's Way athwart Italy joined the Latin Way from Salerno to Rome, their scouts reported that the tail of Bloody John's army had just pulled out of town. Padway snapped his orders. A squadron of lancers trotted out in front, and a force of mounted archers followed them. They disappeared down the road. Padway rode up to the top of a knoll to watch them. They got smaller and smaller, disappearing and reappearing over humps in the road. He could hear the faint murmur of John's army, out of sight over the olive groves.

Then there was shouting and clattering, tiny with distance, like a battle between gnats and mosquitoes. Padway fretted with impatience. His telescope was no help, not being able to see around corners. The little sounds went on, and on, and on. Faint columns of smoke began to rise over the olive trees. Good; that meant that his men had set fire to Bloody John's wagon train. His first worry had been that they'd insist on plundering it in spite of orders.

Then a little dark cluster, toppled by rested lances that looked as thin as hairs, appeared on the road. Padway squinted through his telescope to make sure they were his men. He trotted down the knoll and gave some more orders. Half his horse archers spread themselves out in a long crescent on either side of the road, and a body of lancers grouped themselves behind it.

Time passed, and the men sweated in their scale-mail shirts. Then the advance guard appeared, riding hard. They were grinning, and some waved bits of forbidden plunder. They clattered down the road between the waiting bowmen.

Their commander rode up to Padway. "Worked like a charm!" he shouted. "We came down on their wagons, chased off the wagon guards, and set them on fire. Then they came back at us. We did like you said; spread the bowmen out and filled them full of quills as they charged; then hit them with the lance when they were all nice and confused. They came back for more, twice. Then John himself came down on us with his whole damned army. So we cleared out. They'll be along any minute."

"Fine," replied Padway. "You know your orders. Wait for us at Mt. Tifata pass."

So they departed, and Padway waited. But not for long. A column of Imperial cuirassiers appeared, riding hell-for-leather. Padway knew this meant Bloody John was sacrificing order to speed in his pursuit, as troops couldn't travel through the fields and groves alongside the road at any such rate. Even if he'd deployed it would take his wings some time to come up.

The Imperialists grew bigger and bigger, and their hoofs made a great pounding on the stone-paved road. They looked very splendid, with their cloaks and plumes on their officers' helmets streaming out behind. Their commander, in gilded armor, saw what he was coming to and gave an order. Lances were slung over shoulders and bows were strung. By that time they were well within range of the crescent, and the Goths opened fire. The quick, flat snap of the bowstrings and the whiz of the arrows added themselves to the clamor of the Byzantines' approach. The commander's horse, a splendid white animal, reared up and was bowled over by another horse that charged into it. The head of the Imperialist column crumpled up into a mass of milling horses and men.

Padway looked at the commander of his body of lancers; swung his arm around his head twice and pointed at the Imperialists. The line of horse archers opened up, and the Gothic knights charged through. As usual they went slowly at first, but by the time they reached the Imperialists their heavy horses had picked up irresistible momentum. Back went the cuirassiers with a great clatter, defending themselves desperately at close quarters, but pulling out and getting their bows into action as soon as they could.

Out of the corner of his eye, Padway saw a group of horsemen ride over a nearby hilltop. That meant that Bloody John's wings were coming up. He had his trumpeter signal the retreat. But the knights kept on pressing the Imperialist column back. They had the advantage in weight of men and horses, and they knew it. Padway kicked his horse into a gallop down the road after them. If he didn't stop the damned fools they'd be swallowed up by the Imperialist army.

An arrow went by Padway uncomfortably close. He found the peculiar screech that it made much harder on the nerves than he'd expected. He caught up with his Goths, dragged their commander out of the press by main force, and shouted in his ear that it was time to withdraw.

The men yelled back at him: "*Ni! Nist!* Good fighting!" and tore out of Padway's grip to plunge back in.

While Padway wondered what to do, an Imperialist broke through the Goths and rode straight at him. Padway had not thought to get his sword out. He drew it now, then had to throw himself to one side to avoid the other's lance point. He lost a stirrup, lost his reins, and almost lost his sword and his horse. By the time he had pulled himself back upright, the Imperialist was out of sight. Padway in his haste had nicked his own horse with his sword. The animal began to dance around angrily. Padway dug his left fingers into its mane and hung on.

The Goths now began to stream back down the road. In a few seconds they were all galloping off except a few surrounded by the Imperialists. Padway wondered miserably if he'd be left on this uncontrollable nag to face the Byzantines alone, when the horse of its own accord set off after its fellows.

In theory it was a strategic retreat. But from the look of the Gothic knights, Padway wondered if it would be possible to stop them this side of the Alps.

Padway's horse tossed its reins up to where Padway could grab them. Padway had just begun to get the animal under control when he sighted a man on foot, bareheaded but gaudy in gilded armor. It was the commander of the Imperialist column. Padway rode at him. The man started to run. Padway started to swing his sword, then realized that he had no sword to swing. He had no recollection of dropping it, but he must have done so when he grabbed the reins. He leaned over and grabbed a fistful of hair. The man yelled, and came along in great bucking jumps.

A glance back showed that the Imperialists had disposed of the Goths who had not been able to extricate themselves, and were getting their pursuit under way.

Padway handed his prisoner over to a Goth. The Goth leaned and pulled the Imperialist officer up over his pommel, face down, so that half of him hung on each side. Padway saw him ride off, happily spanking the unfortunate Easterner with the flat of his sword.

According to plan, the horse archers fell in behind the lancers and galloped after them, the rearmost ones shooting backward.

It was nine miles to the pass, most of it uphill. Padway hoped never to have such a ride again. He was sure that at the next jounce his guts would burst from his abdomen and spill abroad. By the time they were within sight of the pass, the horses of both the pursued and the pursuers were so blown that both were walking. Some men had even dismounted to lead their horses. Padway remembered the story of the day in Texas that was so hot that a coyote was seen chasing a jackrabbit with both walking. He translated the story into Gothic, making a coyote a fox, and told it to the nearest soldier. It ran slowly down the line.

The bluffs were yellow in a late afternoon sun when the Gothic column finally stumbled through the pass. They had lost few men, but any really vigorous pursuer could have ridden them down and rolled them out of their saddles with ease. Fortunately the Imperialists were just about as tired. But they came on nevertheless.

Padway heard one officer's shout, echoing up the walls of the pass: "You'll rest when I tell you to, you lazy swine!"

Padway looked around, and saw with satisfaction that the force he had sent up ahead were waiting quietly in their places. These were the men who had not been used at all yet. The gang who had burned the wagons were drawn up behind them, and those who had just fled sprawled on the ground still farther up the pass.

On came the Imperialists. Padway could see men's heads turn as they looked nervously up the slopes. But Bloody John had apparently not yet admitted that his foe might be conducting an intelligent campaign. The Imperialist column clattered echoing into the narrowest part of the pass, the slanting rays of the sun shooting after them.

Then there was a great thumping roar as boulders and tree trunks came bounding down the slopes. A horse shrieked quite horribly, and the Imperialists scuttled around like ants whose nest had been disturbed. Padway signaled a squadron of lancers to charge.

There was room for only six horses abreast, and even so it was a tight fit. The rocks and logs hadn't done much damage to the Imperialists, except to form a heap cutting their leading column in two. And now the Gothic knights struck the fragment that had passed the point of the break. The cuirassiers, unable to maneuver or even to use their bows, were jammed back against the barrier by their heavier opponents. The fight ended when the surviving Imperialists slid off their horses and scrambled back to safety on foot. The Goths rounded up the abandoned horses and led them back whooping.

Bloody John withdrew a couple of bowshots. Then he

sent a small group of cuirassiers forward to lay down a barrage of arrows. Padway moved some dismounted Gothic archers into the pass. These, shooting from behind the barrier, caused the Imperialists so much trouble that the cuirassiers were soon withdrawn.

Bloody John now sent some Lombard lancers forward to sweep the archers out of the way. But the barrier stopped their charge dead. While they were picking their way, a step at a time, among the boulders, the Goths filled them full of arrows at close range. By the time the bodies of a dozen horses and an equal number of Lombards had been added to the barrier, the Lombards had had enough.

By this time it would have been obvious to a much stupider general than Bloody John that in those confined quarters horses were about as useful as green parrots. The fact that the Imperialists could hold their end of the pass as easily as Padway held his could not have been much comfort, because they were trying to get through it and Padway was not. Bloody John dismounted some Lombards and Gepids and sent them forward on foot. Padway meanwhile had moved some dismounted lancers up behind the barrier, so that their spears made a thick cluster. The archers moved back and up the walls to shoot over the knights' heads.

The Lombards and Gepids came on at a slow dogtrot. They were equipped with regular Imperialist mail shirts, but they were still strange-looking men, with the backs of their heads shaven and their front hair hanging down on each side of their faces in two long, butter-greased braids. They carried swords, and some had immense two-handed battleaxes. As they got closer they began to scream insults at the Goths, who understood their East-German dialects well enough and yelled back.

The attackers poured howling over the barrier and began hacking at the edge of spears which were too close together to slip between easily. More attackers, coming from behind, pushed the leaders into the spear points. Some were stuck. Others wedged their bodies in between the spear shafts and got at spearmen. Presently the front ranks were a tangle of grunting, snarling men packed too closely to use their weapons, while those behind them tried to reach over their heads.

The archers shot and shot. Arrows bounced off helmets and stuck quivering in big wooden shields. Men who were pierced could neither fall nor withdraw.

An archer skipped back among the rocks to get more arrows. Gothic heads turned to look at him. A couple more archers followed, though the quivers of these had not been emptied. Some of the rearmost knights started to follow them.

Padway saw a rout in the making. He grabbed one man and took his sword away from him. Then he climbed up to the rock vacated by the first archer, yelling something unclear even to himself. The men turned their eyes on him.

The sword was a huge one. Padway gripped it in both hands, hoisted it over his head, and swung at the nearest enemy, whose head was on a level with his waist. The sword came down on the man's helmet with a clang, squashing it over his eyes. Padway struck again and again. That Imperialist disappeared; Padway hit at another. He hit at helmets and shields and bare heads and arms and shoulders. He never could tell when his blows were effective, because by the time he recovered from each whack the picture had changed.

Then there were no heads but Gothic ones within reach. The Imperialists were crawling back over the barrier, lugging wounded men with blood-soaked clothes and arrows sticking in them.

At a glance there seemed to be about a dozen Goths down. Padway for a moment wondered angrily why the enemy had left fewer bodies than that. It occurred to him that some of these dozen were only moderately wounded, and that the enemy had carried off most of their casualties.

Frtharik and his orderly Tirdat and others were clustering around Padway, telling him what a demon fighter he was. He couldn't see it; all he had done was climb up on a rock, reach over the heads of a couple of his own men, and take a few swipes at an enemy who was having troubles of his own and could not hit back. There had been no more science to it than to using a pickax.

The sun had set, and Bloody John's army retired down the valley to set up its tents and cook its supper. Padway's

Goths did likewise. The smell of cooking-fires drifted up and down pleasantly. Anybody would have thought that here were two gangs of pleasure-seeking campers, but for the pile of dead men and horses at the barrier.

Padway had no time for introspection. There were injured men, and he had no confidence in their ability to give themselves first aid. He raised no objections to their prayers and charms and potations of dust from a saint's tomb stirred in water. But he saw to it that bandages were boiled —which of course was a bit of the magic of Mysterious Martinus—and applied rationally.

One man had lost an eye, but was still full of fight. Another had three fingers gone, and was weeping about it. A third was cheerful with a stab in the abdomen. Padway knew this one would die of peritonitis before long, and that nothing could be done about it.

Padway, not underestimating his opponent, threw out a very wide and close-meshed system of outposts. He was justified; an hour before dawn his sentries began to drift in. Bloody John, it transpired, was working two large bodies of Anatolian foot archers over the hills on either side of them. Padway saw that his position would soon be untenable. So his Goths, yawning and grumbling, were routed out of their blankets and started for Benevento.

When the sun came up and he had a good look at his men, Padway became seriously concerned for their morale. They grumbled and looked almost as discouraged as Fritharik did regularly. They did not understand strategic retreats. Padway wondered how long it would be before they began to run away in real earnest.

At Benevento there was only one bridge over the Sabbato, a fairly swift stream. Padway thought he could hold this bridge for some time, and that Bloody John would be forced to attack him because of the loss of his provisions and the hostility of the peasantry.

When they came out on the plain around the confluence of the two little rivers, Padway found a horrifying surprise. A swarm of his peasant recruits was crossing the bridge toward him. Several thousand had already crossed. He had to be able to get his own force over the bridge quickly, and he

knew what would happen if that bottleneck became
jammed with retreating troops.

Gudareths rode out to meet him. "I followed your orders!" he shouted. "I tried to hold them back. But they got
the idea they could lick the Greeks themselves, and started
out regardless. I told you they were no good!"

Padway looked back. The Imperialists were in plain
sight, and as he watched they began to deploy. It looked
like the end of the adventure. He heard Fritharik make a
remark about graves, and Tirdat ask if there wasn't a message he could take—preferably to a far-off place.

The Italian serfs had meanwhile seen the Gothic cavalry
galloping up with the Imperialists in pursuit, and had
formed their own idea that the battle was lost. Ripples of
movement ran through their disorderly array, and its motion was presently reversed. Soon the road up to the town
was white with running Italians. Those who had crossed
the bridge were jammed together in a clawing mob trying
to get back over.

Padway yelled in a cracked voice, to Gudareths: "Get
back over the river somehow! Send mounted men out on
the roads to stop the runaways! Let those on this side get
back over. I'll try to hold the Greeks here."

He dismounted most of his troops. He arranged the lancers six deep in a semicircle in front of the bridgehead,
around the caterwauling peasants, with lances outward.
Along the river bank he posted the archers in two bodies,
one on each flank, and beyond them his remaining lancers,
mounted. If anything would hold Bloody John, that would.

The Imperialists stood for perhaps ten minutes. Then a
big body of Lombards and Gepids trotted out, cantered,
galloped straight at his line of spears. Padway, standing
afoot behind the line, watched them grow larger and larger.
The sound of their hoofs was like that of a huge orchestra
of kettledrums, louder and louder. Watching these big, longhaired barbarians loom up out of the dust their horses
raised, Padway sympathized with the peasant recruits. If he
hadn't had his pride and his responsibility, he'd have run
himself until his legs gave out.

On came the Imperialists. They looked as though they
could ride over any body of men on earth. Then the

bowstrings began to snap. Here a horse reared or buckled; there a man fell off with a musical clash of scale-mail. The charge slowed perceptibly. But they came on. To Padway they looked twenty feet tall. And then they were right on the line of spears. Padway could see the spearmen's tight lips and white faces. If they held— They did. The Imperialist horses reared, screaming, when the lancers pricked them. Some of them stopped so suddenly that their riders were pitched out of the saddle. And then the whole mass was streaming off to right and left, and back to the main army. It wasn't the horses' war, and they had no intention of spitting themselves on the unpleasant-looking lances.

Padway drew his first real breath in almost a minute. He'd been lecturing his men to the effect that no cavalry could break a really solid line of spearmen, but he hadn't believed it himself until now.

Then an awful thing happened. A lot of his lancers, seeing the Imperialists in flight, broke away from the line and started after their foes on foot. Padway screeched at them to come back, but they kept on running, or rather trotting heavily in their armor. Like at Senlac, thought Padway. With similar results. The alert John sent a regiment of cuirassiers out after the clumsily running mob of Goths, and in a twinkling the Goths were scattering all over the field and being speared like so many boars. Padway raved with fury and chagrin; this was his first serious loss. He grabbed Tirdat by the collar, almost strangling him.

He shouted: "Find Gudareths! Tell him to round up a few hundred of those Italians! I'm going to put them in the line!"

Padway's line was now perilously thin, and he couldn't contract it without isolating his archers and horsemen. But this time John hurled his cavalry against the flanking archers. The archers dropped back down the river bank, where the horses couldn't get at them, and Padway's own cavalry charged the Imperialists, driving them off in a dusty chaos of whirling blades.

Presently the desired peasantry appeared, shepherded along by dirty and profane Gothic officers. The bridge was carpeted with pikes dropped in flight; the recruits were armed with these and put in the front line. They filled the gap nicely. Just to encourage them, Padway posted Goths behind them, holding sword points against their kidneys.

Now, if Bloody John would let him alone for a while, he could set about the delicate operation of getting his whole force back across the bridge without exposing any part of it to slaughter.

But Bloody John had no such intention. On came two big bodies of horse, aimed at the flanking Gothic cavalry. Padway couldn't see what was happening, exactly, between the dust and the ranks of heads and shoulders in the way. But by the diminishing clatter he judged his men were being drawn off. Then came some cuirassiers galloping at the archers, forcing them off the top of the bank again. The cuirassiers strung their bows, and for a few seconds Goths and Imperialists twanged arrows at each other. Then the Goths began slipping off up and down the river, and swimming across.

Finally, on came the Gepids and Lombards, roaring like lions. This time there wouldn't be any arrow fire to slow them up. Bigger and bigger loomed the onrushing mass of longhaired giants on their huge horses, waving their huge axes.

Padway felt the way a violin string must the moment before it snaps.

There was a violent commotion in his own ranks right in front of him. The backs of the Goths were replaced by the brown faces of the peasants. These had dropped their pikes and clawed their way back through the ranks, sword points or no sword points. Padway had a glimpse of their popping eyes, their mouths gaping in screams of terror, and he was bowled over by the wave. They stepped all over him. He squirmed and kicked like a newt on a hook, wondering when the bare feet of the Italians would be succeeded by the hoofs of the hostile cavalry. The Italo-Gothic kingdom was done for, and all his work for nothing. . . .

The pressure and the pounding let up. A battered Padway untangled himself from those who had tripped over him. His whole line had begun to give way, but then had been frozen in the act, staring—all but a Goth in front of him who was killing an Italian.

The Imperialist heavy cavalry was not to be seen. The dust was so thick that nothing much could be seen. From beyond the pall in front of Padway's position came tramplings and shoutings and clatterings.

"What's happened?" yelled Padway. Nobody answered. There was nothing to be seen in front of them but dust, dust, dust. A couple of riderless horses ran dimly past them through it, seeming to drift by like fish in a muddy aquarium tank.

Then a man appeared, running on foot. As he slowed down and walked up to the line of spears, Padway saw that he was a Lombard.

While Padway was wondering if this was some lunatic out to tackle his army single-handed, the man shouted: *"Armaio! Mercy!"* The Goths exchanged startled glances.

Then a couple of more barbarians appeared, one of them leading a horse. They yelled: *"Armaio, timrja!* Mercy, comrade! *Armaio, frijond!* Mercy, friend!"

A plumed Imperial cuirassier rode up behind them, shouting in Latin: *"Amicus!"* Then appeared whole companies of Imperialists, horse and foot, German, Slav, Hun, and Anatolian mixed, bawling, "Mercy, friend!" in a score of languages.

A solid group of horsemen with a Gothic standard in their midst rode through the Imperialists. Padway recognized a tall, brown-bearded figure in their midst. He croaked: "Belisarius!"

The Thracian came up, leaned over, and shook hands. "Martinus! I didn't know you with all that dust on your face. I was afraid I'd be too late. We've been riding hard since dawn. We hit them in the rear, and that was all there was to it. We've got Bloody John, and your King Urias is safe. What shall we do with all these prisoners? There must be twenty or thirty thousand of them at least."

Padway rocked a little on his feet. "Oh, round them up and put them in a camp or something. I don't really care. I'm going to sleep on my feet in another minute."

CHAPTER XVIII

BACK IN ROME, Urias said slowly: "Yes, I see your point. Men won't fight for a government they have no stake in. But do you think we can afford to compensate all the loyal landlords whose serfs you propose to free?"

"We'll manage," said Padway. "It'll be over a period of years. And this new tax on slaves will help." Padway did not explain that he hoped, by gradually boosting the tax on slaves, to make slavery an altogether unprofitable institution. Such an idea would have been too bewilderingly radical for even Urias' flexible mind.

Urias continued: "I don't mind the limitations on the king's power in this new constitution of yours. For myself, that is. I'm a soldier, and I'm just as glad to leave the conduct of civil affairs to others. But I don't know about the Royal Council."

"They'll agree. I have them more or less eating out of my hand right now. I've shown them how without the telegraph we could never have kept such good track of Bloody John's movements, and without the printing press we could never have roused the serfs so effectively."

"What else is there?"

"We've got to write the kings of the Franks, explaining politely that it's not our fault if the Burgunds prefer our rule to theirs, but that we certainly don't propose to give them back to their Meroving majesties.

"We've also got to make arrangements with the king of Visgoths for fitting out our ships at Lisbon for their trip to the lands across the Atlantic. He's named you his successor, by the way, so when he dies the east and west Goths will be united again. Reminds me, I have to make a trip to Naples. The shipbuilder down there says he never saw such a crazy design as mine, which is for what we Americans would call a Grand Banks schooner. Procopius'll have to go with me, to discuss details of his history course at our new university."

"Why are you so set on this Atlantic expedition, Martinus?"

"I'll tell you. In my country we amused ourself by sucking the smoke of a weed called tobacco. It's a fairly harmless little vice if you don't overdo it. Ever since I arrived here I've been wishing for some tobacco, and the land across the Atlantic is the nearest place you can get any."

Urias laughed his big, booming laugh. "I've got to be off. I'd like to see the draft of your letter to Justinian before you send it."

"Okay, as we say in America. I'll have it for you tomorrow, and also the appointment of Thomasus the Syrian as minister of finance for you to sign. He arranged to get those skilled ironworkers from Damascus through his private business connections, so I shan't have to ask Justinian for them."

Urias asked: "Are you sure your friend Thomasus is honest?"

"Sure he's honest. You just have to watch him. Give my regards to Mathaswentha. How is she?"

"She's fine. She's calmed down a lot since all the people she most feared have died or gone mad. We're expecting a little Amaling, you know."

"I didn't know! Congratulations."

"Thanks. When are you going to find a girl, Martinus?"

Padway stretched and grinned. "Oh, just as soon as I catch up on my sleep."

Padway watched Urias go with a twinge of envy. He was at the age when bachelors get wistful about their friends' family life. Not that he wanted a repetition of his fiasco with Betty, or a stick of female dynamite like Mathaswentha. He hoped Urias would keep his queen pregnant practically from now on. It might keep her out of mischief.

Padway wrote:

Urias, King of the Goths and Italians, to his Radiant Clemency Flavius Anicius Justinian, Emperor of the Romans, Greetings.

Now that the army sent by your Serene Highness to Italy, under John, the nephew of Vitalianus, better known as Bloody John, is no longer an obstacle to our reconciliation, we resume discussion for terms for the honorable termination of the cruel and unprofitable war between us.

The terms proposed in our previous letter stand, with this exception: Our previously asked indemnity of a hundred thousand solidi is doubled, to compensate our citizens for damages caused by Bloody John's invasion.

There remains the question of the disposal of your general, Bloody John. Though we have never seriously contemplated the collection of Imperial generals as a hobby, your Serenity's actions have forced us into a policy that looks much like it. As we do not wish to cause the Empire a serious loss, we shall release the said John on payment of a modest ransom of fifty thousand solidi.

We earnestly urge your Serenity to consider this course favorably. As you know, the Kingdom of Persia is ruled by King Khusrau, a young man of great force and ability. We have reason to believe that Khusrau will soon attempt another invasion of Syria. You will then need the ablest generals you can find.

Further, our slight ability to foresee the future informs us that in about thirty years there will be born in Arabia a man named Mohammed, who, preaching a heretical religion, will, unless stopped, instigate a great wave of barbarian conquest, subverting the rule both of the Persian Kingdom and the East Roman Empire. We respectfully urge the desirability of securing control of the Arabian Peninsula forthwith, that this calamity shall be stopped at the source.

Please accept this warning as evidence of our friendliest sentiments. We await the gracious favor of an early reply.

by MARTINUS PADUEI, Quæstor.

Padway leaned back and looked at the letter. There were other things to attend to: the threat of invasion of Noricum by the Bavarians, and the offer by the Khan of the Avars of an alliance to exterminate the Bulgarian Huns. The alliance would be courteously refused. The

Avars would make no pleasanter neighbors than the Bulgars.

Let's see: There was a wandering fanatical monk who was kicking up another row about sorcery. Should he try to smother the man in cream, as by giving him a job? Better see the Bishop of Bologna first; if he had influence in that direction, Padway knew how to make use of it. And it was time he cottoned up to that old rascal Silverius . . .

And should he go on with his gunpowder experiments? Padway was not sure that this was desirable. The world had enough means of inflicting death and destruction already. On the other hand his own interests were tied up with those on the Italo-Gothic State, which must therefore be saved at all costs . . .

To hell with it, thought Padway. He swept all the papers into a drawer in his desk, took his hat off the peg, and got his horse. He set out for Anicius' house. How could he expect to cut any ice with Dorothea if he didn't even look her up for days after his return to Rome?

Dorothea came out to meet him. He thought how pretty she was.

But there was nothing of hail-the-conquering-hero about her manner. Before he could get a word out, she began: "You beast! You slimy thing! We befriended you, and you ruin us! My poor old father's heart is broken! And now you've come around to gloat, I suppose!"

"What?"

"Don't pretend you don't know! I know all about that illegal order you issued, freeing the serfs on our estates in Campania. They burned our house, and stole the things I've kept since I was a little girl—" She began to weep.

Padway tried to say something sympathetic, but she flared up again. "Get out! I never want to see you again! It'll take a squad of your barbarian soldiers to get you into our house. *Get out!*"

Padway got, slowly and dispiritedly. It was a complex world. Almost anything big you did was bound to hurt somebody.

Then his back straightened. It was nothing to feel sorry for oneself about. Dorothea was a nice girl, yes, pretty, and reasonably bright. But she was not extraordinary in these respects; there were plenty of others equally attractive. To be frank, Dorothea was a pretty average young woman. And being Italian, she'd probably be fat at thirty-five.

Government compensation for their losses would do a lot to mend the broken hearts of the Anicii. If they tried to apologize for treating him roughly, he'd be polite and all, but he didn't think he'd go back.

Girls were okay, and he'd probably fall one of these days. But he had more important things to worry over. His success so far in the business of civilization outweighed any little failures in personal relationships.

His job wasn't over. It never would be—until disease or old age or the dagger of some local enemy ended it. There was so much to do, and only a few decades to do it in; compasses and steam engines and microscopes and the writ of habeas corpus.

He'd teetered along for over a year and a half, grabbing a little power here, placating a possible enemy there, keeping far enough out of the bad graces of the various churches, starting some little art such as spinning of sheet cooper. Not bad for Mouse Padway! Maybe he could keep it up for years.

And if he couldn't—if enough people finally got fed up with the innovations of Mysterious Martinus—well, there was a semaphore telegraph system running the length and breadth of Italy, some day to be replaced by a true electric telegraph, if he could find time for the necessary experiments. There was a public letter post about to be set up. There were presses in Florence and Rome and Naples pouring out books and pamphlets and newspapers. Whatever happened to him, these things would go on. They'd become too well rooted to be destroyed by accident.

History had, without question, been changed.

Darkness would not fall.

far away places . . . visitors from other worlds . . .
the wonders of ancient civilizations . . .
the ancestors of Man . . .

from **Ballantine**

ANCIENT ENGINEERS, by L. Sprague de Camp.
From the pyramids of Egypt and the Great Wall of China to the "no parking" signs at Nineveh and the water alarm clock of Plato.
From the author of **Citadels of Mystery**   **$1.75**
As fascinating as **Chariot of the Gods**

TEMPLE OF THE STARS, by Brinsley le Poer Trench.
An examination of Mankind's ancient link with visitors from distant stars as seen in astrological theories.
By the former editor of **Flying Saucer Review**   **$1.50**

PILTDOWN MEN, by Ronald Millar.
Here is the story, as fascinating as a whodunit, of how the Piltdown skull came to be discovered; how the hoax was exposed; and who the hoaxer may have been.   **$1.75**

IN SEARCH OF THE MAYA, by Robert L. Brunhouse.
The wonder, the disbelief, the unfolding of the idea of a unique culture as sophisticated as that of the Old World was a genuine discovery and as fascinating an adventure as any that can be found in exploration or archeology.   **$1.65**

SELECTIONS FROM THE PUBLISHER
OF THE BEST SCIENCE FICTION
IN THE WORLD

To order by mail, send $1.25 per book plus 25¢
per order for handling to Ballantine Cash
Sales, P.O. Box 505, Westminster, Maryland
21157. Please allow three weeks for delivery.